THE LAY OF THE LAND

The Lay
of the
Land

DEAN CRAWFORD

VIKING

VIKING
Viking Penguin Inc., 40 West 23rd Street,
New York, New York 10010, U.S.A.
Penguin Books Ltd, Harmondsworth,
Middlesex, England
Penguin Books Australia Ltd, Ringwood,
Victoria, Australia
Penguin Books Canada Limited, 2801 John Street,
Markham, Ontario, Canada L3R 1B4
Penguin Books (N.Z.) Ltd, 182–190 Wairau Road,
Auckland 10, New Zealand

First published in 1987 by Viking Penguin Inc.
Published simultaneously in Canada

Grateful acknowledgment is made for permission to reprint
an excerpt from "I Left My Heart in San Francisco"
by Douglas Cross and George Cory.
© 1954 (renewed) Colgems-EMI Music Inc.
All rights reserved. Used by permission.

LIBRARY OF CONGRESS CATALOGING IN PUBLICATION DATA
Crawford, Dean.
The lay of the land.
I. Title.
PS3553.R2788L3   1987   813'.54   86-9200
ISBN 0-670-80155-0

Printed in the United States of America by
R.R. Donnelley & Sons Company, Harrisonburg, Virginia
Design by Marysarah Quinn
Set in Electra

For Darin and Rob

"These brief lays, of Sorrow born."
TENNYSON

Part One

Part One

My sister and I have always been a bit in love, though you couldn't call it incest. We never touched. "We're not demonstrative," my sister said when we were already grown, an occasion when she was leaving or I was leaving and in either case we should have been kissing. "We're not demonstrative," my sister said and then she started to cry and I started to cry and her two children, great sympathizers, gazing up at our grins and tear-streaked faces, joined in too. Then we all touched, as I remember. As a foursome, we were safe enough.

It hadn't always been safe enough for my sister and me. We never spoke of it, but still there was no quibbling between us in our shared knowledge that in some dark, deep-seeded way we'd each have liked to burn down the bed with our natural, unnatural lust. Natural enough, the shrinks would say, sibling incest fantasy, precoital, postoedipal, parte-wombal, recombinant Sigmund-Freudal. But this is different, I maintain. My sister and I were convinced that we shared the same consciousness, inhabited the same soul. We were never silly enough to articulate it, not as adults at any rate, but still, in our precognizant lobes we thought we were twins, *Siamese* twins, severed before the womb, then staggered six years in our respective earthly births.

Coming together again and again, we discovered that we'd shared the same thoughts, traced the same experiences, and if those ex-

periences were inverted as boys' and girls' tend to be, the emotional
residue was always, inextricably, the same. When one fell sick or
wounded, the other one phoned: "What's the matter? What is it? I
can tell there's something wrong..." Decisions, taken separately,
set us once again on the same paths, and when time came for
recounting, we learned that we'd each stepped in the same puddle,
sheltered under the same elm, gotten sopped by the same kind of
storm, though our passings were years or miles or worlds apart.

Leading us together again:

I watched for the familiar flash of my sister's taillights. Always
Leslie used her blinkers, even when there wasn't another car on the
road, and in my mind's eye (more like a dark lens, more like the
curving face of an early TV) I can see her now, somewhere hours
or days ahead of me on the road, crooked over the steering wheel
of her late-model VW bus, checking first the side mirror, then the
rearview, then remembering the blind spot over her shoulder, before
tripping her turn signal on a stretch of open highway where she
hadn't seen another pair of headlights in almost an hour.

My sister, the fugitive. She never looked like a dangerous character to me. A good driver, except sometimes when she was alone
in the car. A devoted mother, but not only a mother. A great sister,
in spite of those occasions when I might have wanted more.

My sister and I drove tandem across the country in 1974, re-
migrating from Connecticut to California in our modern-day covered wagons: mine an aging Dodge van with seven great American
cylinders churning, one popping; hers a menagerie on four wheels,
crammed to the roofrack with boxes and crates, stuffed animals,
children (Barbara and Mat), cats (Baby and Flower), turtles (Hortense
and Calisher, for those who could tell them apart), and one delinquent Irish setter (Blazes Boylan, the child-biter). My sister and I
returned together to the land of our births and childhoods, fleeing
the East for all the familiar reasons—parents, divorce, poor crops,
the rising cost of heating oil. We chose independently to move
together, and once again I found myself following in her tracks,
looking far ahead for the blink of her lights as I passed the same
smokestacks of Pennsylvania and Ohio she'd passed four days before,

skirted the same turgid outskirts of Indianapolis and Chicago she'd
skirted three days before, sweltered through the same interminable
heartland plains of Nebraska and Iowa she'd sweltered through not
more than a day or two before me. And finally breaking out into
the West, I scanned the wide horizons of the rowdy cow country of
Wyoming and Montana where I knew I'd catch her if only I could
project myself into her car, her thoughts, her whims. Most of all
her whims. Les would want to stop off at Aaron's farm because he
was an old boyfriend and she'd want to alarm him. She'd be drawn
to the Black Hills for Bob Dylan's sake, to Livingston, Montana, for
Pete Pardieu's sake, to Mount Rushmore and Salt Lake for the
children's, and New Mexico for her own sake. Would she be sensible?
Would I know it if she suddenly changed her mind? As it happened,
my sister and I crossed the continent in leap-frogs, passing and
repassing each other on the same lengths of highways without ever
knowing it. It took us each about a week.

Which would be plenty of time for recounting, I assured myself,
and a recount was just what the little resurgent Jesuit in me had in
mind—a private, furtive reappraisal, stripping away my self-delusions
like so much sunburnt skin while driving across the country alone
in a derelict vehicle. Hadn't I deserted both wife and mistress? Hadn't
I scandalized a perfectly nice little southern town? Guilty as charged.
And since I was leaving as well as returning, rediscovering as much
as starting anew, it seemed only fitting that I should suffer for my
sins and perverse self-denials, even as I indulged them. My van was
really a hair shirt by Detroit, designed with the driver's seat perched
right over the front axle for maximum effect of road upon kidneys.
I imagined the long and gloating nights and miles, my orgiastic feats
of guilt and urethral retribution while the ribbon of broken white
line slipped down the asphalt beneath me, unrolling, leading inex-
orably toward truth, self-awareness, final freedom from delusion,
that moment of crazed agonized vision when, the blinders finally
ripped away, the self revealed, I beheld . . . Would I lose control of
the car? Attain great wisdom? Go mad from the flash of too-sudden
insight? Be reincarnated as a cow?

I never knew because predictably I hardly gave myself an honest thought for those three thousand miles. Instead I thought of Leslie. Surely my sister's life was the shadow-line of my own, and if I could retrace her steps, if I could perceive the pattern, then I might know my own steps—past, present, and for the next six years. Hadn't we both gone south and married hastily, taken the plunge for the sake of plunging and then kept on sinking for the next five years? I was now "separated"; Les had been free for six years. So what came next on the agenda? More descent, darker lovers, lost weekends of pills and booze? Les had her kids to check her fall, but what would save me, without children for buoyancy? I wondered, I wasn't asking seriously.

I could have picked out Dudley's apartment from the Cross-Bronx Expressway. Dudley Do-Right, who once showed me how he could pick off any car on the road from his bedroom window. He even had the gun to do it. Dudley was one of Les's old beaux—the only one of that club who was also a member of the Black Panther Party. I remembered he'd given Les some opium once (how could I forget?), and we'd smoked it together, she and I, that night we nearly took our own little plunge. No, I wouldn't stop to see Dudley. I was only an hour out, there was never a safe spot to park in his neighborhood. Anyway I didn't want to be the one to tell him that Les had left for California without saying good-bye.

   She'd done that to me once, when she ran away to get married. Here on the Pennsylvania Turnpike she'd ridden the Greyhound bus in January 1963, being carried toward the Oklahoma hills and Hank Jakes, escape and elopement, first betrayal of her little brother, two lovely children-to-be, and a web of deceit and disaster. My sister, riding forth on a Greyhound bus in the winter of a preconscious age: nineteen years old, 1963. What was she thinking about for three days on a bus, falling through space, staring out the window at this procession of grain elevators and white corn towns? Lonely, lost, impatient, vacant as a cupboard in a vacant house? Did she feel like Satan? Or like Dorothy on the road to Oz (without her little Toto, me)?

   In a box in a drawer of the bureau in the back of my van, I

carry the relics, posed photographs from that era, the very month, January 1963. They show Les huddled in a Victorian chair. She's an immigrant, just off the bus. Is poor little Leslie yearning to breathe free? Then why did she run away? It's clear she's submitting, first to the photographer's set, but that's not all she's submitting to. Leering above her is the all-American specter, a Stanley Kowalski with a crew cut and rolled-up denims, the stub of a Camel between his grimy fingers and a smirk across his brutish face. That will be Hank, my sister's intended, her husband-to-be. Hank leans, you can see he's about to grope her, but he doesn't hold her. In fact, she ran to him. Something else is holding my sister. What? The twinkle of that microscopic diamond on her ungloved hand? She's not pregnant *yet*, is she?

Here then is the great enigma, the knot to blame for all my sister's woes, the one act so divergent no loving (or lusting) brother can understand. Why did she throw herself away on this man?

Still, she might be vacant, without a motive in her head. From the look of her, my sister might be waiting for a bus. She's got her coat on, you can see. Her hands and one loose glove are stacked neatly on her purse, which is resting on her knees. She looks like she's waiting, at the bus station, or a train station, any transit depot, ready to leave. My sister is really just a nice girl waiting, nothing more. Any minute now they're going to call her bus: "All aboard for St. Louis, Kansas City, Cincinnata and points east, not excluding little brothers waiting at home! All aboard now!" But she cannot, will not leave.

The longer the fall, the better, I suppose. I dug out this photograph when I stopped for gas. I stopped for gas to dig it out. I knew it was there. I knew where to find it, even though it was Les who'd packed it. I hadn't seen her pack it, I hadn't seen the photograph in years and years. The left hand is twin to the right, though. It galls me just to think about this picture, the twists of those mouths, this Leslie who doesn't look like Leslie, who doesn't act like Leslie, who might as well not—for all practical purposes—have been Leslie.

There are other snaps, easier to live with, in the same box and drawer. Here's one of Leslie in an outsized bonnet that looks like one of our grandmother Gum's. Little Leslie is leading me by the hand. In another, Les is halfway down the slide, smiling like a kamikaze pilot as she aims her feet for the camera, with our grandfather's face fuzzed angelically out of focus at the top of the slide. I found a whole nest of snapshots in that drawer, and I replayed them, like scenes from half-forgotten dreams, heading west.

In the photograph we are frozen, my sister and I, children of Sunshine and Fog. Les is ahead of me on the beach, of course, of course, and her eyes are slammed shut for the camera. Half-turned toward the picture-taking parent (is it Sunshine or Fog?), she's making her monkey face. Of me, one can see only my broad little back, my stubby legs and outstretched arms. I'm three, already in headlong pursuit of my sister.

The locale for this immortal shot, this three-by-five glossy Grecian urn, is a California beach—San Gregorio, Pescadero, one of those buena vistas near Half Moon Bay. Rocks are in the picture, that's how I know it's not Half Moon Bay, the beach itself, a stretch of seaweed, shale and sand and horse manure, but no rocks. Thanks to mother love and Mother's love of water, we came often to the shore: downshifting the Ford with a grind and a clunk for the long hill on Cañada Road, the terraced lawns and gardens rising steeply from the road, the ticklish scent of mimosa and acacia hanging in the hot air as we wafted by; then winding up through the redwoods and eucalyptus to the crest of the hills where the rattling dry smell of sage collided with first sight of the ocean, first knowledge of whether the beach would be warm or fogged in; and finally topping the hill, holding our breaths while the car gushed downward, past the pumpkin patch, past the roadside stands, past the hothouse orchids and the mortuary that we couldn't smell, then whizzing past the old house with walls made entirely of doors, all sorts of doors, our first landmark of a foreign place, we burst out, "House of doors! House of doors!" Our voices echoed for two dozen years, "House of doors!"

But there were lots of trips and snapshots, so let me place this particular picture in time. If I'm three, Leslie must be nine, and the historical moment must be the drab fifties, our national infancy, when the Gerber baby was the president, when normalcy was perceived as a virtue and folks dressed to match their cars. Cars! In the fifties, we were mad for cars, especially in California. My cousin Jersey, who lived in Colma, a city comprised as far as I could see of orchards and the vast graveyard where my grandfather ended up as ashes in a box, had about the best job I could imagine. Cousin Jersey sold cars, a Dodge dealer in fact. I saw him on television, selling cars, and anytime he wanted he could drive any of a thousand new cars: pink Polarises, cozy DeSotos, wide-hipped land cruisers whose names I've forgotten that would float across the desert to Vegas in a hum, a whisper, a croon. Pat Boone's smile. Everyone wanted a Bing-cherry-red convertible to glide down the boulevard and slip into drive-ins, where carhop girls would cantilever over the side.

Our own car was concrete gray. We lived on "the Peninsula," a string of suburbs of San Francisco. My father, whose name was Francis (we called him Fog), commuted by train to work as a "figure juggler" for a large corporation, the name of which is engraved on my memory as if in stone: Merrill Lynch Pierce Fenner and Beame.

"What do you do at work all day, Dad?"

"I juggle figures," he told me as he painted the garage.

"Like the circus?"

"Don't be stupid, son."

"All right. You mean like arithmetic then?"

"Yes, that's closer. We call it speculative addition."

I waited for him to continue, but he didn't, which was the problem with Fog. Even now, my shoulders start to round and ache, and I slouch in my seat when I think of the drudgery and deadly addition he sustained in order to give us, Sunshine and Les and me, the split-level in a safe and quiet burb, the death-gray Ford, the dishwasher, the wash washer, overcooked lamb chops on the dinner table, summers at Donner, and afternoons at Half Moon Bay.

But for sheer martyrdom, old Fog could never hold a candle to Sunshine (née Bernadette), dear Mater. I remember one night, deep in the Dark Ages, the miasmic fifties, when my mother lay like a flute on the bed and whined out of key. Fog had done it again, something terrible, I didn't know what. Had he forgotten to take out the garbage? Blanked on an important anniversary? Referred to Rita Hayworth as an attractive woman? (I always took my father's part.) He'd already slammed out of the house, and now Sunshine was emitting weird noises in the bedroom. She kept it up until Les and I came in to check.

"We thought maybe you were doing something to the cat," Les said.

"Oh, my *God!*"

"What's the matter, Mom?" Les and I spoke in one voice, the voice of reason, of sanity, of sound mental health. "What's the matter, Mom?"

"Your *father...*" she began, but didn't continue.

"Dad *what?*" I asked defensively.

Sunshine didn't answer. "No," she said finally. "You're too young. Some things... It wouldn't be fair to tell."

Mother had us where she wanted us now, chained to her bedside, captives of curiosity and guilt. She started to rock and moan. The light was a purgatory gray, her dress and her skin an elegant match. Mother's eyes were wide and visionary: a catechism saint.

"Dad *what?*" I asked again, hot tears welling up in my eyes, but still I got no reply.

"Are you all *right*, Mother?" Les asked. "Is there anything we can do?"

"Leslie!" She fluttered her hand.

"Yes, Mother."

"Leslie!" She seized my sister's arm. "Leslie, go into the kitchen, the third drawer from the refrigerator on the left. Bring me the knife, the long one with the walnut handle. I have to kill myself!"

I looked to my sister. Her face didn't flicker. "Okay," she said. And went. Les was an old hand, and she had always been a delightfully literal child. I knew that about her even though I was six years the younger (and exactly six at that). I knew that from the snapshots alone. "Leslie! Turn around, dear!" someone would holler. And Les turned every time. "Say cheese!" A coaxing voice. And Les would screw up her face, every time. It was just like clockwork, the automatic response.

Leslie fetched the kitchen knife, the monster with the wooden handle. "Here's the knife," she said as she laid it on the spread.

Sunshine scrutinized the knife shrewdly, appraising it through her puffy eyes. Time slowed. Clocks stopped ticking. When Mother opened her mouth, I thought she was going to make an offer (two and a half because it's stainless but not a penny more), but she didn't. Her eyes filled up again as she looked at Leslie. Then her throat heaved as though she couldn't bring herself to speak. She turned away. "You don't care," she said in the direction of the wall. "You don't love me. No one does."

I felt Les stiffen. She didn't say anything, but she swayed, tottering on the verge of either slapping our mother or falling over backward. Then she turned on her heel and left the room, leaving me to minister to my mother's melodrama.

And minister I did, although I wanted to fly as fast as my PF Flyers would fly me. I did as I should, as I always did. Miserable if you do, guilt-crazed if you don't. Sunshine was gasping for air between her sobs. She started to hiccup. For a few minutes, I allowed myself to observe her impassively, from the scientific viewpoint. I saw a woman basking in her own tears and miseries. Then I picked up the carving knife, the one I was never allowed to touch, not even when I dried the dishes, and set it gently on the floor. I touched my mother's lifeless arm. "Mama," I said, already aware of the power in a name. "Please be our mama."

Sunshine relented. She blinked back her tears and cracked a smile, raw like an egg. "You should be a diplomat," she said with a lift to her chin. She dried her eyes on the bedspread. "The secretary of state. You have such tact. What natural tact you have."

I wonder now if Sunshine truly imagined that world affairs were carried on in the same spirit of melodrama and good sportsmanship that characterized our family quarrels, that Joseph Stalin could be shamed into returning the Baltic States, that great nations came together to play games of gentlemanly manipulation: "Two points for a crying jag!" "Chest pains! Good move! Czechoslovakia is yours, and you deserve it!"

But whatever the rules of world statesmanship, Mother was without question the Machiavelli of our house, the John Foster Dulles of the dinette. Brinkmanship: vague threats of suicide and divorce, accusations about the unpaid bills. We played guilt like hot potato, and I learned early (before I can remember, perhaps before I talked) that it's much better, infinitely preferable in fact, to be the Victim, the Sap, the Fool.

Sunshine wasn't Jewish. She was Irish Catholic, if not in pure blood, then certainly in temperament. When you mix a fine dry gin with Irish whiskey, you taste the whiskey every time, and so it went for Sunshine. She was Anglo-Irish, I suppose—half a twig from some dead limb of a colonial family tree, and half Gum (Great Gum!), my maternal grandmother.

Gum was born with the girlish name of Annie Mahoney, but by the time I knew her she was already a shriveled old woman, a near-midget of superhuman strength. Every Sunday we drove across the bay to Oakland to visit Gum and Papa. She drew us to her by magnetic force, then served drinks and cheese and crackers while Papa slipped away from the gathering to play with Les and me. We could still hear her, though. Great Gum held forth, her voice rasping absolute on any subject, though her favorites were the ethnic groups. Often she began with a familiar joke: "Now take the Germans . . . please!" And she loved to turn a nasty phrase: "So he says to the rabbi, he says, 'Go fly a *kike!*'" In Gum's presence, Sunshine visibly shrank, and Fog passed the hours crossing and uncrossing his legs, just as his gray namesake passed the days playing venetian blinds along the coastal hills. Together on the low sofa, my parents sat up to their waists in overstuffed cushions while Gum towered above them on a straight chair.

For dinner, we ate chicken, inevitably—breasts baked until the tender flesh metamorphosed into rock and then began to fissure. The family sat down solemnly to eat: We come to bury this meal, not to praise it. At the age of six or seven, though, I was still too young to hack through shards while keeping mindful of Emily Post, and once, when I tired of sawing, I forced my knife point into a crevice in the meat and started prying along the fault line. It snapped; parts of chicken hurtled from my plate and ricocheted across the table. Gum stopped talking in mid-sentence. All adult eyes turned to glare at me; only Les turned away. She was staring at her milk, which had been forced on her, even though she'd given it up a few months before. We both stared at her brimming glass. "Can't he even cut his meat?" Gum asked. No one answered; it wasn't a question. "When I was his age, I was fixing dinner for a family of eleven. But then I was a girl, and girls are so much faster than boys..." Suddenly Les's glass began to rattle. No one was touching it—Les's hands were in her lap—but still it rocked from side to side, then pitched over sloshing milk into the brussels sprouts.

I can't remember much of the scene that followed, except that I was accused of kicking the table, then Les was. And maybe she did, first estimating the length of her leg and the distance to that one spot under the table, then correcting for error before giving the coup de grace, a perfect kick right under the milk glass. I never believed that, though, and neither did the rest of the family. Sunshine decided that we'd just had an earthquake, a highly localized one (right under the milk, that is). "Aren't we very close to the Hayward Fault?" she asked ingenuously.

"We'll have to rename it the Leslie Fault," Gum groused.

Normally, Gum and I didn't speak to each other, except when she was accusing me, or when I was starting to gag on the food and had to ask for something to drink. As my family arrived or departed, she would offer me her cheek, and occasionally she commented on my recent growth with a touch of annoyance in her voice. Gum liked boys no more than men, and possibly less. Men at least had been trained to cut their meat properly. But being a child, I enjoyed even in Gum's presence some of the child's prerogative of dumb persistence, and several times asked why it was Gum wasn't eating dinner, the meal she'd prepared herself, along with the rest of us. Maybe I was curious. More likely I was suspicious. Often I had to repeat the question in order to get an answer. Gum looked up and smiled as tolerantly as she could from the depth of her affliction. She survived entirely on potato chips, old-fashioneds, and Raleigh cigarettes. "No, thank you, dear," she said with smoke pouring from her mouth like a dragon. "I couldn't keep it down."

Gum had been a convent girl. She never spoke directly of her experience, and as far as I could tell (or anyone else could tell me), the only things she'd learned at parochial school were the abhorrence of sex and Italians, were the only ethnic group Gum ever allowed herself to malign directly. She liked to refer to the church dances as "wop hops," and whenever Papa offered to do the shopping, she asked him first, "You're not going to that Guinea grocer again, are you?"

Although she herself attended mass only on Easter Sunday and Christmas Eve and hadn't stooped to make confession since she'd married Papa—a Methodist—in 1915, Gum enforced Catholicism on the rest of the family with her tiny iron fist. Sunshine was sent to convent schools. To her credit, she hated them: the lives of the saints, the enforced modesty, and the uniforms most of all. She married my father outside the Church, and when Leslie was born, Sunshine declined to have her baptized in the Catholic Church. Gum must have raised the roof, but since it was wartime and Sunshine was living in Chicago, the old lady's tyranny was diminished. Then Fog was sent overseas, and Sunshine, young wife and mother, was having trouble making ends meet. Poor in Chicago in the wintertime, what could be worse? She appealed to Gum and Papa for a loan.

"Why, of course, dear. You don't think we'd let you do without. We'd be only too glad to help... just as soon as little Leslie has been properly baptized. Of course, she'll need a saint's name. Elizabeth? Ann? Or shall we just call her Mary? It's my duty as a Catholic grandparent, I'm sure you understand."

Sunshine's resistance must have crumbled once Les had been officially splashed and the family was living again within scolding distance of Gum. I can't say that Sunshine fought the good fight exactly, but at least she made the initial effort. By the time I came along, Les was already enrolled at Immaculata, the Convent of the

Purple Heart, listening to lectures on the spiritual benefits of wearing scratchy underwear and denying the pleasures of the flesh.

Family chronicles are as riddled with contradictions as families, though, and here I must admit to one, admit the contradiction although I can't explain it. Who knows what wild thoughts ran through Mother's mind? Maybe she thought that the active ingredient of Catholicism, the contagion, was contained in the holy water itself, and that, once splashed, Les might as well be made to go the distance: convent school and missals, First Communion, Confirmation, and CYO. Or maybe she just let Gum push her around. Yet Mother balked once more when it came time to baptize me. Pridefully, I've always wondered if I weren't the occasion of Sunshine's Great Rebellion, her first and final assertion of herself. No quick dip on the way home from the delivery room for me; I grew to be one, two, three years old, still as dry and heathen as the day I was born.

Then my mother contracted polio. Les and I were sent to stay with Gum and Papa. Polio was epidemic that summer, and Mother's ward was strictly quarantined. You had to be an RN or an MD to get past the door. ABSOLUTELY NO VISITORS—ONLY AUTHORIZED PERSONNEL BEYOND THIS POINT. Fog rented a ladder and propped it against the hospital wall beside Mother's window. He stood on the top rung of the ladder and spoke to her through the glass. Mother couldn't move her head, couldn't see his face or anxious tears, only hear his voice. I wonder what he said.

Her only visitor was Dr. Miller, pediatrician to Leslie and me; to our mother, patron saint. He came as soon as he heard, or maybe he was already on the ward. The point is he was there the night she was admitted, and he sat at her bedside through the critical hours of the fever, talking to her softly, never mind the words. My mother was too delirious to respond, but she heard his voice and remembered, according to her own lights.

According to Mother's lights, late in the night, when she felt herself slipping, sliding pleasantly into something like a dream, Dr. Miller grabbed her by the shoulders and shook her. "Don't you dare die!" he screamed into her ear. "You've got two children to raise and I won't let you die! You hear me? I won't *let* you! Wake up, you bitch! Get mad! Wake up and *fight!* Do you *hear?*"

There's another thing my sister and I share: reverence for Dr. Miller. Like the Old Testament God.

In the meantime, one day when Fog was hanging on the ladder or Dr. Miller was screaming in Mother's face or maybe later when my mother was struggling first to swim then to walk again, Gum snuck me down to the local parish church to be dipped in holy water. *"Carpe diem,"* the priest intoned. *"Dominus vobiscum."* By the time Les and I were finally allowed to come home, I had turned four years old and a stutterer, and Les was burdened with a secret about Gum that she could never tell. Sunshine's convalescence was long, but her recovery complete, or nearly so. She lost her backhand, but she always hated tennis anyway. Publicly, the family maintained that Sunshine's polio started my stutter, but privately she and I shared an unspoken understanding that it was the cold shock of baptism that caused my disfluency.

Gum done it. If pressed, I'd have to allow that the old lady might have believed the dogma, particularly those parts promoting virginity. Who knows? Maybe she actually believed in an abstract God, although she never mentioned His name in my presence. Or maybe she wanted (less than consciously) to make her female offspring tough man-haters like herself and she knew that the convent schools were the right place to start. Certainly Gum never suggested that *I* be sent to parochial schools. I caught only a glancing blow from the Catholic Church. Les was the one hit full-force with the nuns' guilt and terror. "The convent is proper training for young girls," Gum often remarked. "Look at me. It didn't do me any harm. A little hellfire and damnation never hurt anyone."

More likely, my grandmother was hedging on religion out of innate practicality. She was selling short against eternity and wanted to share this sound investment tip with those she cared most about, the female members of her family. I'm sure Gum had it figured to some advantage. Living up there in the clouds as He did, God simply couldn't comprehend the exigencies of day-to-day life: the importance of good manners and the white lie, the presence of those loud-mouthed Italians in church.

But if Gum was a realist and a hypocrite, then Papa was the dreamer, Saint Christopher in a salesman's suit. Each day he ventured forth from the apartment on Mead Park. He scratched, frisked, patted, and stroked the dog, then pecked Gum on the cheek. She grimaced, and he was off to the city to sell. Papa could sell anything to anyone. As it happened, he sold pharmaceuticals to druggists, friends mostly of thirty years or more. The business transaction was a simple by-product of their friendship. Papa winked, smiled, wisecracked. Everyone adored him. Sometimes he even forgot to close the deal.

Once on a Saturday I was allowed to accompany him. I don't remember exactly how old I was—sometime between the age of reason and ten years. My grandfather was, without question, my favorite creature in the world. At seventy, he was still jittering with excitement, still driving ferociously. The traffic was heavy on the Bay Bridge, and Papa changed lanes as though playing checkers, as though the piece he was driving could move only along a diagonal. Three passenger cars moved abreast, and Papa tailgated each in turn.

The fog was just beginning to lift from the clock and the Hills Bros. coffee sign on which a two-dimensional ethnic type, an Arab dressed in a bedsheet, was trying to slurp from a cup that jerked up and down on a mechanical arm. The City of San Francisco was "under construction," an erector-set state of affairs which I childishly regarded as permanent. Papa poked one long finger toward the ferry building. "That's how we *used* to get across," he said. "Folks in Oakland were so grateful to be visited that they sent the trolley halfway cross the bay to meet the ferry." Papa swerved across three lanes of traffic and leaned on his horn. Now we were tailgating a delivery truck labeled HOFFMAN'S CHIPS. He leaned out the window. "Move it, you Kraut potato farmer!" The truck wallowed on unperturbed, and he turned to me. "The family couldn't imagine why your Uncle Bob and I would want to spend our Sunday afternoons in Oakland, of all places!" Papa chuckled, remembering his suspicious sisters and Bob, his long-dead twin and cohort. "But you see, there were these two fräuleins who lived right off Grand Avenue. Sisters they were, and both of them real lookers. My mother would have howled if she'd known that we were stepping out with German girls. She would have raised the hair on the dog. So we never told her. Bob and I dressed to a T, and oh, mama, were those fräuleins ever glad to be visited." Papa slipped the car into a hole and swerved around Hoffman's Chips. "But you don't have much use for girls yet, do you?" he asked me.

Naturally, I hated girls and told him so. Papa arched an eyebrow. "What about Leslie?"

My mind seized up like a motor on that contradiction. Les was a girl, I had to admit. Yet she was also not-girl. She didn't whimper when her shoes got muddy, and she liked to terrorize tarantulas with a BB gun. I tried to resolve the question with adult authority and grown-up diction. Between Les and other girls, I could see nothing but the obvious similarity, and I'd seen that only once. "Les is an entirely different situation."

We crossed the bridge from Oakland to San Francisco in record time. Lights turned green for us, as they always did when my grandfather was at the wheel, and in no time we jolted to a halt beside a fire hydrant on Polk. But when I asked about the hydrant and the possibility of a ticket, Papa winked. "The cop on this beat is Gum's cousin," he whispered. "The Irish! They're all cousins!"

Gum remained at home. She never worked, never learned to drive a car. She farmed the household chores out to "ladies of color," usually black or brown. But although she was leisured, sheltered absolutely from the crass pursuit of money, housework, and what it does to your hands, there wasn't an innocent bone in all of Gum's fragile frame. She was a woman of impossible contradictions and mountainous hypocrisies, but no illusions. Grasping the motive was a movement as natural to my grandmother as plucking an extra transfer on the Presidio bus.

Gum never took a cab. She could recite the bus and trolley schedules like the passages of poetry she'd never troubled herself to learn in school. "Sit in the middle," she instructed me on the Presidio bus, going out to the Legion of Honor. "I'll be right along."

I could hear the snap of her voice behind me as I staggered down the alley of stockings, dresses, and hats towering like so many church steeples high above my head. I couldn't have been more than five or six, costumed in my navy blue sailor suit. A shopping day with my grandmother was an ordeal comparable only to a .trip to the dentist or my tuba lesson. Most of all, I hated the sailor suit.

"How's that guinea son-in-law?" Gum was asking the bus driver. "Has he gotten a job yet?" The driver replied in a lilting brogue, but I couldn't make out the words. I found two seats together and jumped up. "Well!" I heard Gum bark behind me. I wheeled quickly in my seat and felt a hot rush of relief after determining that her remark was not directed at me. Gum leaned further over the driver's shoulder and spoke in a lower voice. Then they both laughed. Gum straightened. I watched her body flutter with the roll of the bus like a flower stalk jittering in your hand. Gum's velvet hat was the blossom on the end.

Then she turned and slowly made her way up the aisle. I continued to watch while Gum greeted every second passenger along her route. There was no denying her popularity, and in all fairness, I had to admit that she addressed the silk dresses and scrub clothes alike. Gum was a lady (and a native San Franciscan, she was proud to say), but to me she looked like another child playing dress-up in white gloves and grown-up clothes.

two

I reached the outskirts of Chicago tired but exhilarated. My odometer was poised at 99,993, about to flip up zeros and start counting anew. It was the turn of the century as far as my van was concerned; by local time, it was only mid-evening, eight-thirty or nine o'clock, September fifth. I pulled off the interstate to make the time go slower and found myself on the "alternative business route," a four-lane miracle mile of car dealerships, gas stations, and fast-food eateries that proclaimed their particular edibles in the shapes of great ice cream cones, hot dogs, and triple-decker hamburgers, all depicted in neon lights. The road was packed with slow-moving cars: jacked-up Falcons and Camaros, "Kozy-Kar" vans with flaming dragons painted on their hoods, "4 × 4" pickups with roll bars and gun racks and oversize tires. Were these people watching their odometers, too? I doubted it. Here on the outskirts of Chicago, it was Friday night, date night, that timeless teenage institution, while for me it was 99,995.

Under the circumstances, what would Leslie do? Stop for champagne? I looked around for a 7-Eleven store, wondering whether they stocked party hats and little paper whistles.

Where was Leslie? Any moment now my odometer would roll up goose eggs like a slot machine, and the moment would be wasted, worse than wasted, if I lived it alone. I needed a sister, soulmate, twin. Only Leslie could be counted on for just the right reaction, the exact combination of irony and Vegas joy, like the moron who's just won the bedroom suite on "The Price Is Right."

Les would take this as a sign. "It's cosmic. It's a whole new ball game," she might say, never having taken the slightest interest in baseball. "It's the bottom of the ninth and the scoreboard has just gone kablooey and erased everything, *everything*. So you've got a clean slate, a *tabula rasa*. Don't you feel *reborn?* Don't you? Don't you believe me, Jeremy?"

"Yes!" I say aloud. "I feel like the owner of a brand-new automobile!"

"Close enough," she'd say. "That-a-boy." Then Les might do anything—pop the cork on a bottle of champagne, kiss me, or lean out the window and start talking to strangers. Stopped at a traffic light like this one, she was fully capable of turning to the carload of teenagers idling alongside. "This car has just been born again," she'd announce, possibly in a southern accent considering that I was sporting Georgia plates. Her children in the back would cringe and duck behind the seat, embarrassed because teenagers were their elders, too. I'd be embarrassed too, but laugh, only wishing that I were capable of suspending reality as readily as my sister could. The teenagers would stare at her, of course: a lady with wild auburn hair, she might as easily be a madwoman or somebody's mother. And Les was fully capable of going on from there, rolling her eyes to the heavens and slapping the door of the van. "You see this car? This here car has just been *born again!* Brothers and sisters! Praise the Lord! In the name of the Father and the Son and the Holy Ghost, not to mention the fruit of thy loom, Jesus Christ! Young man? Son? That's right, I'm talking to you boy. I just want to ask you something. I just want to ask you one little all-important, earth-shattering question. Have *you* taken the Lord Jesus into your heart like this here rattledown automobile . . . ?"

My sister wasn't a pallid personality. She might appear demure with boys and later with men because that was her training growing up in the fifties, but Les was really the bold one. I was the carbon, she the original. I envied my sister even as I idolized her, emulated her, pretended she was with me when she was not.

My sister could have gotten beneath the surface of this strip. All I could do was drive it. She could have gone right up to those four black guys on the corner. She could have leaned out the window at that light. She could have ducked into any of these bars with neon lintels above the doors and struck up a conversation. In fact she wouldn't even have to do the striking up. Men would come right over to her, ask her where she came from, offer to show her around the town. They might not be cute or interesting or even single, but they'd be natives. The real thing. How can a man ever hope to know a place like a woman, who can open her legs and submit to all the archetypes: Stanley Kowalski, Honest Abe, Buffalo Bill, Geronimo, Popeye the Sailor Man? How else can you know America, if not by being fucked by it? The double standard works against men, or so it seemed to me. We may be freer to debauch ourselves without being seen as damaged merchandise, but what kind of freedom is that if the only way really to know your native land is to get down in the muck and slither around? The fact is no man can degrade himself the way a woman can, not unless he takes it up the ass. That's why I envied women, I decided, and wanted to be one, able to *sin*, to steal away from our father's house, sneak downtown, and take on a whole carload of blacks, rednecks, or juvenile delinquents.

"I'd never do that. I never wanted to."

"Come on, Les. You can be straight with me."

"No, I can't, not about that. But even if I could, I'd say the same thing. Girls don't want to be gang-banged."

In spirit Les rode beside me down the strip, and I didn't even notice when my odometer flipped up zeros. No lights flashed, no bells rang, no nickels came pouring out from under the dash. When the miracle mile rejoined the freeway, so did I. I followed the signs for Joliet, the home of the Illinois State Pen, driving into the night and feeling more than ever alone.

Nineteen forty-seven is the year of my favorite snapshot, showing father and daughter, a four-year-old Les gaily waving one hand and one foot as though caught in mid-step of the Charleston. Father holds daughter like a dance partner, one wide hand on her tiny back.

They both smile and squint into the sun. The scene is a stretch of empty beach. On the back of the photograph is scribbled "Mokoleia," a meandering beach with a reef of the same name on the north shore of Oahu, but from the look of it, this could be any Pacific beach in the same year, 1947.

It could be one of the Bikini group. "Watch out!" I want to warn them. I'm not even born yet, but I want to scream into this blissful scene, "Watch out! An A-bomb's about to fall on your heads!" There's an A-bomb poised above my father's and my sister's heads, but the A-bomb has yet to fall.

All this happened before my birth: Sunshine, doll-child, toddled off from home, first to convent, then to college, then to married life and war, with nun-forbidden ribbons in her hair and in her head a worldview she might have gotten out of a Cracker Jacks box; Fog, born golden, grew ashen and disgusted, corporate at twenty-six; and Leslie, precursor, big sister, was already disapproved of, a disappointment before she was five.

How could it be otherwise? Les hated ribbons. Scowling, she tore them out of her hair as soon as Sunshine was out of sight, and sometimes even before. Les maimed her dolls, every one of them except the string of paper dolls she'd carved herself, saving that for my disposition later on. "A doll for a doll," Sunshine said, presenting Leslie with a doll, hoping against hope that that twist she saw in her daughter's mouth didn't mean what it had always meant in the past. Les styled herself on the family dog, Classy, a wild Irish setter. To begin with, they had the same color hair.

At four, Les was finally allowed her first haircut, and she carefully gathered the fallen strands from the barbershop floor. Everyone stopped to watch and smiled. "How darling!" Sunshine exclaimed, proud mother, able at last to identify in her daughter a cute and girlish trait, imagining the scrapbook page that read "My Baby Hair" with arrows pointing to the obvious, some auburn curls scotch-taped to the construction paper.

But Les had no intention of sentimentalizing her hair. The truth is she'd never wanted to be a little girl in the first place. She'd wanted

to be a wild and painted Indian, and when she didn't feel like being
an Indian, she wanted to be a dog. So Sunshine needn't have been
so surprised when her daughter appeared at the breakfast table the
following day, naked except for the hair taped to all parts of her body
and refusing to speak except in barks and whimpers and howls.

How could it have been otherwise? When Sunshine had been
such a pretty prissy child herself, grown now into a girlishly pigeon-
toed adult whose disapproval was only the iceberg tip of her total
miscalculation of what Leslie, as girl-child, was destined to be. As
for Fog, he despised inefficiency, and having to pick up his barking
daughter and unleashed dog after they'd been apprehended playing
bow-wow in the reservoir was precisely his idea of a needless chore.

How could it have been otherwise in the postwar era, when the
regularity of bowel movements and family roles and tooth decay and
TV reception and steady rise of GNP were the desperate ideals of
national health? In the first bloom of corporate love, when cheerful
moms and dads, the postwar (and forgetful) blithe spirits, craved and
saved for the new washers and dryers and federally secured home
loans, when the good life was upon us, right there on the cover of
Life (No, don't look back!), embodied by new roadsters, station
wagons, and bassinets! How could it have been otherwise in the
height of the baby boom, when we had to be able to tell our girl
babies from our boy babies or at least from our dogs and cats and
wild Indians, than that a wanton and wild-headed little girl who
wanted to be anything except a girl would be misunderstood, an
embarrassment to her parents as they strolled down the avenue or
had to pick her up at the pound?

Les was wild from birth, so the question of rebellion becomes
one of chicken or egg. Which came first, the narrow expectations
for little girls or Leslie's infant unwillingness to conform? The answer
would be moot since Les was born into a world already gone dreary,
where rebellion was the only alternative to laundry detergents and
Doris Day.

But surely there was still magic in the pictures of the toddler
Les, screaming down the beach, pursued by her glad dad, not quite
yet Fog, bespectacled but still brown and slender and just beginning

to molt. He called her Chief, whether for her affinity to Indians or her bossy ways we were never sure.

Sunshine beams out at the camera in her golf skirt, in her tennis togs, in her bathing attire—fashionable but absurd. Looking at these snaps, it strikes me that she's not a mother but a mannequin, a clothes dummy with a fixed and painted smile. No, she's a model (more consciously cool and artificial for possessing free will) contemplating herself, gazing back at the lens as though it were a mirror, knowing all too well the appeal of beauty in remoteness, having eyes only for herself. It's not surprising that it's the clothes I notice, not the mom. I see the face of Hepburn above the golfing pleats, Bette Davis looking less buxom today in her tennis dress, Lucille Ball trying to be sexy in a two-piece with a jellyfish fringe. Fog looks well beside her. He's a handsome man, but not so dazzling that he might distract. Together they gaze out from the snapshots as though from the pages of a magazine: The Good Life, Drink Tanqueray. It's a set piece, a vacuum, unlivable if it ever could exist. And fortunately for the human race, into this pose crawls little Leslie, shaggy dog, chewing on a beachball. Les is the incongruous element, the peg which is neither round nor square, the cowlick which defies the comb. She is wearing her "clo," the bottom half of a bikini, the only article she'll willingly put on.

"I don't wear clothes," she says. "I wear clo!"

"Oh, how darling," Sunshine says. "Now let's stick a dress on her."

"No!"

"Come on, darling. Of course you want to wear this pretty dress. Isn't this just a darling little pretty dress?"

"No!"

"Come on. Don't you want to look pretty for Daddy?"

"No!"

"The kid's a walking one-liner. Who needs one?" Fog asks in jest, sliding into an exasperation that will one day calcify in disgust. "You reach for her, she snarls. You touch her, she's likely to bite your hand. Who needs one?" he keeps on asking after the joke has worn off. "We've already got an untamed dog."

That was in '47 or '48 when we were living in post-Paradise. (We: I include myself, the unborn.) After the war, Fog settled the family in Hawaii, as was customary, as he'd been planning on doing for almost four years. The island boy returns to the islands. But Hawaii had changed and so had he. Honolulu was no longer a sleepy town, Hawaii no longer a colony, one big country club for haoles. His high-school sweethearts, the Mineri sisters, had married servicemen and moved away, one to San Diego, one Spokane. Everyone that Fog met seemed like a stranger to him now, his old friends most of all. He hadn't been home to the islands since he left for college before the war. Still, he couldn't say he was surprised by the changes—the sheathed corpse of the *Missouri* in the harbor, the vast cemetery that had sprung up on Diamond Head, the honkytonks stacked up in quintuplicate on Hotel Street. He'd expected the changes and steeled himself, yet he was disgusted by them. Everyone talked about the war, and Fog just wanted to forget it, to luau at the beach house on the north shore, strum his ukelele, drink and sing the pidgin songs, and watch his cousins hula in the sand. He'd come home with a dose of malaria from occupation duty in the Philippines, and for two years afterward he awoke in the night with chills and cold sweats, symptoms he was only too willing to attribute entirely to recurrent attacks of the fever.

Sunshine accepted that explanation for a little while. She was young, and forgetfulness was the fashion in the postwar era. But when the attacks persisted, her natural inquisitiveness was aroused. And when Fog refused to see a doctor, she started to suspect there might be buried secrets to dig up. "Frank dear, what are you dreaming about when you get these attacks?"

"Nothing."

"You must be dreaming about *something*."

"No. You know I don't dream."

"Everyone dreams. You just don't remember yours, or maybe you don't want to tell me . . ." Sunshine bided her time, waiting for the right moment, the next time Fog started to shake and moan. "What do you see?" she whispered in the ear of his troubled sleep. "What does she look like? What's her name?"

"Run! Quick! The buffaloes are coming!"

"*What?*"

"The buffaloes are coming!"

"What buffaloes?"

"The ones right in front of you, dummy! Run, run! The buffaloes are coming!"

Over the next two years, Fog's attacks of malaria subsided, but Les developed asthma. The family was living in Wahiawa, the wettest town on Oahu, in the house given to them as a wedding present by Granny and Grampy Fog. It was awfully convenient, right next door. Sunshine and Fog saved their money, but by the time they'd bought their narrow lot on the dry side of Diamond Head, Leslie's condition was critical. They could remain in the islands only at the risk of their daughter's life.

So the family picked up and moved to California the year before I was born. Sunshine wasn't sad to leave the clammy world of cousins and private pidgin language, where she would always be the wife, a mainland girl. She, too, was smothering in that climate. As for Fog, what was there left of paradise to lose? A stranger in his own land, he was already paling to a haolier shade of white. So the family moved east, retracing the first steps in their backward migration, and Fog took a job with an up-and-coming firm of stockbrokers, with whom he would put in his twenty-odd years.

Years later, when Fog was well past hearing, his old firm would come out with an ad campaign in which a husky corporate voice announced, "Merrill Lynch is bullish on America!" as though there could be no buts about it. Then a herd of cattle would stampede across the screen, alarming the unwary viewer. But I knew better than bullish, as my father's dreams had foretold. Merrill Lynch was *buffalo-ish* on America. "Run! Run!" he'd called out to us from his sleep. "Don't you see them, dummy! The buffaloes are coming!"

Many times I've wondered if we don't live our lives more than half submerged, with only our little heads bobbing up above the surface of our sleep.

Even as a child, I saw life as a swimmer in the sea. I've always been a sucker for the high-flown metaphor, but that's what I was as a child, a swimmer, after all. If ever Sartre and Camus and Saint-Exupéry had come to me smoking Gauloises and asking, *"Et tu, mon petit*, who are you?" I would have had to tell them, *"le Nageur."* Like Les before me, I'd been racing since I was five, and when I slept I rolled in the swells, fluttering my little feet and flailing my arms.

But if we're all of us lone swimmers on the sea, then what about direction? Fate? Free will? The diety himself? my child's imagination asked. The answer seemed plain enough to this diminutive philosopher. On a placid day, you can see the lighthouse; in rough weather, only the next wave, unless of course it lifts you up for a look around. As for currents, carrying you away to a fate that could be plotted on a chart, I didn't really believe in them, or at least not in their power over me. I was a good swimmer, and a cocky one.

But what about the demons we all know are undulating just below the surface of the sea? As a child, I'd read no psychology, so what I had in mind were sharks, which I was terrified of with an obsession that could only be sexual. I saw my legs dangling in the water like tender young bananas, tempting on the vine, and never, not even in the freshest of fresh water, would I close my eyes for an instant lest the monster fish sneak up on me.

At nine or ten, I'd already read much of the literature on sharks and could recite the species like a baseball roster, complete with batting averages and likely totals of human lives consumed. Almost daily I interrogated my father about the incident on his surfboard in the Molokai Channel, and when they caught a big mako off Santa Barbara, slitting its stomach open to discover the partially digested arm of a man, I nearly shivered out of my skin. I watched it all on TV—the rocking boat, the white underbelly, the knife—and then rehashed the event so often in my memory that I confused the image and the incident with a Timex commercial that was popular at the time and began in my replay to hear the voice of John Cameron Swayze announcing triumphantly as he held up the decomposed and disconnected arm: "It's still ticking!"

But about currents I knew nothing. I probably thought I could outswim them or somehow buck their flow, and it was just this kind of arrogance that made my parents careful whenever they took me to the beach.

We're at the beach in 1959, all four of us at San Gregorio for a balmy family outing on a Sunday afternoon. Any month now, we'll all board a plane that will transport us to that Devil's Island on the Connecticut shore, Tory Hole, but for now it's a Pacific afternoon. The fog has lifted, its damp chill burned away. Sunshine is basking in this California sun, perhaps for the last time, while Fog shields his bald spot with a napkin on his head. The day is hot and almost airless, with just enough breeze to lift a napkin. My father has to sit with one hand clamped over the top of his head.

I'm nine and not allowed to swim in the ocean when the surf is up, as it is today, but there's a small river feeding into the breakers where I can console myself in the brackish water, trying to stand on a slimy log. Sunshine and Fog are watching me from the bank, just in case I conk my head or make a break for it, try to slip away downriver to the sea. I scull over to the bank and beach myself on the sand at their feet, asking for the umpteenth time, "Can't I *please*, if I promise not to go out over my head?"

Sunshine looks to Fog to play the heavy. "No," he snarls. "And that's *final*. Period. *Capisce?*"

Les is swimming in the surf, out where I yearn to be. I can't see her because the ocean lies around a dune, but I know she's out there, learning to body surf, having a wonderful time. I drift back out on my log, watching as the napkin lifts from my father's head and floats away on a breath of air. He reaches for it, but it's gone.

Leslie is swimming out through the surf. In my mind's eye I can see her now, since I have the advantage of hindsight. No one is watching her from the shore (no one else) because everyone is watching me, but Leslie is a strong swimmer, sensible most of the time. She's fifteen, almost sixteen, old enough. The waves today are too erratic for body surfing. They're coming in as a tangle, toppling over one another, breaking in fragments rather than lines.

Leslie is swimming out just one more time, then she's going to call
it a day.

In the lazy swells beyond the surf, she stops and bobs for a
moment looking out to sea: all that water rolling from here to Japan.
Cold, cold ocean. Cold Japan. Les feels a chill and turns to face
the land, the bright sand, the cliffs and dunes fuzzy with the suc-
culent life of plants. Slowly she reaches out an arm to stroke. Then
she gives a kick to get herself started, and that's when she feels it,
something rub against her leg.

Leslie starts to scream. She twists to look behind. She stares at
the water all around her trying to see through its gray surface the
looming shape before it strikes.

Then, not ten yards away, up bobs a harbor seal, bewhiskered
and bright-eyed, treading water. Les laughs, more with relief than
humor. "You know what I thought *you* were," she says to the seal,
who fails to reply. The two of them gaze at each other. "Well, are
you just going to sit there?" Les asks finally, and cocks her head to
mimic the seal's. Gently she starts to breaststroke toward the seal.
"It's all right," she says soothingly, as though to a nervous dog. "I'm
not going to hurt you. It's all right. Do you mind if I call you Sam?
Sammy the seal," she coos.

But Sammy maintains his interval. Without appearing to move,
he is constantly receding before her, drawing her out to sea. Then
he dives, and when he surfaces a moment later at her side, he
starts to roll like a dolphin through the swells. Sammy stops in
front of Les again, still watching her with his shoe-button eyes.
Les tries the rolling motion, and when she comes up beside the
seal, he repeats the demonstration. Again. And again. Les feels
as though she's a dolphin or a seal herself, swimming faster and
easier through the waves than ever before, intoxicated by her own
motion, free.

But when she stops again to look for the seal, he's gone. "Sammy!"
she calls. "Sammy!" Les looks all around her, and only then does
she notice how far it is to the shore. On the up-bobs, she can see
the surf like a feather. In the troughs, she can see nothing at all.

"Oh, my God," she whispers, knowing the reason already and refusing to accept it as true.

Les swims hard for the beach, and when she stops to check the distance, she sees that she's no closer and maybe farther than before. Her face sets in anger, and she starts to swim even harder. Maybe in the quiet with her face underwater, she can hear the instructing voice: "Never try to buck a riptide. Swim always *across* its flow, in a direction parallel to the shore." Maybe Les can hear the voice, if so her own. She wants to heed it, she wants to, but she can't. Maybe, she kids herself, it's not a riptide after all. But when she stops again, she knows now that she's farther out than she's ever been, and she feels the fear rising up in her chest, agitating her legs, even as the current draws.

She's kicking harder than she needs to to tread water, and she knows she's wasting precious strength. She sees a figure on the shore, gazing out to sea. Les waves. It looks like a boy. She waves again, more desperately. The boy sits down in the sand.

Leslie dimly remembers beginning to swim again, but she doesn't remember how long or even what stroke she swam. She remembers only the terrible leaden ache in her muscles, then nothing more.

Les remembers nothing until she wakes sitting in the surf alone. She can remember: the seal, the swimming, and the shore moving away from her, the boy sitting down to watch (if there really was a boy, if she didn't dream that part), and that's all. How did she get here? How did she get out of the riptide? Did it just drop her off? Even if it did peter out though, how could she possibly have had the strength left to swim to shore?

Les looks around. She sees cliffs, a rocky point. This isn't even the same beach she started swimming from. Did she dream the whole incident? Is she dreaming now? Les tries to stand, but her legs give out and she flops back down. She sits, she doesn't know how long, but she remembers worrying about the tide. She tries to crawl across the sand. Then she hears above her head the sound of Fog's voice calling her, calling her name. She looks up at the sky and squints and waves an arm, but before she can make out the figure of her father on the cliffs, he's already down and splashing through the shallows. "Chief! Chief!" he is saying, "I thought we'd lost you!" Then he is holding her fast, dragging her up the sand. Les slumps against him. Fog is crying, but she is too wet herself to feel his tears.

three

From Chicago I drove on through the night, stopping for infusions of coffee and pie every two or three hours. Gas-station attendants and waitresses in coffee shops were the only people I'd spoken to in thirty-six hours, and I'd never been very good at talking to them. I felt autistic. I felt estranged. I felt sour, like my father's son. My father, who specialized in humiliating waitresses, also demeaned in smaller ways the boys who offered to wash his windshield when he stopped for gas. "Can I check your oil for you today, sir?" asked an all-American cherub with a streak of motor oil down his applecheek. "If you think you can handle it," was my father's customary reply.

Shortly after midnight I had to face a cherub of my own. I stopped at a food and fuel exit, and, after loading up on coffee and apple pie with a cup of sugar in the cinnamon sauce, I decided to fill up on gas, too. The attendant was sixteen or so, his hair as limp and golden as the silk on an ear of corn. "Hi! How're you doin' tonight?" he asked me.

"Fine. Fill it with regular, please."

"Sure thing! Comin' right up, sir!" He bounced away toward the pump. I followed more slowly, stretching and bending my back, which felt like a mass of small, tight coils. I was wired on stimulants, caffeine and sugar, and felt not only capable of ripping this bright red gas pump out of the ground and flinging it across the lot, but so inclined. My young attendant was already washing the rear window of my van—a considerate thought but not a very useful one since the windows were blocked on the inside by boxes of clothes. "Where ya from?" he asked enthusiastically, but his eyes dropped to my license plate before I could reply. "Oh, I'm sorry. I mean, I coulda just looked for myself, I mean. Come on, shit-forbrains." He knocked his head against the side of the van. "I can be a real dummy sometimes... You know what I mean?"

I didn't say anything. I was waiting for him to think of washing the front windshield, which was streaked with insect guts.

"So you're from Georgia, huh?" My license plates were from Georgia, it was true. I was not "from" Georgia in any of the usual meanings of that expression, since I hadn't been born there, and had lived there only a year (a pretty rotten one at that), but I didn't feel like explaining. "The Peach State, right?" he asked. Contrary to what it said on my license plate, South Carolina exceeded Georgia in the production of peaches, but I didn't really want to explain that either. "I never met anybody from Georgia before! I met folks from twenty-seven states—Oregon, New Mexico, Alaska, Hawaii, even that real tiny one..."

"Texas."

"Naw! You're just kiddin' me!"

"Rhode Island."

"Right," he said. "Rhode Island. But you're my first from Georgia, the Peach State."

"Well, I 'spect us crackers don't git around much anymore," I said in my best Southern accent, which wasn't very good.

The kid was ecstatic, grinning and bobbing his head. "Crackers, Georgia crackers! I hearda them! I hearda them on the television..."

I smiled back at him. Suddenly I knew what would happen next and watched as his eyes dropped again to my license plate. The smile drooped from his face. His mouth hung open like a dog's. What he was looking at was the county-designation sticker on my plate. Georgia required that every license bear the name of the county of residence, and as it happened, I'd been living in White County. "Is that...? Oh jeez. Are there other licenses that say... you know..."

"Colored? Sho 'nough, son. How else ya think we gonna recognize the darkies when they're in their cars at night?" Gum would have been proud of me that night.

I had hoped to make it across Iowa under cover of darkness so that I wouldn't have to look at the state in the light of day, but at three in the morning I noticed that the engine temperature was beginning to creep up toward the red line. God was getting back at me through my car. I'd felt nothing driving away from that poor disillusioned gas-station attendant—no humor, no remorse. My radiator started to boil at four A.M., and I pulled into the first rest area, parking between two tractor-trailer rigs in the hope that their great bulks, like Wall Street, would shield me from the hot morning sun. It was as dark as a canyon in there when I shut off the headlights.

First cousin to meanness is fear because meanness so narrowly defines the range of human decency: mercy, compassion, the kindness of strangers, all the usual virtues. That night I shut all the windows and locked all the doors and stretched out on the backseat with a hunting knife close at hand. Here I was at a rest area on the major interstate artery of the mid-Midwest, the heartland both actually and metaphorically of America, terrified of what might be hiding in the amber waves of grain. Ours is a violent country. Charles Manson might have been paroled since the last time I'd read a newspaper. And even if he hadn't been, there were thousands of others of Charlie's bent in our great land (the center of which was my rest stop in Iowa), and when the latest backwoods fiend came slouching down from his hideout in our purple mountains majesty, his eyes purple, too, from close reading of the Old Testament, waving his double-bladed axe of divine retribution (known as a "Maine axe," I sounded it out myself) and arriving first at the bumper of my sinful van, I knew I could count on no help from my neighbors, these teamsters, sleeping their soundless Nebutal sleep.

I fell asleep sooner than expected and awoke drenched in sweat. The truckers were gone, and the sun beat down scornfully on my shut-in van, making it a hothouse. I felt like a delicate flower, an orchid, my petals wilted and stuck to the plastic seat. My first thought was a shower. My second, human companionship. I decided to stop at Aaron's farm just outside of Omaha. Aaron was one of my sister's best old beaux. Les might even be stopping there herself. I didn't have Aaron's phone number, but I knew how to reach him if I arrived in Omaha between nine and five, Monday through Friday. I could look him up in the telephone directory, under "U.S. Govt., FBI."

I made it to Omaha late in the day because the van had started overheating again and I'd had to rest it through the hottest hours of the afternoon. A receptionist answered the phone: "Six six three, six six six three."

"I'd like to speak to Aaron Mendel, please."

"May I ask who's calling, please?"

I hesitated for a second, debating whether to play it straight or coy. "Tell him I'm a close associate of 'the Magpie,'" I finally said.

"If you'll hold, I'll check to see whether we have an Aaron Mendel working here," the receptionist said drily.

I didn't have to hold for long. "Leslie?" Aaron asked. "Is that you, Leslie?"

"No, but you're close. It's Jeremy."

"Well, Jeremy. How are you? *Where* are you? Is Leslie there with you?"

"No, sorry. I'm right here in downtown Omaha. Nebraska. Les ought to be around here somewhere, in the Midwest at least. I mean, she's driving across the country right now and she's a few days out, about the same as me. I thought she might have stopped at your place for a day or so . . ."

"No." He sounded disappointed.

"Oh well, she might have missed you then. Maybe she called and you weren't home."

Aaron's voice brightened at the suggestion. "Maybe. You almost missed me, too. I was just about to leave for the day."

"Then I was lucky, I suppose. I don't have the number at your farm."

"That old place? Didn't Leslie tell you? I'm not living out there anymore. I bought a condo here in town."

"A condo."

"You know, a condominium. I got sick of all those mangy chickens and goats."

I tried to check the disappointment in my voice. "You sold the farm?"

"No, not exactly. I still hold the deed for tax purposes, but I've got a tenant farmer now, and I lease out the acreage he can't handle to some other people in the area."

"Sharecroppers, that's nice," I said as mildly as I could. "Listen, Aaron, I thought maybe we could meet for a drink or something. I'm just passing through town."

"You mean you won't be staying the night?"

I wondered if the tone I heard in his voice was relief or disappointment or some doublethink version of the two. "No, I'm on a very strict night-driving schedule designed to spare my motor and break my neck, but if I could impose on you for a shower..."

"Sure thing, sport. Come on over to my place. I'm leaving the office now."

Aaron's directions were infallable, an ability I've always connected with a person's capacity for objectivity, his surefooted observation of the world. Aaron lived in a rabbit warren of rustic beachfront dwellings that backed up to the riverbank east of town. He came to the door looking younger and trimmer than I'd ever seen him, this in spite of the salt making headway against the pepper in his hair. We shook hands manfully and then grinned at each other and hugged. I realized that Aaron and I had never been together without Les around. I felt shy, doubly so since I stood there in the doorway clutching at my change of clothes, my small but insistent bundle of neediness. "You look great, Aaron. You've really been keeping in shape," I said, thrusting a bottle of Scotch, which I'd picked up on the way over, into his hands.

"Thanks," he said with a pardonable vanity in the lift of his chin. "I jog, play a little racquetball, and squash of course. I try to keep fit." He opened the paper bag just enough to peek at the label, then twisted it shut again. "A drink? Scotch all right, I suppose?"

"Terrific."

"Please, sit down," he said, motioning toward a sunken living

room and a sofa that didn't even reach to my knees. Aaron fetched
ice from the kitchen, returning without the bottle that I'd brought.
He poured the drinks at a little fold-out bar, which was really an
antique secretary converted to contemporary use. Handing me a
glass and then sitting down himself, he said, "Tell me all about your
sister first."

My antenna tingled. Les and I had always had an unspoken pact
to clam up entirely whenever someone questioned one of us too
closely about the other one; solidarity had been our only defense
against Sunshine and Fog. "Les is just fine," I said finally. "She's
quit smoking, you know. And she's been swimming a lot. Les has
really got her act together, I think."

Each of us sipped warily. "Tell me more," Aaron said.

"She *looks* great, very svelte. Of course, I only saw her briefly
before she left."

"Left for where?"

"California. Didn't she mention it?"

"Many times." Aaron glanced around the room, his hooded eyes
moving over every object, all of them possessions. "So, she's finally
doing it. Good for Leslie. And what about you?" he asked suddenly.
"Just bumming around?"

"No, I'm moving out to California, too. I'm starting graduate
school at Stanford this fall."

"Good school. Good area. Good for you." He looked me up
and down. "So you're moving out there together . . . doing it in
duplicate."

"Quadruplicate would be more like it, if you count Barbara and
Mat—"

"I always counted them."

"More than that if you count the animals."

"Oh, don't tell me your sister is still keeping that rabid dog—
what's his name?"

"Blazes Boylan."

"Jesus, what a liability." Aaron shook his head. "Speaking of
funny names, what about that black dude she was running around
with, the married one?"

"I'm not sure I know whom you mean."

"How many are there? I mean Sultan, the one who ran a night-club. You see, I do know his name."

"What about him?"

"Well, is your sister still running around with him?"

"You'd better ask my sister."

"She's not here, that's why I'm asking you."

"I don't know. I've been living in Georgia, remember? Not Tory Hole."

"Yeah? Even so, I thought you kept in touch . . . Come on, what are you afraid of? Afraid she'll yell at you if you divulge too much?"

"No."

"What is it with you two? There's always been something funny. You always were as thick as thieves."

We withdrew to our respective cocktails. "Mind if I take that shower now?" I asked after an interval.

"Sure thing, sport. First blue door to your right. Towels are hanging on the wall."

Even the bathroom was decorated. All the fittings were brass. The sink had been fashioned out of an old spittoon. The mirror looked like it had once done service as a porthole on a sailing ship. I tried to remember when Les had last come out here to visit, sometime recently? She might have used this bathroom, stripped off her clothes and looked at herself in this same mirror, just as I was doing now. Our bodies were almost the same—long arms, long legs—except for her extra padding here and there and the differences in our plumbing fixtures. Les might have stood right where I was standing and touched herself as I was, except she wouldn't have had to strip in the bathroom. She'd have used the bedroom. What had she ever seen in this man?

Coming out of the shower, I saw that Aaron had changed into fresh clothes, too—painter pants and an aloha shirt, as was fashionable at the time. He'd already poured us two more drinks. "Short ones. Then we're going out. I know a little place, right around the corner. We can talk there." He seemed excited, pacing the room.

"A restaurant?" I asked, worrying about the expense, but Aaron had already ducked into the bathroom.

On the way out the door, Aaron laid the bottle I'd brought, still in its twisted paper bag, on top of my bundle of dirty clothes. "Listen, why don't you just hold onto this? It was nice of you to bring it, but it's your brand, not mine."

"I don't have a brand," I said.

Aaron's little place had a bar decorated as a fisherman's shack with nets and buoys hanging like great cobwebs from the walls and ceiling, supported by old posts and beams that still showed the stains where the rusty nails had been extracted. The bartenders wore striped T-shirts like French sailors, and the cocktail waitresses looked a little like London fishmongers, except they smelled of perfume and were wearing hose. Around the bar was a cluster of men and women dressed like Aaron or in the female equivalent, halters and tank tops. Taken together, they looked like groupers, working their lips underwater and slowly sculling with their tails and fins. Two steps down from the bar was a dance floor where strobe lights pulsed throbbingly. The name of the place was Fisherman's Wharf.

"What is this, a single's bar?" I asked dumbly.

"Something like that. Maybe you'll be good for my luck."

"I don't want to . . . pick anyone up."

"Relax. There's nothing to be afraid of. It might be good for you to get your line wet."

That expression stopped me. I had to smile. I hadn't heard it in years. "I don't think you understand—" I began, but Aaron was way ahead of me, pushing through the crowd. "Aaron? Aaron?" I finally caught up with him at the bar. "You don't understand. I don't want to get laid, I want to get *out of* Nebraska tonight."

The crowd surged around us. Aaron pretended not to hear me. "We can't talk here!" I screamed, then: "Strobe lights bring on epileptic fits, you know."

"What?"

"Strobe lights cause seizures." I mimed an epileptic fit, shaking my arms and shoulders, rolling my head to one side, sticking out my tongue and pretending to chew on it. "It's just a matter of hitting the right frequency."

"You're not an epileptic. Don't be such a nerd."

"Petit mal!" I screamed through the background noise. "How do you think I got out of the draft?"

Aaron stared into my eyes, examining my pupils, I supposed. "All right, sport. You win. We'll sit in the other room then, where it's quieter."

The other room was a screened-in porch where the air was fresher at least. We sat in captain's chairs at a table that had once seen duty as a wire spool and since been sanded and varnished to a high sheen—with marine varnish, no doubt. "Have a seat, relax, settle down. What are you afraid of?" Aaron repeated, positioning himself so that he was facing the female occupants at the next table. He spoke without looking at me. "Leslie told me you and your old lady were splitting up, right? So get your line wet. Go fish. Why not? A little adventure might be just the thing."

A little "adventure" in the company of one of my sister's boyfriends, along with the male camaraderie that went with it, was exactly what I was afraid of. It seemed downright incestuous to me. "Getting my line wet, as you put it, is exactly what's gotten me in trouble in the first place..."

Aaron didn't seem to hear me, though. His attention was concentrated on the cocktail waitress, who was tall and lithe and honey-haired and wore an orchid behind her ear. "Hi," she said. "What can I get you guys tonight?"

"Two Dewar's White Label, over easy," Aaron said. "You don't mind if I smell your flower, do you?" He was up before she could object. With his nose in the orchid, he then whispered in her ear. The cocktail waitress's expression didn't flicker. She just turned on her heel and walked away.

I wondered what Aaron had said in her ear. Whatever it was, it didn't seem to have worked. When she returned with the drinks, she stepped well back from the table before announcing the price. Aaron waved my money away and handed her a ten; she counted out the change, plunked it down on the table, and quickly swished away. Aaron was undaunted, though. "What do you say about those two?" he asked with a lift to his eyebrows, indicating the table next to ours. "Fish or fowl? Sturgeon or starling?"

"Or magpie?" I asked.

"No, no. That's a nickname. I'm talking generically now. Birds fly away, but fish take the bait and *swim around*, and *thrash*, if you know what I mean..."

"I'm afraid I do."

"So what do you say? Salmon or mackerel? Caviar or catfood?"

I glanced over. One of the young women was short, the other tall. One was dark, the other blond. One wore an orchid above her ear just like the waitress. She looked up at me and smiled. I looked away automatically. "They're kind of pretty, if that's what you mean."

"'Kind of pretty!'" Aaron repeated, loud enough for them to hear. "I think they're knock-outs! Foxy's not *nearly* good enough to describe these two ladies!" He finished his outburst with his arm extended and his gaze fixed on the two girls.

One giggled. The other scowled.

"Aaron, please..."

"Excuse me," he continued booming. "Pardon me, ladies. I wonder if you'd be kind enough to settle something for us. My friend here says you're both 'kind of pretty,' while I maintain that you're the cat's peejays. How would you describe yourselves?"

"Piss off," the scowling one said.

The giggling one smiled. "Kind of pretty," she said, dipping the orchid behind her ear, apologizing with that gesture to the world.

Aaron sighed and sat back in his chair. "All right, if you say so, then that's the way it is, I guess. Though I still say you underrate yourselves. What do you say? Can we at least buy you pretty ladies a drink?"

"Piss *off*, I said," the scowling one said. I thought I detected an English accent.

"Oh, are you from Australia, love?" Aaron asked, putting on an accent of his own. "Where *is* that bloody barmaid? I want to buy this Sheila a bloody drink." He waved to the cocktail waitress, who looked right through us.

The friendlier girl smiled at me and held up her full glass. "Aaron, they don't want another drink," I said. "Neither of them needs one yet."

"Well, I do. Do you *believe* the service around this place?"

"I'll go get them," I offered and dashed off toward the bar.

It was a relief to get away. The bar was less crowded than it had been when we first arrived. Our waitress was there at her station, making a point of not looking at me. "Dewar's over and a cup of coffee please," I said to the bartender.

"In a minute," he said irritably.

The fellow standing at the bar beside me turned in my direction and announced in an ominous tone, "Bad times are ahead between the sexes." I nodded and inched away. "I tell you it's going to be *rough times* for male-female relationships . . ." I moved a little farther away. The fellow was in his late twenties and looked a lot like Neil Diamond, except there was something wrong with one of his eyes. "You married?" he asked me.

"Separated."

"Then you know what I'm talking about. You know what I mean. Me and my old lady been together nine years, *nine fucking years* if you count our senior year in high school, and since we were living together, *practically living together* our whole senior year in high school, why the hell not count it?"

"Why the hell not?" I agreed pleasantly.

"Got any rug rats?"

It took me a moment. "No. No children."

"You're lucky. We got one. My old lady ran off and stuck *me* with the rug rat!"

"Where's your kid now?"

"I just got through telling you! Don't you listen? The kid's with *me!*" He thumped his chest with his thumb for emphasis. I noticed that one of his eyes seemed to be roaming, checking out the "ladies," while the other was angrily trained on me.

I had to look away. "I mean, where's your kid right now, this evening?"

He ignored the question. "We had this band. You know, this fucking *band...*"

"Oh?" I said, distracted by the sight of our waitress whispering to the bartender and pointing at me. "A rock-and-roll band?"

"Yeah. What'd ya think I meant, a rubber band?" He turned his head so that his other eye was momentarily glaring at me. "I'm a musician. I play lead. *She* played backup. She *used* to play backup, I mean. I'm not letting her play anything anymore..."

"Your rug rat, you mean?"

"My *old lady*. What the fuck's the matter with you, man? You mentally impaired or something? Anyway, you know what my old lady did? You know what my old lady *did to me?*"

"I wouldn't want to speculate."

"She split with the drummer, that's what she did. And you know what else?" He paused—rhetorically I thought—but then he didn't continue. I looked up at him finally only to see that both his eyes were wandering. "Guess."

"I don't want to guess," I said, looking desperately at the bartender for my drinks.

"You could never guess—not in a million years—so you know what I'll do? I'll tell you. The drummer was a *chick*. That's what else. My old lady run off with another *chick*, for christsake. Can you believe it? Isn't that *incredible?*"

"Bartender!" I said, motioning wildly.

"Dykes. Fucking dykes," my new friend concluded. "I tell you, man, this is war, the war between the sexes."

Returning with the drinks, I noticed that the scowling English girl had turned her chair completely around so that her back was toward our table. I felt a kinship with her. Sipping my coffee I thanked Aaron for the shower and the Scotch and said that I needed to get going if I expected to make Wyoming by daylight. He nodded. He didn't seem to care whether I decided to stay or go. He had his eye on the giggling girl with the modest self-image. A wise choice, I thought.

"Answer me one question before you go," Aaron said, glancing at me for a second before returning his gaze to the girl. "What does your sister have against me, anyway?"

"Against you? She doesn't have anything *against* you..."

"Sure she does. Come on, be straight with me for a minute. Is it because I look so... you know, Jewish?"

"Of course not, Aaron. Leslie isn't like that, not *at all*. You know that."

"Well," he said with a little snort. "I know she likes black all right... but that's something else again." I rose to go. "Did you know I asked her to marry me?" he continued. "Her and the kids, the whole shebang. Cats, that hound of the Baskervilles. And you know what she said, don't you? She shot me down."

"No, I didn't know that," I lied.

"Oh, she didn't even mention it? Happens all the time? Do me a favor, will you, sport? Just don't gloat."

"I'm not *gloating*. I just don't have the answers that you want."

"Kid me not. Just do me one more favor, if it's not too much trouble for you. Tell Leslie to give me a call."

I left then because I was afraid he might start to cry. Walking back to my car, though, I remembered another Aaron from three or four years before. As with Nixon, there was an old Aaron and a new Aaron, except the old version wasn't so bad. In the daytime, he'd been a public defender. The rest of the time, he was trying to write his dissertation on Rimbaud. Aaron's apartment was a seedy studio under rent control, just off Greenwich Avenue, heading east. He was burglarized like clockwork between the first and fifth of every month, but Aaron (the old Aaron) never seemed to mind. The burglars were nice enough to wait until he was out, and after the first few times, he hadn't much left to lose. Anyway, he'd explained, the burglars were probably junkies and therefore desperate. One time he came home to find the door forced and a quart of milk missing from his refrigerator. Nothing more. Another time, all they took were the Stouffer's frozen entrees from the freezer and few early Beatles albums, which were less of a loss than they would have been if the stereo hadn't been stolen a few months before. When he took this job with the Feds in

Omaha, Aaron had announced that he was buying a farm and "fixing" to raise chickens and goats. "For my karma, for balance," he'd explained. Then he'd asked Les to marry him. Over the years, he'd asked a number of times. Aaron wasn't such a bad sort, I decided, just a little modest in his self-appraisal. He could have settled for so much more.

Zigzagging vaguely west from Omaha, following the little roads that ran past cornfields, over cattle grates, and through sleeping towns, I eventually rejoined I-80, the main transcontinental drag. My plan was to cover the rest of Nebraska that night. After that, I thought I might veer north through Wyoming to the Grand Tetons, Yellowstone, and Gardiner, Montana. Gas was cheap. I had time and a credit card. Gardiner was the little town where another of my sister's old beaux, Pete Pardieu, had once spent a few years on a "ranch"—or so he'd told everyone. Les might be drawn in that direction, too. She'd always been curious about Gardiner, and she'd always been given to midnight whims, especially where men were involved. Driving through the night, I imagined the Dewar's profiles for the men in my sister's life:

Aaron Mendel (beau): Occupation: Fed. Hobbies: Keeping fit, picking up girls. Most Notable Achievement: Growing up the only son of a blind, widowed, orthodox rabbi and learning to swim in the mainstream. Last Book Read: *Fear of Flying*, by Erica Jong. Favorite Scotch: Dewar's White Label.

Jay Gladden, aka "Bluejay" (number-two beau): Occupation: Photographer. Hobbies: Drinking, playing darts (East Coast Championship Runner-Up, 1969, 1972). Most Notable Achievement: Delaying the onset of alcoholism until age thirty-nine by drinking only beer. Last Book Read: *Under the Volcano*, by Malcolm Lowry (Leslie made him read it). Favorite Scotch: Ballantine Ale.

Dudley Dumas, aka "Do-Right" (black beau): Occupation: Member, Black Panther Party. Hobbies: Staying alive and out of jail in spite of membership in Black Panther Party. Most Notable Achievement: See "Hobbies" (above). Last Book Read: *The Autobiography of Malcolm* X (chapters 1–3). Favorite Scotch: Southern Comfort.

James Johnson, aka Sultan, aka Abdul X (married black beau): Occupation: Night Club owner. Hobbies: Having an affair with my sister, being nice to her kids. Most Notable Achievement: Loving my sister in spite of her white skin. Last and Only Book Read: The Koran. Favorite Scotch: Nehi Orange.

Hank Jakes (ex-husband, father of her children): Occupation: Self-Made Man. Hobbies: Self-Made Man. Most Notable Achievement: Self-Made Man. Last Book Read: *How to Win Friends and Influence People,* by Dale Carnegie (in 1959). Favorite Scotch: A can of Bud.

Pete Pardieu (first lover): Last Known Occupation: Gigolo in Miami Beach. Hobbies: Small-time extortion, roller disco. Most Notable Achievement: Giving my sister crabs at the same time he popped her cherry. Last Book Read: *Boys in Bondage,* author anonymous. Favorite Scotch: Someone else's.

Frank Morgan, aka "Fog" (father): Occupation: Stockbroker. Hobbies: Painting the garage. Most Notable Achievement: Lifetime of loyalty to a heartless corporation. Last Book Read: *How To Prepare Your 1973 Federal Income Tax Return.* Favorite Scotch: the one with the clipper ship on it.

Bill Cannon, aka "Papa" (grandfather): Occupation: Salesman (retired). Hobbies: Driving without his glasses, putting a nickel on the nags. Most Notable Achievement: Living a long and harmless life. Last Book Read: *The Last of the Mohicans,* by James Fenimore Cooper. Favorite Scotch: Old Crow.

four

The weather was mild when we boarded the jetliner in August 1959. The sun was shining but the breeze was cool, blowing out of the west and over the hills, right through the fog before it reached the airport. Our natural air conditioning, columnist Herb Caen was already calling it in 1959. I was barely ten years old and had never set foot in an airplane, much less a jet. I remember feeling a hot-air kind of vacancy, only amplified by the steady wind bending the long dry grass, which suddenly flattened when a plane came gliding by, trailing a hurricane of hot air and a whine so high I wanted to be a dog so that I could howl. Fog was sitting right beside me, though. He'd dressed me up that morning in a jacket and tie. I knew he wouldn't tolerate any son of his baying at the incoming flights. And I wanted to please him, naturally.

As a younger child, I was allowed to sit by the window, and I stared first at the blond hills topped with the cresting wave of fog that looked like Kookie's hairstyle on the television program "77 Sunset Strip." "There are jackrabbits living between the runways," my father said.

I looked down at the grassy strips. "Don't they get run over by the airplanes?"

"They do sometimes. But rabbits multiply, and their only natural enemies out here at the airport are the planes. It's Malthusian. If the one thing doesn't get them, then the other will. There's only just so much for rabbits to eat, you see. So if the planes didn't squash a couple of rabbits every day, then some of them would starve. You wouldn't want them to starve, would you?"

"I guess not," I said warily. I understood only a little of what my father was telling me and even that reminded me inappropriately of my hamster, Henry the Eighth, who was hidden under my seat, but I knew better than to ask my father any stupid questions. Instead I prodded Henry's wicker basket with my shoe and was reassured to hear him react with a flurry of frantic rustling. Henry was my eighth hamster because of attrition from such natural causes as gnawing on electrical appliances, falling from great heights (table tops), drowning in bath water, and failing hearts due to obsessive running around on the rodent wheel. "Dad, if you were a rabbit, which would you rather, starving to death or getting smooshed by a jet plane?"

Usually Fog had little patience with this kind of speculation, but he was in a good mood today. The brokerage firm was promoting him to the home warren in New York. "Oh, I'd much rather take my chances with the planes than just sit around in my hole waiting to starve."

"Me too, Dad," I agreed in my best Beaver Cleaver voice, although afterward, watching the rabbits zigzagging across the tarmac and scurrying for cover whenever a plane whined by, I wasn't so sure.

Flying from west to east, one passes directly into night with no sense of gathering dusk or gentle waning of the evening light. One second I was watching the sun glinting off Missouri lakes like so many new pennies; the next, darkness slammed down on us like a manhole cover and the stewardess brought around dinner on a tray.

Later, the world below us began to light up again with small glittering dots and the dots began to congeal into Milky Ways along the Eastern Seaboard, but even before that, Sunshine began to hum. At first we could hardly hear her. Then slowly we recognized the tune. She was humming "California, Here I Come." "I know, it's absolutely ridiculous!" she said gaily. "But I can't help it, I can't get

it out of my mind! Here we are flying *east*—you see, dear, I do
realize what direction we're going—*away* from San Francisco, toward
New York, and I'm sitting here singing 'Open up your pearly gates'—
no, I mean, 'golden gates—'cause California, here I come!'" She
giggled. "I can't get that tune out of my mind! Maybe I should try
another song, hair of the dog that bit me . . . That always seems to
work for you, dear. What do you think?" She turned to Fog, who
was reading *Sports Illustrated* and trying to pretend he'd never seen
this woman before. "Shall I try 'I Left My Heart in San Francisco'?"

"No," he said in a harsh whisper. "Anything but that—"

Heedless in her excitement, Sunshine broke into song. "'I left
my heart—in San Francisco—high on a hill—it calls to me. Where
all the little cablecars—go halfway to the stars . . .' How am I doing,
gang? Isn't that the way it goes?"

"You know I can't stand Tony Bennett!" Fog hissed through
clenched teeth.

"Oh. I forgot. I'm sorry, dear. We'll just sing the other one then.
Come on," she suggested to Les and me. "California, here I come—
right back where I started from . . . !'"

The airplane began its descent. We buckled our seatbelts, then
I remember a sinking sensation as the glittering lights and big black
spaces and my stomach rose up to meet us. Fog turned his back on
us. He probably would have liked to change his seat, but Sunshine
and Les and I didn't care as we giggled and sang our way down to
the ground at Idlewild Airport. We were so giddy as we taxied to
the gate that we almost forgot to grab my hamster in his basket
under the seat.

"Henry!" Sunshine said when we were nearly to the exit door.
We rushed back down the aisle to retrieve him. "Henry!" He scurried
around in his basket by way of reply. "We can't forget Henry, he's
irreplaceable! Who wants a Henry the *Ninth?*" she was saying as
we stepped off the airplane, where temperature and moisture and
air pressure had all been delicately balanced and controlled to sim-
ulate California, into the heat and humidity of August in New York.

• • •

Much attention has been paid to the shock of movement from warmth into sudden cold and its effect on chafing dishes. Also to the shock of being yanked headlong into the delivery room after knowing only that perfect habitat, the womb. But little thought is given to backward movement, travel from, say, the cool of the evening, skimming across the land in a convertible with the wind blowing through your hair, into the fetid atmosphere of a Turkish bath that hasn't been cleaned in thirty years, teeming with immigrant peoples like a big jar full of fruit flies, and without even the benefit of a midwestern transition.

The world closed in around us. The very air weighed us down. I remember that both the temperature and the humidity stood poised near the stasis point, ninety-nine, and it was already eleven at night when we landed in New York. We were dripping—whether from sweat or condensation we couldn't tell—before we reached the gate. The gates at Idlewild were still wooden then, long and low like cattle chutes and crammed shoulder-to-shoulder with loud, boisterous people who might as well have been speaking cow for all I could understand. They were speaking Spanish, Les told me. They were from Puerto Rico, Fog said. Yet they fit right into the scene. It was our little planeload of arrivals from the city by the bay that stuck out like so many sore white thumbs, gazing around helplessly. Most of the people around us at the gate appeared to be arguing. Most of them were also holding babies, who cried, and shaking off bigger children, who clutched and whined. I remember going back for my hamster. I remember the shock of heat and humidity and the herd of fervid humanity. But as though caught in a current, I was swept along and remembered nothing after that until I woke up the next morning staring at a radiator in the Plaza Hotel.

It's not easy for me to justify the magnitude of the shock we sustained. I for one had never seen a radiator before. As California kids, neither Les nor I had been good readers, which is one way to know the world. Nor had television prepared us for this sudden change. Admittedly, it wasn't a tragic shock—but still the reason for our initial trauma has always eluded me, as I go over and over

Dean Crawford

the mild and meager details. Here we are singing "So open up your golden gates, 'cause California, here I come!" as we land in New York. We step off the plane still worrying about a pet hamster and find ourselves suddenly in the Amazon. Then just as suddenly, we're whisked off to Manhattan and wake up the next morning to the hoot of taxicabs seventeen stories below our fine old twelve-pane window in a hotel with a better sense of self than any of us might ever hope to have ourselves. Although in time I would see Venice, Paris, and Rome, the ancient ruins of Stonehenge, and a lot of old castles on the Rhine, when I think of the "Old World," I'll always be reminded first of the radiator at the Plaza Hotel.

The next day Les and I took a walk in Central Park and saw a decrepit old man scrounging through one of the wire trash bins. Like other first-timers to New York, we wondered what the poor man had lost in there. Later, while Sunshine was shopping, Fog took us out to "someplace famous" for lunch: Horn & Hardart. Then we caught the afternoon local out to Tory Hole. Fog thought we might prefer the slower, scenic route, stopping in every hamlet and bedroom town, getting what he called "our bearings" and "the lay of the land." The train was old and rattled. Probably it had been chosen for the local run because it couldn't go any faster than that. In our carriage alone, I counted nineteen cracked or shattered windows, each bearing a printed sticker that read: THIS WINDOW WAS DAMAGED BY VANDALISM.

When we arrived at our new house, I found the same sticker on a broken window in the garage. Our new house was a hundred years old and looked every day of it. The bedrooms were designed for little people (Fog explained that people were considerably smaller in the century before), and there were other, even tinier rooms at whose function we could only wonder. In fact, for a child the house was full of wonders: walled-up chimneys, storage closets that turned into tunnels as they went back under the eaves and narrowed like a wedge, great rumbling noises that rolled across the ceiling and made the whole house shudder. In my bedroom the wallpaper was peeling, layer upon layer back to before the Civil War, and lying awake at night I would uncover living history with my fingernail.

But if the house was a wonder for Leslie and me, it was a nightmare for Sunshine and Fog. Fog started painting as soon as we moved in, and he didn't stop until we moved. The house was like an old person plagued by certain persistent ailments and a great many more complaints. The garage, for instance, soaked up groundwater like a dry sponge, and the paint peeled almost as fast as Fog could slap it on. And on the inside, the house seemed even more mysteriously alive. Sunshine regarded it as "dirty," like an orphan child with some serious complexion problems. "This house has dirt in every *pore!*" she repeated as she stalked from room to room. We were never happy in that house.

Like an omen, Henry the Eighth died the day we moved in. It seemed he'd caught a cold from the shock of moving suddenly from temperate California to equatorial New York. "Pneumonia," the vet said ominously, herding him back from the edge of the treatment table with a tongue depressor. "It's gone into his lungs." We all watched as the vet gave Henry an injection and placed him back in his cage to spin like a windup toy. Henry ran around and around for thirty seconds like so much accelerated hamster film, then he fell over, twitched, and died. "Heart failure," the vet concluded in the same even tone, dropping my hamster into one of the cardboard boxes of various sizes he kept close at hand. "I'm sorry, son, but there was nothing we could do to save him."

I buried Henry in the backyard beneath the forked elm tree. Then I climbed up into a low branch and brooded about English history. There had never been a Henry the Ninth. After an hour or so, Sunshine came out and stood beneath my branch. "We'll get you another hamster, I promise," she said.

"There aren't any more Henrys."

"We'll call him Hotspur then," she offered.

"I don't want another hamster," I said inconsolably. "You're standing on Henry the Last."

Sunshine shrugged and went back into the house, and after a while Les came out, jingling the car keys. She'd gotten her license only a few weeks before. "Let's go for a ride," she suggested. "Let's cruise the strip."

"You're standing on King Henry the Eighth," I said, even though she was standing in an entirely different spot than my mother when I accused her.

"Sorry there, 'Enery, Your Highness, Lowness." Les moved two steps away, until she was standing on top of Henry's actual grave. "Come on, Jeremy. You're not really that sad about Henry, are you? You didn't cry when Henry the Second chewed through a wire and blew out his transistors, and he was very sweet. Henry the Eighth was the meanest of *all* your hamsters. He was probably the meanest hamster I've ever *seen*. I'm not even sure he wasn't a she. Come on, didn't he bite you almost every day of his life? Tell the truth now." Les was right. Henry had chomped great bloody divots out of my fingers whenever I'd reached into his cage. "Dust to dust, Jeremy. Let's go for a ride. We can put the top down..." she coaxed. I slowly climbed down from the tree.

We had a red convertible that we'd prevailed on Fog to buy as a consolation prize for leaving California. Les fluttered her foot on the accelerator pedal, keeping time with Chuck Berry on the radio. She pulled out a pack of cigarettes—the first I'd ever seen her smoke. In California Les had gone to a convent school, where they didn't even allow the girls to wear hose. Les explained that these were the mildest cigarettes on the market: Springs. Their slogan was "Just a breath of fresh air!" Reluctantly, Les allowed me to light her cigarette. "But you have to promise first, you won't start smoking till you're at least eighteen. Promise?" I was ten. I promised.

We drove slowly through downtown Tory Hole. All the stores looked alike to me, all from the century before. The latest controversy raging before the zoning board was whether to allow Howard Johnson's to build a restaurant with an orange roof. Even the local moviehouse called itself a "playhouse," implying something very different to me, and it sported no marquee.

"I'll show you the Tory Hole beaches. The good beach and the bad one," Les offered. The first beach she showed me was on an open bay. Its bathhouse was large and clean and new without being noticeably new or in any way ostentatious. It blended tastefully into the sand, which was also a soft shade of white and perfectly rock-free. The lifeguards were all blond. Most of the bathers were also blond, and those that weren't were at least tall and good-looking. Even the overweight mothers with little skirts on their bathing suits looked less fat than statuesque. The place reminded me of L.A. and its soulless winning baseball team, the Dodgers, which I hated as only a Giants fan can.

The other beach looked much older, set in a narrow harbor that was at that moment almost devoid of water since it was low tide. There were slabs of mud between the water and the shore. It smelled bad. The bathhouse and concession were painted an army-surplus shade of green. Even the sand looked second-rate, coarse and clumped like brown sugar and containing all the rocks from the other beach plus its own.

"What do you say?" Les asked after we'd seen them both. "Which beach do you like better?"

"This one. I feel sorry for it."

"Yeah, me too. This is the bad beach. That other one was where the 'in' crowd goes, except the best beaches of all are the country club beaches and the private beaches behind people's houses—mansions, I mean. That's where the *really* 'in' crowd goes. They've got sand that's so white they have to give you special glasses to look at it, like a three-D movie. Harriet says they have special cleaning people who come in and bleach it every night. You don't believe me, do you? But it's true. That's the real reason they don't allow Negroes to join the country clubs. They're afraid they'll leave black marks all over the sand just from walking on it..."

We laughed about the hierarchy of beaches, not yet aware that everything in Tory Hole was hierarchial: the churches, schools, country clubs, and grocery stores. Not to mention accents, not to mention cars. George III might as well have won the war. In fact, there really was a Tory Hole, a little cave where the royalists had ducked in whenever the revolutionaries were passing through town. It looked something like a primitive root cellar, and reminded me, as a newcomer right off the plane, of the holes that the jackrabbits hopped into whenever a jet plane came screaming down the airport runway. Tory Hole was perfectly Malthusian. Watching the commuters, morning and night, I could see only one kind of adult male. He wore a fedora and charcoal-gray suit and buried his nose in the financial section while riding the train daily to and from New York, where he had to dash and zigzag across Madison and Lexington and Wall, trying not to get smooshed by a cab or a member of the board. Surely Thomas Malthus could have described the rules of the world on which the wealth of this town was predicated, above which Tory Hole was erected like a village built on stilts. On its way into Grand Central, the commuter train passed through some of the worst slums in the New World, but the passengers didn't see them from behind their uplifted copies of the *New York Times* and the *Wall Street Journal*, like so many morning- and afternoon-blooming plants. Tory Hole was a bedroom town for the New York commercial class, yet it remained more loyalist to a strict interpretation of the term "New England" than any little township in New Hampshire or Vermont. It was English without the English love of eccentricity. It was Dickensian in its snobberies and pretensions, Jane Austerian in its narrow expectations, and—though we might laugh at the elaborate stratifications of the society that prevailed, it was the only game in town.

The local bully's name was Tobias. During the first week of school, he cornered me beside a hedgerow and forced me to the ground. Then he sat on my chest, pinning my shoulders into the damp earth with his knees. Tobias was two years older, so he must have been about twelve at the time, but he seemed gigantic looming over me, bouncing on my stomach. I could barely catch my breath. I felt sure that any moment he was going to dribble spit on my face, stuff worms in my mouth, or rub mud into my nose, but instead he leaned way over and demanded, "What does your father do?"

"Lots of things..."

"For a living, stupid. What kinda job does he have?"

"He works in a business."

"*Course* he works in a business, everybody's father does that! What kinda business? What's he president of?"

"My father's not president of anything."

"All right, *vice* president then!"

I was starting to cry, more for my father than for myself. "My father's not vice president of anything."

"You're lying!"

"No, I'm not!" I screamed back, doubly offended since by my religion he'd just accused me of a sin. "Let me up now! You'd better let me up!"

"What's my name?" he demanded with fresh resentment. I tried to struggle out of the question, but he pressed me even tighter to the ground by putting his weight on his knees. "I'll let you up if you tell me my name."

I tried to doublethink the question. What would I want to be called if my name were Tobias? "Toby?"

"Wrong!" he screamed, and tears sprang to his eyes. "My name is Tobias, don't call me nothing else!"

Sometimes when I read John Cheever, or when nostalgia bites, I can recall a fondness for certain moments in Tory Hole—the smell of burning leaves in the autumn air, the branches growing together to form a green leafy tunnel of Long Neck Point Road, the clear musical note reverberating under a frozen pond as a child tries bashing a hole in the ice with a stick. But when I think of Leslie, I feel only bitterness for the town. Like the Catholic Church and our parents, Tory Hole was never so hard on me as it was on my sister. We moved there when I was still young enough to make friends. I had more of what we think of as "the advantages"—good schools, a clear complexion, engraved invitations to the debutante balls—and if I'd chosen to, I could have gotten myself a gray suit and a fedora and ridden the commuter trains into New York. I probably wouldn't have proven any good at business, but success is not the point here. I had the option to reject.

Les never was accepted by the rich kids or any other kind of "in" kids in Tory Hole. Nor did she get the chance to go to a boarding school, as I did. Maybe if she'd been born on Nob Hill and spent her summers in the south of France, maybe then she might have had the option in her hands. And Les would have certainly rejected the Tory Hole option. My sister was a born rejecter of everything and everyone except the downtrodden and the despised, whom she passionately embraced. Nevertheless, the essential thing, the thing we can never quite compensate for later in life, is being offered the local option while we're still in high school, whether or not our rebellion is forgone.

Les made what friends she could from the leftovers, and possibly her friends were more interesting for being the relative dregs of Tory Hole High School. There was Harriet, who had hair the color of a fire engine and wore it teased into a beehive on top of her head. Harriet's skin was so fair that she tanned only when her freckles started to merge, and she liked to keep people posted on their progress toward that end. She used to lie all day on the beach getting a terrible sunburn and rattling on and on in a flat tone, making fun of her body. "Will you look at that? Varicose veins, and I'm only sixteen. Can you imagine what my legs are gonna look like at forty? I'll be walking around on two road maps of New Jersey." You could listen to Harriet or not, it didn't seem to matter.

Les's closest friend was Maria Bertolli (no relative to the olive oil). Not that it would have done Maria a lot of good if she had been heiress to an Italian canned-goods fortune. In a town where the realtors were careful never even to show a house to a Jew or a black, it was bad enough to be Irish-Catholic, let alone a wop. No doubt Maria had it rough long before we moved to Tory Hole. Her father was a policeman. Her oldest brother lived at home and raised pigeons, even though he was almost thirty. Until my sister came, none of the kids from "nicer" families would even talk to her. Maria worshiped and fawned over Leslie. She came over all the time. We thought Maria couldn't be more harmless, when in fact she was nurturing a foul resentment like a boil or a secret abscessed sore. Maria would go on to a life of heavy breeding and pasta dishes, interrupted only by a remarkably treacherous attempt to steal my sister's husband in 1968, but at this time she was just sweet Maria who tagged after Leslie, never letting her alone.

Of my sister's Tory Hole boyfriends, I knew only Pete Pardieu, and I didn't meet him many times. Pete rode a motorcycle, which would have been reason enough for Fog to hate him even if he hadn't worn a leather jacket with diagonal zippers, combed his hair into a ducktail, and "acted smart" when he came to the door. Actually, Pete didn't come to the door but once or twice before Les was forbidden to see him anymore. After that, she had to start arranging their dates under cover of CYO meetings or nights spent at Maria's. They met in dark places—theaters, pizza parlors, and the beach after dark.

I was mainly interested in fishing for eels at that time. Maybe that was why I was kept in the dark; maybe not. But when Les suddenly stopped seeing Pete, then dropped out of college only two weeks after registration, came home, and a few months later eloped with some guy she hardly knew, I was aware that some currents moved her, even if I didn't understand at the time what they might be. Les, who'd always told me everything, would take years to tell me about her romance with Pete Pardieu, and by then I'd already know all about it from his little sister, Lucy.

Lucy Pardieu was more than my informant. She was my objective correlative, the closest I'd ever get to Les with Pete, besides being my own forbidden fruit. Their whole family was out of bounds after what Pete had done to Leslie—which was too horrible to go into but "You can take it from me, buster, I've got a good reason, so just steer clear of any and all Pardieus. Do I make myself thoroughly understood?"

It turned out that I was as forbidden for Lucy as she was for me, so it was almost biblically ordained that we'd get together. Kissing, petting, and tempted on to further things, we felt as if we were reenacting something, like *East of Eden*, which neither of us had read. Whether our heat was entirely our own or fanned by our fathers' disapproval or only the reflected glory of older siblings' fire didn't really matter. It was hot enough.

I was a lifeguard that summer at Longneck Point, which was the bad beach, and I remember this girl smiling at me for days before we met. I thought she was too young for me. Lucy was barely sixteen. I was seventeen, almost. "Aren't you Jeremy Morgan?" she finally asked me.

"That's right. Is there something I can do for you?"

"Your sister went out with my brother, Pete."

"Pete Pardieu?"

"Par-doo," she corrected me. Then she stuck out her hand. "My name's Lucy. Glad to meet you."

"Lucy," I repeated, trying to look her in the eye. She was sitting on the sand with her long legs stretched out in front of her. Lucy wore a two-piece bathing suit of normal proportions, but her body was so long that the suit seemed smaller in comparison. Why hadn't I noticed her before? "You know, in French your name would be pronounced as Par-dieu..."

"Our name is Par-doo."

"Do you know what it means?"

"No. You tell me what it means," she said flirtatiously.

"'By God.' That's what it means, 'By God.' It's an oath, like 'Oh, my God,' 'Christ on a crutch,' or '*mon dieu*.' I read it in *The Three Musketeers*."

"That's very interesting," she said politely. "How is your sister doing?"

"Fine. She's married now. She has a little girl. She's living in L.A."

"How old's her little girl?"

I had to count. "Two. Going on three." Lucy nodded. "Did you ever meet my sister?" I asked her.

"Nope, but I sure heard enough..."

"What did you hear?"

Lucy smiled and turned over on her towel. "Same stuff you heard. Plus what Pete told me, you know, that she was neat and everything. They were pretty close, for a while there."

I may have been a shy teenager, but I wasn't retarded. Even then I had a yen for forward women, and Lucy was alternately forward and demure. Some nights she was already waiting by the mailbox when I pulled up in front of her house. Then she'd slip into the car and say, "Let's go. Squeal it. Let's go somewhere and park." Other times Lucy would be prim, though, and hardly say a word all evening. Or she'd ask me formal questions, about my courses and my school. I never questioned her. It was obvious that she was miserable at home.

The Pardieus had five children, all of them beautiful, all of them wild. The family was French-Canadian, a people who seemed to me violent, vulgar, and terribly exciting, at least where I saw them in the narrow social alleys of Tory Hole. Papa Pardieu was an alcoholic. Mama Pardieu was a walking victim's profile. Their oldest daughter became a call girl and died of a drug overdose long before that came into style. The other two girls, Isabelle and Lucille, made hasty marriages while they were still in their teens, and the boys found their own ways to escape. Pete cut a romantic figure, working as a ranch hand and a model and ending up as one of those handsome, well-dressed young men familiar to the hotels in Miami Beach but with no visible means of support. His younger brother, Michael, shot a liquor-store clerk in the course of a robbery and was already serving a longish sentence for murder by the time he was eighteen. After scandals like these, the Pardieu family never had a chance in Tory Hole—not that they'd had one before. Why didn't they just move? This question must have been asked again and again by the town fathers at informal sessions of the zoning board, the planning board, the school board, and the selection committee meetings of the country clubs. "We've kept out the Jews and the Negroes, how could we have overlooked these trashy French-Canucks?" "Don't you remember, Teddy dear? It was because of the *Hugo*nauts and Bumpy Worthington's great-grandfather Dupis..."

Lucy wasn't willing to talk about her family, so I didn't talk about mine. We spoke vaguely about our older siblings, Les and Pete, wondering where they hung out on their dates, what songs they listened to, whether they drank beer, Ripple wine, or Southern Comfort, but more often I just blithered on ad nauseam about Deerfield, which I pretended to hate but loved to talk about, or translated words into Latin or French to impress her. I called her "Lapin." Lucy really did look like a rabbit in a coquettish way. Come hither, her beauty said, hitherer and hitherer. Her attraction was undiminished by her bunny-rabbit nose and skittish eyes.

If anything, the suggestion of fright only deepened Lucy's allure.

We went out the rest of the summer—out for pizza, to the movies, the drive-in, often just to the cemetery to park. Sometimes we gravitated down to the beach where we'd sit on the picnic tables under the trees, teasing each other sexually or just looking out from the darkness into the relative light. All the loose nuts of Tory Hole gravitated to our beach after dark, and if we were wearing dark clothes, we could watch them, invisible ourselves in the shadows under the trees.

I knew a few of the oddballs from the daylight hours I spent at the beach—Joe Conforte, who worked as a janitor and claimed to have a nephew in the Mafia, Mrs. O'Mara, the first selectman's mistress (retired), Manny, who ran the concession stand and was rumored to have an extra Y chromosome, and the guy in the blue Falcon, who drove down to the beach every night and never got out of his car. But Lucy knew them all. She knew which guys sniffed glue and how many grades they'd had to stay back in school. She pointed out the girls who'd gotten pregnant in junior high school. She even knew a lot of the cops, which ones would take a twenty in lieu of a traffic ticket and which ones spent their shifts trying to screw teenage girls.

"Why haven't you ever tried it with me?" she asked suddenly.

"Ever tried what? Bribery? Sniffing glue?"

"No. You know..." she said, blushing. "Ever tried to fuck me."

"Well..." I said, embarrassed. I thought *fuck* was a boys' word. "I don't know, but that's an oversight I can correct right now." I grabbed her playfully around the waist and started wrestling her back onto the picnic table.

"No, seriously..." she giggled, and I could see that she was serious. "I'm not saying I'd let you 'cause I wouldn't, I was just wondering why you never *tried*."

I left my arm around her waist, which seemed suddenly boyishly slender to me. "It's because you're so young. I'd feel as though I was taking advantage."

"We're the *same age*, Jeremy. We're both sixteen."

"I'll be seventeen any minute now."

"So?"

"So that makes me a year older, almost."

She counted on her fingers. "Nine months."

"All right, nine months then. Maybe that's the reason..."

"Boys don't have anything to worry about," she said sullenly.

We were silent then, gazing out from under the trees. I was annoyed. I realized that it was my role as a red-blooded American male to try to get laid whenever and wherever I could, except in a case where, say, my best buddy's honor was involved, but I didn't think I should have to talk about it, especially not with a girl. The fact was I was still a virgin, but I'd formed some definite ideas. Assuming that the girl and I were evenly matched, my game was to be all hands and rush the net (gently); hers was to hold the line (firmly). Lucy and I were hardly evenly matched, though. She was younger. Her family was poor. She didn't even know how to play tennis. I would have felt too guilty if we'd gone all the way, and guilt was one of my greatest fears of all.

"Do you mind if I ask you another question?" Lucy asked after a while.

"Shoot."

"You don't have to answer it if you don't want to."

"What's the question, Lapin?"

"Do I really look like a rabbit?"

I laughed. "A little, but only in the prettiest possible way."

"That's not my question. My question is, why don't you ever introduce me to any of your friends?"

That stopped me for a second. "How long have you been wondering that?"

"Oh, not very long. It just occurred to me, I guess. Never mind, though. It's not important. Let's just forget it, okay?"

"No, I don't mind answering it. The fact is, I really don't *have* any friends in Tory Hole, except for a guy named Malcolm who's away for the summer."

"Oh," she said quietly. "Away where?"

"He's in Italy."

"Is he Italian?"

"No, his family just has a place there—"

"You mean you have friends who go to Italy for summer vacation?"

"Just Malcolm. He's an old friend, and kind of a special case. Now it's my turn to ask a question. Why don't you ever let me come to the door when I pick you up for a date? Because I'm not presentable?"

"You know . . . It's because of your sister. And Pete."

"I know they went out together. Five or six years ago."

Lucy was silent, as though waiting for me to finish. Finally she asked, "What about *your* parents? What do they think?"

Now it was my turn to hesitate (again). I'd never told my parents that I was going out with Pete's younger sister, Lucy Pardieu. "They don't usually ask me who I'm going out with, and I don't usually tell them."

"I see."

"Do your parents know you're seeing me?"

"No." She smiled faintly. "They think I'm going out with a guy named Tony Marino, who's too shy to come to the door."

Maybe talking about good fortune really does tempt fate, or maybe my nerves were inflamed by the conversation and that was what made my skin break out, a condition noticed by my mother, a women with an uncanny ability to sniff out a secret. Whatever the reason, the evening of my next date with Lucy, Sunshine suddenly demanded to know the name of the girl I was seeing. I told her. Sunshine took a step backward and caught her breath, but I'd always known that my mother enjoyed a moment of melodrama. I thought little of it until a few minutes later when Fog came crashing down the stairs like a herd of buffalo. He was only halfway changed from the office, clad in wing-tip shoes, knee-high socks, and undershorts. "You are *not* going out on this date, and that's final! Do you read me, loud and clear? *Comprenez-vous?*" He yanked the telephone receiver up from its cradle and thrust it at me. "Now break that date! Call her!"

As a matter of principle, I refused.

Fog held his position on the stairs, where he could still look down on me. "Don't you principle me, twerp. I'll give you principles, I'll read you chapter and verse! Now I'm warning you for the last time, *call her!*"

"No, I won't. It would hurt her feelings."

"Christ on a crutch," he said through his teeth, waving the receiver in the air like club. "I don't believe this kid, I don't believe my ears!"

Sunshine stood behind him on the stairs, scowling over his shoulder. "Do you realize what that horrible Pardieu boy did to your sister? Do you have any idea how he . . . he . . . treated her?"

"No, Mother, I haven't the foggiest. No one has ever seen fit to tell me. I seem to be the last person in Tory Hole to know how he-he-he treated her. So why don't you just tell me?"

Sunshine narrowed her eyes at me, but didn't answer. "You just never mind about that!" Fog bellowed. "I won't have you talking this way to your mother. You'll show some respect around this house, or else you're not going out with anyone! Do you read me? Am I getting through to you, mister?"

"I can hear you, Dad."

"Then do as you're told and call the goddamned girl!"

We argued for almost an hour, right up to the time I had to leave to pick up Lucy, but Fog was fighting with one arm tied behind his back (and in his underwear). He couldn't prevent me from going out with Lucy without divulging what exactly Pete had done to Leslie, and he considered that a breach of family security.

So I kept my date and, shortly after that, went back to school, where I had what must be called a failure of nerve or principle or taste. I lost interest in Lucy Pardieu. Thus we win the battles and lose the war. I wrote to her once or twice, and she wrote back in big round script with circles over her *i*s, apologizing over and over again for her grammar and spelling, but I didn't call her over Thanksgiving, Christmas, or Easter. I thought I was in love with a girl from Miss Porter's named Biddy and I asked her, not Lucy, to the Senior Formal. She seemed the more appropriate choice.

• • •

The next summer I worked at Merrill Lynch, not at the beach. Fog had gotten me a job as a messenger in the office they'd just opened in Tory Hole. It was August before I got around to giving Lucy a call. Then we went out to a movie about a couple of suave diamond thieves in a Pygmalion situation. It was something Lucy had seen before, but wanted to see again. She seemed changed—more confident, more filled out, more cold. Neither of us had a very good time.

Then Malcolm, who'd come home for the last week of August in order to get ready for college, decided to throw a party while his parents were still in Italy, and I remembered Lucy's question of the summer before. I saw this as my chance to redeem myself, if only for when I looked in the mirror.

Malcolm greeted us at the door. He was dressed in an open silk shirt, a linen jacket, and white pants, and he was trying to grow a thin mustache. "Oscar Wilde, right?" I asked him.

"Why, yes," he said in a clipped, haughty tone. You would have had to know Malcolm to know that he was joking.

The house was large, the driveway lined with lindens, and the entrance flanked by lions carved in stone. Lucy was awed. I told her that I'd only used the front door once before in my life, but that information didn't seem to help her. "I wish I'd worn a dress," she said. She didn't speak more than another two words for the first hour we were there. A few couples danced (hardly moving their shoulders at all), but most of the guests just stood around drinking and talking about Saint Paul's, Choate, and Groton, Nantucket versus the Vineyard, and the Electric Circus, which was a discotheque on Saint Mark's Place. Lucy stood very close to me, looking more the frightened rabbit than I'd ever seen her before.

"Like to get a breath of fresh air?" I asked her after a while.

"Yes, please!" she whispered desperately. We took a bottle of champagne with us and walked out onto the lawn, which sloped gently down to the water. Malcolm's house was located on a little inlet called Winter Cove. The tide was full, a state I've always associated with true luxury, the excess of warm water promising something sumptuous and undeserved. Across the cove, we could see a house lit up like the Gatsby mansion and its lights playing over the water almost to our feet. "Now I know why you never asked me to any of your friends' parties," Lucy said.

"That's not fair. There weren't any parties, and these aren't my friends. This isn't my world. I don't even know these people, or only one or two of them..."

"Just Malcolm," she prompted me.

"That's right, just Malcolm. He's really the only friend I've got in this town, and he hasn't given a party since his birthday when he turned thirteen."

She shrugged. "Still, all this is Malcolm's. This house, this lawn... Just feel how thick the grass is. You know, I've got an uncle who's a professional gardener. He *mows* this kind of lawn."

We sat down together on the lawn. "You've got to remember this is really Malcolm's parents' place, not his. They're pretty old and stuffy, but nice, for rich people, I mean. I always felt like Horatio Alger in their house."

"Who's that?"

"Just a guy who wrote boys' stories. Rags to riches, the poor boy who makes good."

"*You're* not poor," she said contemptuously.

"It's all relative—"

"Balls. Give me a swig of that, will you?" Lucy leaned back, tilted up the bottle, and started swallowing rhythmically. I watched her throat contracting. "I still like you, though, even if you're not poor," she said coming up for air. "Anyway, Malcolm's not the *only* friend you've got in Tory Hole."

"Thanks," I said softly. We drank some more champagne. "You seem so much older, more sophisticated, than last summer," I said after a while.

"You mean I'm drinking like a fish?"

"That too." I laughed.

She rolled over onto her stomach. "It's been a long time."

"Almost a year."

"Year's a long time."

"Yeah, I guess it is. I'm sorry I never called you, Luce."

"Come on. Give me a break. I never expected you to call. I figured soon as your parents found out..." She made a noise with her mouth. "Well, anyway, I was surprised to hear from you at all."

I didn't say anything. The excuse she already believed was a good one, better than the truth. I didn't want to hurt her feelings by trying to explain.

She finished the champagne, then passed the empty bottle to me, and flipped over on her back. "You still think I'm pretty?" she asked, stretching out her arms, running her fingers through the grass.

"Even prettier, sexier."

"Then why don't you... you know, make your move?"

Lucy really *had* acquired a certain savoir faire. She kissed and rolled and rifled my clothes with much more adept fingers than ever before. Then, when we were panting, she rolled off and knelt beside me in the grass. I was expecting her to say something conventionally negative about cooling our jets, not getting carried away, but instead she started unzipping her pants. "Tonight, you're gonna get laid."

"Oh yeah?" I heard my voice crack.

"Yeah!" She giggled. "You're not a virgin, are you?"

"Not exactly," I said, telling the approximate truth.

"Me neither, *par dieu!* Hey, why aren't you taking off your clothes?"

Lucy had already pulled off her shirt and her pants and was arching her back fetchingly to reach the hook on her bra. Then she shrugged it off too and flipped it away. I saw her silhouetted against the high water, reflecting back the lights all around the cove. I don't know how I mustered the nobility to utter a word of objection, but that's what I tried to do. I was going to tell her I'd be leaving for college in less than a week and didn't know when or if we'd ever see each other again. "But Leslie—" I began, then stopped, shocked that I'd mixed up the names.

"You don't have to worry about *that*," she said, looming above me and beginning to descend. "It doesn't run in the family, you know. Relax. You won't get anything from me but a good time."

Some of us can't help profiting from the misfortunes of others, whatever they may have been exactly. "I don't deserve this!" I said after she rolled off of me and I lay there gasping for dear life.

"That was for Leslie," she said.

"Oh yeah? If I died right now—"

"Not before we do it again. The next one'll be for ourselves."

five

*L*ucy had knocked my socks off, so naturally I tried to reach her all that last week before I had to leave for school. Once her mother answered (she sounded scared), but the other times I just got a brother or a sister or one of their friends. "She's not here!" they echoed one another, then slammed down the phone. Every time I called I was afraid that Lucy's father would answer. First he'd say, "Who wants to know?" like Edward G. Robinson. Then I imagined he'd find some way to reach out and bludgeon me with the telephone.

The night before I was supposed to leave for college my mother came up the stairs and announced, "There's a young woman who would like to speak to you on the phone. I didn't ask her name, and I'm only letting you speak to her against my better judgment, I want you to know. Your father—"

But I was already past her, running down the stairs. "Lucy?"

"Hi, how're you doing? You all ready for college?"

"I'm supposed to leave tomorrow. I've been trying to reach you all week..."

"Yeah, well, I haven't been around too much. Can I see you tonight? Just for a little while?"

"I'll be right over."

"No. I'm not home right now. Meet me at the beach, okay? By the flagpole?"

I reached the beach before she did and started walking around the flagpole. Suddenly I felt guilty, as though I were running out on something. This beach, the "bad" beach, where the relative outcasts came to let their freckles merge? What was I supposed to do, stick around and become a local, selling reefers to the high school kids and riding around town on a motorcycle? It wasn't in the cards, I knew that, but still I felt a tug. Lucy had been lying in the sand not ten feet away from this flagpole the first time I'd met her. She'd looked a little like a flagpole, too, like someone you might call "sis." How many hours had I logged at this beach, first as a kid, then as a lifeguard, and finally making out with Lucy on the picnic tables? How many hundreds of hours? I knocked my knuckles against the flagpole. It rang hollowly. It seemed silly to be getting sentimental when I wasn't even gone yet.

A dented VW bug with a souped-up engine pulled up to the curb. It idled for several moments before Lucy got out of the passenger side and the car roared away. "Hi," she said and threaded her arm around my waist in a way I found fond, almost wifely in what it took for granted. She started walking toward the picnic tables at the end of the beach. "Let's sit over there."

"I've been trying to call you all week. Didn't you get my messages?" Then I remembered that I hadn't left my name. "Didn't anybody tell you some guy who wouldn't identify himself was trying to call?"

"I haven't been around," she said.

"Where have you been?" I turned to look at her under the floodlight and that's when I saw the strawberry bruise on the cheek she'd been holding away from me. "Jesus, what happened, Luce! Did *he* do that to you?"

Lucy hesitated, unsure which he I was referring to. "That guy? No, he's just a friend. He just gave me a ride down."

"Your father then?"

"Please don't ask me any more."

We sat in our old spot, on the picnic table under the elms. I didn't think I'd asked her much at all yet, considering, but I didn't want to press, so I waited for her to speak. "Jeremy, how would it be if I came down to see you at your school?"

"Fine. I mean, sensational! I'd love it, really. I was going to ask you anyway, except I haven't had a chance."

She nodded without looking at me.

"Will you really come?"

"Yeah, maybe."

"When?"

"I don't know yet. But write me. And maybe I'll come."

"And stay for a while?" I asked eagerly.

She glanced at my face, then looked away. "Maybe. We'll see."

Lucy didn't look anything like a college girl. Her clothes were wrong, too neat, too cheap (and not in any hippie way), but I told myself that didn't matter to me. "I think I'm falling in love with you, Luce," I said, but she didn't look up at me even then. Maybe she was ashamed of her bruise, or just surprised. I lifted her chin and kissed her, but she didn't respond except politely. Romantic love was a luxury she probably felt she couldn't afford. I let her go and she put her head on my shoulder. "Once you get to Washington, you can catch either a bus or a train right to Charlottesville. It's not too far."

"Maybe I'll fly."

"Fly? There's not much of an airport in Charlottesville. Fly down to Washington you mean?"

"Yeah, I guess so." She dropped her head again. I could feel her shrinking away from me. "I'll just take the bus, I guess."

"But you will come?"

She nodded.

"Promise?"

"Yeah. I'll try to. I promise."

That was the last time I saw Lucy Pardieu. I wrote to her as soon as I got settled at U.Va., and when I was home at Christmas I called. Her mother told me, "She doesn't live here anymore," and then hung up the phone. I called back, introduced myself, and asked politely whether Lucy had received my letters and how she might be reached. "I don't know," Mrs. Pardieu said in a frightened voice. "I can't talk now. Lucy's gone."

The next summer, I tried once more. This time Lucy's little sister answered the phone. "She's not here. Who's this?" she asked.

"Jeremy Morgan. Also known as Tony Marino," I said.

"Oh, hi, Jeremy. This is Belle. 'Member me?"

I remembered Belle as an even bigger coquette than Lucy, a gorgeous little dark-eyed girl and still very much a child. "Of course I remember you, Belle. How are you doing?"

"Pretty good. You know, Jeremy, I've changed a lot since the last time you saw me. I'm sixteen now, almost."

I had to laugh. "I don't believe it." Even if she'd been older than she looked, Belle couldn't be more than fourteen now.

"It's true!"

"Then you must be a knockout, Belle. Listen, when you see Lucy, will you tell her that I called?"

"She's married now. She's got a little baby, too."

"When? How old is the baby, I mean?"

"Oh, it's little. She just had it, I think."

"When exactly? What month was it born?"

"*I* don't know. Listen I gotta get off now, and you better not call anymore either. Lucy's *married* now."

I often wondered whether Lucy got any of my letters, whether anyone ever told her that I'd called. Probably I should count myself lucky that she didn't come to visit me at U. Va. Getting married was the only way out for a girl like Lucy in 1967 (or Les in 1963), and taking the plunge into a disastrous marriage was just the kind of help I might have been tempted to provide.

Second semester of my freshman year, Les's marriage to Hank collapsed like a house of cards, and she came home to live with Sunshine and Fog. The end had come suddenly. One week they were getting along as usual, more or less; the next Hank was gone, and he'd taken the car—which is a little like taking the horse when you're living in a desert like L.A. Les had only the telephone, so she called Tory Hole. Seven months pregnant with Matthew, she had nowhere else to go. She even had to lie to the airline about her due date before they'd let her on the plane.

Mat was born prematurely, just three weeks after Les had flown in from L.A. Fog drove her to the hospital. I was sitting in my dorm room when he called. "Your sister just had the baby!" he hollered into the phone.

"Great! How's she doing?" I hollered back.

"Great! She's a champ!"

"How are *you* doing, Dad?"

"I'm shaking like a leaf! She had the baby fifteen minutes after we got here, *fifteen minutes*, and it's a thirty-minute drive! I thought I was going to have a heart attack! Her pains were coming right on top of each other before we got halfway!"

"That's terrifying!"

"You're telling me!"

"You know, I love you, Dad!"

"Love your sister!" he screamed back at me. "She's the one who's just given birth to a child!"

How I wished that Les could have seen Fog then, or even heard him, but she was otherwise engaged at the time. She was always otherwise engaged. Of course, I told her later what he'd said, and at first she seemed pleased. But then she shrugged: Jeremy the Peacemaker again. "Why didn't he come in to see me in the recovery room if he was feeling so proud? He could have come right into the delivery room, as far as that's concerned. There were other fathers in there."

I had a job lined up as a lifeguard on the Maryland shore, but changed my plans and came home to work in Tory Hole the summer after Mat was born. I'd seen Les only once in the five years she was married to Hank, and that time she'd seemed so skinny, so nervous, and so painfully submissive I'd hardly recognized her. I hadn't wanted to recognize her. Now was our chance to get reacquainted. Fog set me up in business, as he called it: the concession stand at the beach at Longneck Point. "You can handle the books now, after your experience of last summer with us." The "us" referred to Merrill Lynch Pierce Fenner and Smith, but whatever I might have picked up there didn't help me serving up hamburgers and french fries.

Keeping the books was the smallest part of my job. Between the griddle, the deep-fat frier, and the hotplate for the coffee urns, it was an inferno in that hut, and I had to keep a fly swatter handy beneath the counter to slap the candy-grabbing fingers of the beach urchins. The paperwork was easy, and the flies hardly bothered me at all.

My family moved into a larger house at the first of the summer. Besides the addition of Les and Barbara and Mat, there was Papa who'd come to live with us two winters before when Grandmother Gum had died. Papa was seventy-six at the time, still working and driving crazily when she died. Then he aged twenty years. I know of a medical theory that differentiates biological age from chronological age and maintains that a person is only as old biologically as he looks. Before Gum died, Papa looked no older than sixty. His hair was hardly gray. Within a week, he looked eighty. He had a heart attack; he retired; his hearing, then his eyesight, began to fail. Always a jovial man, Papa grew bitter and morose. He blamed the doctors for Gum's death. My grandmother weighed sixty-eight pounds at the time of her death. A head cold would have finished her off. But Papa had to blame someone, so he blamed the doctors.

To get back at them, my grandfather became an outspoken advocate of socialized medicine. From there, he became a socialist. Then his health began to improve. Papa read W. E. B. Dubois and Rosa Luxemburg. He read Emma Goldman. "You know, this old bird could write," he once told me. He even read a little Marx. After that, he started reading everything in sight. He ran through my parents' books in a month and a half. Then he started beating down the doors of Tory Hole's pitiful public library, which he exhausted in a little over a year. So he got himself a card for the New York Public Library. Once a week, he rode in on the train for more books. While the other passengers read the *Wall Street Journal*, he read *The Daily Worker*. He loved the Fifth Avenue branch of the public library. "I can sit outside with the lions," he confided to me. "Also the pigeons and the teenage girls. Maybe you'd care to come along sometime?"

We were four generations in one house the summer after Mat

was born. It was 1968: the summer after Martin Luther King was shot, the summer of blacks rioting in every major city and quite a few minor ones, the summer of the Democratic Convention in Chicago and peace demonstrations everywhere, the summer when Bobby Kennedy was killed. I was working in the concession hut when I heard on the radio that he'd been shot. It was 9 A.M. I'd just opened up. I remember there was a child at the counter proffering six cents, which might have meant two pretzels or three pieces of Double Bubble gum. I said to her, "Bobby Kennedy's been assassinated." The child looked up at me stricken. She started to cry. Then I did what Les would have done. I left the hut unattended, walked over to the flagpole, and started to lower the flag to halfmast.

I was still wearing my apron covered with hamburger grease. One of the lifeguards was watching me from the shade of the boat-house. His hair was golden, his skin was tan. He'd just been transferred over from the good beach to the bad. I remember noticing that the hairs on his legs were almost white. This was the Yalie with the Apollo complex. I was spending the summer growing a ponytail. "What the fuck do you think you're doing, douchebag?" he called out to me. That was the way people talked to each other in 1968.

"What does it look like, motherfucker? I'm lowering the god-damned flag."

"Oh, no, you're not." He covered the distance to the flagpole in three huge bounds. "Who do you think you are? We don't let every homo short-order cook decide what to do with the American flag!"

"Then *you* lower it. Bobby Kennedy's just been killed." He stared at me. "Well, what are you waiting for? Orders from the Pentagon!" I reached for the rope. Apollo and I got into a little scuffle then, but the other lifeguards quickly broke it up. Neither of us was even bruised, but for the rest of the summer, Apollo had to bring his lunch in a paper bag.

Politically, it was an evil time. Events that summer set a lot of people at each other's throats; not in our family, though, oddly enough. We all mourned Kennedy and mourned even more for what we were left with when he died. Papa announced his support for Eugene McCarthy early on. Sunshine said she preferred McCarthy but had to vote for Humphrey because we couldn't risk letting Nixon slip in; then she voted for McCarthy anyway. Fog was disgusted by the choices and refused to vote at all—or so he told us at the time. And Les was so ecstatic to be free and single and over twenty-one that she forgot to go to the polls.

She went to peace rallies, though, just as she went to see *Hair* three times that summer—for the sense of awakening, new beginning, liberation widely shared. Les woke up more than anyone I knew. Her slumber had been longer, she'd been waiting all her life. Like Papa, she blossomed almost overnight, and then she teased me unmercifully for what she termed my "preppiness," my lack of spontaneity. Often in the evenings she brought Barbara and the baby down to the beach. We were still getting reacquainted. Barbara splashed around and Mat gurgled while Les and I talked. Then I fried up hamburgers all around and shut up shop. We dropped the kids off at the house and drove on into New York.

I liked to go to the movies or a quiet bar in the West Eighties where they made margaritas, but that was too tame for Les. She'd suggest that we stop off in the South Bronx and score some reefer, then cruise downtown to a place in the West Village not far from Aaron's. Les had two boyfriends that summer. Besides Aaron, who was Jewish, there was Dudley, who was black. And the place she liked in the Village was a gay bar, gay in both senses of the word. It terrified me. I think that was why Les insisted on dragging me there all the time.

"Would you order me a Cuba libre while I make a call?"

"No, wait! A Cuba libre, what's that?"

"The waiter'll know what it is."

"Please don't leave me alone here, Les!"

"*Relax*, bro. What are you afraid of? I shouldn't be gone too long."

Les was always gone too long, and when she got back to the table, I was always flushed a bright, indignant shade, staring at my fingernails to avoid any chance of eye contact anywhere in the room. "Well," she said, plopping down across from me again. "You liberated yet?"

"What do you want from me?"

"I haven't decided yet."

Liberation is a merciless state of mind, but it cuts both ways. I told my sister all about Lucy, and she grew a little glum. And later, when I asked about Pete, she had to tell me everything. "That's ancient history. Come on, I can barely remember, it's been so long."

"What happened? What was the horrible secret Sunshine and Fog would never divulge?"

"Secret?" She blushed. "All right. All right, I'll tell you. I was a virgin . . . until then, with him . . ."

"Is that *all?*"

"No. He also gave me crabs. Are you satisfied now? You do know what crabs are, don't you?"

"Yes."

"Well, I didn't, and they're horrible."

Leslie was a virgin until the summer before her sophomore year in college when she finally gave in to Pete Pardieu. He plowed her underneath a picnic table, one of the same picnic tables where Lucy and I would later sit at Longneck Point. It was supposed to be their last date, the last of the summer and the last forever. Les planned it that way. She was writing to a guy she'd met at college. He lived in Colorado. She said she no longer cared about Pete.

Les had decided: she'd give Pete what he'd been trying to get for three years, let *him* spill the blood and the tears. Her friend Harriet had told her, "The first time is a wash-out anyway. It's from nowhere, what a mess!" So Les surrendered her virginity underneath a picnic table, a space designed for feet. She found the act less painful, less momentous, and less messy than she'd been led to believe. Then she went back to school.

Within a week, she started to itch. "You know, down there. At first I thought I'd just gotten poison ivy. The skin's pretty sensitive, after all. But then I spotted the little creepers. I flipped out."

Les had no one to turn to. She couldn't trust her roommate, and all her closest friends were male. When she went to the infirmary, the nurse refused to let her even see a doctor until she'd given them a list of names. So she decided to drop out of school. "What else could I do? I couldn't very well go to class and spend the whole time scratching between my legs. I had my reputation to think of, after all."

The registrar called Fog. Fog called Leslie. "What the hell do you think you're doing down there?"

"Daddy, I'm dropping out of school."

"The hell you are . . ."

"I have to, Daddy. You don't understand."

Fog flew out to see her. Les had to tell him something. "Pack up. I'll see you at home," he said. He left her a plane ticket. He didn't even stay the night.

The campus of the University of Arizona is modern with just enough Spanish flavor to remind a lapsed Catholic that he hasn't been to church. It's a large school and sprawls over dozens of city blocks. The campus is not enclosed or comforting in the way we tend to think of college—the small New England school with a fireplace in the library and ivy on the walls, the dean in his office, and everything right with the world. Flying in or out of Tucson, what one notices first and then compulsively afterward are the blue dots. There are tens of thousands of blue dots in Tucson. Closer to the ground, they enlarge and take on shapes—rectangles, ovals, and kidneys. Tucson is a desert city, stranded from the sea. The dots are its swimming pools.

For some people it feels like home, but Tucson is no oasis. Water is piped in, mainly from the Colorado. Beyond the city limits lies desert all around. In the winter, the desert blooms miraculously, but for the rest of the year it's too hot for most forms of life in the daylight hours, and too cool at night.

It's difficult to exaggerate the sensations of freedom, vacancy, and silent, otherworldly beauty one feels flying out of Tucson. The desert runs flat and empty up to meet the mesas. The mesas turn on like neon in the waning light of day. Looking down on the desert past the pale silver wing of the plane makes the traveler want to check his supplies of food, water, and air.

What my sister couldn't tell me that liberated summer—even in the gay bar and even as she told me every other embarrassing detail—was that she'd slept with the guy from Colorado, the one she'd liked so much, between the time she returned to college and she spotted her first little white lice.

A bottle of prescription ointment was waiting on her dressing table when Les got back to Tory Hole. Fog never mentioned it, and neither did Sunshine once she knew. Les got a job as a salesgirl. Fog went on a long business trip. The firm had been after him for some time to go to Brazil. He hardly spoke to Leslie, she hardly saw him, from the time she came home from Arizona until she ran away.

What I knew at the time was nothing. I knew that my sister had quit college because she didn't get the courses that she wanted that year. I knew she worked in Juniors at Lord & Taylor, came home in the evenings and shut herself up in her room. I knew she didn't appear for dinners, but came down later and ate cold leftovers, after everybody was in bed. I knew that Les never took me for rides anymore. She was dating a guy from Oklahoma who'd just gotten out of the Marines and was staying for a while with a Marine buddy who lived next door to Maria in North Tory Hole. The guy's name was Hank. I didn't even know that Les was gone when she ran away.

"Where is she?" Sunshine asked.

"I don't know," I said forlornly.

"Yes, you do. You're just lying to cover up for her, give her time to make her getaway. You always were as thick as thieves."

The month was January 1963. We were still living in the house commonly referred to as the Old Grimm Place, but only because we couldn't find a buyer. I sat on the edge of the pink bedspread watching Sunshine rifling my sister's drawers. Les's room was claustrophobic, its ceiling sloping steeply with the gable, the wallpaper pink, too, to match the pillows and the bedspread. Sunshine had had the room redone while Les was away at college. "Make it easy on yourself," she said. "First, I want you to admit to me that you knew she was running away. You insult my intelligence when you say she didn't tell you anything."

"She didn't. She didn't tell me anything," I repeated again and again throughout the evening. Les had gone away without telling me, without saying good-bye, without taking me along. It hurt just to say the words, that I hadn't known she'd gone.

Afterward, I could see why she couldn't take the risk of telling me. Sunshine was sure to grill the little brother, and I was only thirteen years old. Les realized I couldn't have stood up to a mother's interrogation: the harsh light of the bedside lamp, the pink glare off the walls and bedspread, incest fantasy—the guilt of every adolescent since Freud. Any fool could have figured out why Les had run away. Coming home with crabs to this girlish room was reason enough to make anyone run screaming out the door. Forget the daily horrors of Lord & Taylor. Forget the prospect of being an outcast forever in Tory Hole. As for where she'd run to, who besides Hank had Les been seeing? Who'd just gone home to Oklahoma not a month before?

"Either Arizona, Oklahoma, or Montana," Mother muttered. "Somewhere out West. I'll call that other Marine, that friend of Maria's. She'll have his number. What's his name? Bob?"

"The Blob," I said, since that was the way Les had always referred to him.

"That's right. Bob the Blob. I'll call him right away."

Bob came right over, looking concerned like an Eddie Haskell who'd put on about 150 pounds. Mother offered Bob a beer. "Don't trouble yourself, Mrs. Morgan. I'll get it," he said. He came back with two cans.

Sunshine seated him on the sofa, where he seemed to puddle. She sat in a straightbacked chair, something the Puritans had probably made. Mother looked lovely, like a spider. Bob looked like an overweight fly. I watched them from the corner until I was noticed, then eavesdropped from the top of the stairs. Working on his second beer, Bob said he might have Hank's address somewhere at home maybe, he'd have to take a look. Mother asked him to do so please.

Bob said Hank was a pretty good guy and smart, except he was kinda Southern, you know, backwards, not educated real good. His family were sorta hillbillies, he thought. Hank would be staying with his mother in Oklahoma. The name of the town—the nearest town, that is—was Zena. He had a brother living there too. Hank's father was living in southern California somewheres. Yeah, his parents were divorced, kinda. Matter of fact, he wasn't sure they'd ever been exactly married, 'cept common law. On his way out the door, Bob offered in a low tone to come back that same night with Hank's address. He'd just remembered right where he'd stuck it. Mother asked him just to phone.

Bob the Blob married Maria Bertolli the following spring in a big church wedding, a relief to all concerned. That summer, they moved out to Los Angeles to be closer to their best friends, Hank and Leslie. Hank and Les, for their part, had tromped down to the local courthouse on a bitter, windblown January day to tie the knot. Then they'd had a few pictures taken at the Old-Timey Picture Parlor, where Les had huddled in her winter coat, looking a little like Bonnie to Hank's Clyde. Les wrote in May to tell us they were living in Gardena, California, and expecting a baby in October.

Sunshine didn't take the news very well. She was going to be a grandmother, and there was nothing she could do about it. There wasn't even anyone for her to talk to, to let off steam. Fog was away more than not that year, and I was hardly more than a child myself. Sunshine attacked the housework with a sense of mission, and when I started sprouting a few pimples and blackheads she went after me with the same zeal. "There's dirt in your very pores!" she exclaimed as she gouged my skin with a two-headed instrument of torture, slotted on one end, conical on the other, tooled from the finest Nazi steel.

I fled to the backyard, my Garden of Eden. Without Les around, life had become dangerously imbalanced. There was only Mother and me. In the daytime, I played outside while she scoured, but at night we sat together in the demimonde of the television room, with the yellow light coming through the window shades and the moths forever circling the bulb.

Fog was away for two and three months at a time. He was still working in Brasilia. Studying the atlas, I discovered that Brasilia was not only located on another continent two hand's-lengths from New York on the blow-up map, it was also in the opposite hemisphere where winter was summer, spring was fall, and (I figured) bad was good and night was day. My father served for short periods of time as president, vice president, and treasurer of various companies down there. At one time, he held all three offices simultaneously.

I found it little consolation that my father was president of something after all. My mother was acting more and more like a crazy woman as the summer wore on. Dirt seeped out of the woodwork, mold grew from the cracks in the bathroom tiles. There was rot in the walls, internal corruption, and, if we sniffed hard enough, we could smell it. Mother's nose was hypersensitive, since she'd just quit smoking. She traced the source of the stink to the library. Mother was convinced that a rodent had died in there, probably inside the walls but perhaps only behind a row of books. Before we brought in the carpenters to start excavating, though, she decided to search the room one more time, and enlisted my help to check the topmost shelf.

I stood on the first six volumes of the *Encyclopaedia Britannica* piled on top of a chair. Sunshine watched me from below, her heart in her hands, her hands clamped over her mouth. I tilted. I stretched. There, behind the end book was a funny shape, a white paper napkin that had opened like a poisonous flower, budding great green tufts of mold. I stared at the napkin, fascinated and appalled.

"What is it? What have you found?"

"Nothing," I sighed. "There's nothing up here."

"Of course there is. I saw you staring at *something*."

"No, nothing. You're welcome to climb up and look for yourself."

Mother's eyes narrowed to slits. She was afraid of heights, but she was stubborn. She'd wait me out, that's what she'd do. Then the telephone rang, and her face looked suddenly stricken. I could see that Mother was cruelly torn. She could either let it ring and never know who was calling or answer it and give me a chance to

hide the smelly secret someplace else. "Don't you move a muscle."
Mother scurried to answer the phone.

No sooner had she left the room than I swallowed my revulsion,
stuffed the moldy wad in my pocket and replaced the books on
the shelf. I opened the napkin later in my hollow under the elm.
Inside was a furry mass. The smell was supernatural, like some
unknown form of life. Prodding it with a stick, I separated the
mass and identified its component parts: seven brussels sprouts. I
buried them beside my hamster. Les had always hated brussels
sprouts.

What Les had loved were chocolate bars, especially Peter Paul Almond Joy, but these she'd been forbidden, even at age nineteen, on
account of her complexion. Sunshine and Fog had paid some steep
bills from the dermatologist on account of her complexion. That
summer after Les ran away, Sunshine probed deeper and deeper
into the crevices of the house, scouring. And I made my own, parallel
search. Soon after discovering the brussels sprouts, I crept deep down
into Les's closet, afraid of what I might find. Her closet went back
under the eaves even further than mine. Behind the suitcases and
the boxes diminishing in height, I squirmed on my stomach and
felt with my fingers for the ruffled clumps of paper like plants that
bloom in the dark. Secrets. These I dragged out into the light of
day. They were candy wrappers, dozens of them. Milky Way, Mars
bars, Snickers, and (saints preserve us) Peter Paul Almond Joy. Worse
yet, I found two empty jars of macadamia nuts, and that made even
me mad. Every Christmas, Fog's mother in Hawaii shipped us a
box of macadamia nuts, and we shared them all equally, counting
out the half and whole nuts.

I could hear Sunshine rumbling from room to room in other
parts of the house and wondered what ugly secrets I might have
hidden away inadequately. Sometimes I could hear my mother
muttering. Sometimes I could hear the Hoover howl. The house
itself still shuddered and moaned with the agonies of the previous
owners (the Grimms), on top of our own. It was an altogether
auditory year.

It was also a lonely one. Fortunately, I was already too old to come down with autism, but I exhibited a number of the symptoms: private, furtive play, self-inflicted stimulations. I didn't masturbate yet because I didn't know how, but, alone in my room, I enacted elaborate dramas with a deck of cards in which the fresh young queen of diamonds was forced to submit to that peasant, the three of spades, and sometimes his brother, the five. I had no one to talk to. My friend Malcolm was away for the summer in Italy. My mother was clearly deranged. Only the backyard could draw me out of my room. Mowing the lawn was my responsibility, but I delayed it because I liked to think of the backyard grass as a haven for rabbits and other animals, a jungle where the yellow eyes of leopards peered out of the dense undergrowth.

We had a cherry tree in the backyard that was plagued every summer by raucous birds. The birds couldn't share the tree, not with the squirrels, not even with each other. Hopping from limb to limb and pecking, the larger ones drove the little ones from the tree, and from all around the yard in a ring came the envious shrieks of other birds while one fat crow or bluejay feasted. The shrieks rose in pitch as the cherries ripened, until by August the tree was swarming with frenzied birds, pecking and screeching at each other, tearing at the cherries, their greedy mouths red with the pulp and juices of the fruit. At first they'd seemed to me a parody of a family fight, then something more. Watching them eat became a carnal, a religious experience. The whole tree shook with the fury of their feeding.

The first summer we lived in the house we'd tolerated the birds since they were there before us, but the second year we decided to save the cherries for ourselves. Fog netted the tree. The birds tore through the netting almost immediately. The next summer, we offered to compromise and netted only one limb, but the birds were not to be appeased or reasoned with. They tore through and invaded our limb before the rest of the cherries were even half consumed, and that was when Sunshine agreed to let me guard the tree with my BB gun.

The crows seemed to be the meanest birds, the most disgusting,

Dean Crawford

selfish and obscene, so they were the only ones I aimed for. All the others—robins, blackbirds, sparrows, jays, and finches—I just tried to scare away. It was easy enough to miss. The sight on my gun was inaccurate. If I aimed about a foot to the right and dropped six inches, I had a chance of hitting something. If I aimed directly, I always missed.

Hunters maintain that crows are among the smartest birds because they can tell whether you're carrying a gun and if it's loaded. Maybe the hunters exaggerate, but it's true that it's very difficult ever to get a clear shot at a crow. First I tried the back porch. No crows went near the tree. Then I built a blind in my hollow, where I might have been hidden from the house and the tree but was plainly visible from the air. Finally, I settled on my upstairs window. I slipped the barrel of my BB gun out of a slit in the screen, and the darkened mesh concealed me. Crows came to the tree and ravaged the cherries every hour of the day. I shot with little chance of hitting anything because the range was so long, but I got used to taking deadly aim—a foot over and six inches down.

Throughout most of the summer, I popped away heedlessly. I didn't hit anything until August. Then I was aiming at something black, and it fell from the tree. I ran downstairs and across the yard to find a blackbird flipping in the grass. I'd crippled his wing. The blackbird stared at me with one eye, then started flipping more frantically. What had he seen in my face to frighten him more? He seemed more alive now in his injured condition than before when I'd been aiming at him in the tree, but the bird couldn't fly. He couldn't even climb to his feet. It was clear to me what I had to do. I pressed the barrel of the gun to his head and fired. Then again. I pumped and fired long past the time the bird lay still, until I imagined his head was no longer a head at all but just a mass of tiny brass balls, like a ball bearing encased in a skull.

A hush had come over the yard. For the first time that summer, the birds were silent. I carried the dead blackbird off our property and buried it as deep as I could dig in the vacant lot next door. Still gripping my gun, I came in the back door and didn't even hear my mother calling me by name. Steadily I tromped through the kitchen, dining room, living room, and up the stairs, still not hearing my mother calling, "Jeremy, answer me! Is that you?" I met her at the top of the stairs. Seeing me she fainted away, and only then did I realize that I hadn't lowered my gun but held it pointing straight ahead of me.

The saga of the Morgans and Pardieus doesn't end there, though. Les and Pete met one more time. It was the very end of the summer of '68, when I was working in the concession stand. In the middle of a hotter-than-normal August afternoon, a dark-eyed girl walked up to the counter and said, "Hi."

I said, "Hi. What can I do for you?" Then I smiled because she was very pretty, even if a little on the young side.

"You're Jeremy, aren't you?"

"The same." Everybody knew me at the beach. I was the guy who fried their hamburgers.

"You don't recognize me, do you, Jeremy?"

I looked at her more closely, but it didn't help.

"I'm Lucy's sister, Belle."

"Belle! That's incredible! You *have* grown up, haven't you?"

"Yeah," she said, checking the top of her bathing suit (her straps were down). "Well, I'm glad I recognized you. Now I can tell Lucy what a hippie you've become."

"Is Lucy here somewhere?"

"'Course not. She lives in Philadelphia, with her husband. He's in executive training school. And she's got her little boy."

"How old is he now?" I asked casually.

"'Bout a year and a half."

I flinched, and she saw me. "What can I get for you, Belle? Hamburger, hot dog, french fries?"

"Just a bag of Cheez-its and a Coke, I guess."

I gave her her order and waved away her dollar bill. "On the house."

"Well, thanks, Jeremy. See you around, I guess." She was still watching me and smiling as she backed away. "Oh, and one more thing. I was just teasing about the baby's age. Lucy wanted me to tell you that he's a Cancer. You know, that means he was born the end of June or in July..."

Les and Pete met at the beach about a week later, but it wasn't accidental. I didn't know which of them took the initiative and called, but it was arranged somehow.

I was hosing out the concession hut when Les arrived alone, without the kids, and announced that any minute now she was going to be meeting Pete Pardieu. "I won't stop you. Are you sure he'll show up, though?"

Les hesitated. It had been six years since they'd seen each other. "Yeah, but he's late. As usual."

"Can you tell me *why* you're meeting him? You never really cared for him, you said."

"I didn't. It's more that he changed my life. You could say I'm curious, I guess." At that moment, a large blue car, a Ford maybe, came gliding across the parking lot. We watched its slow progress in our direction. When it finally slowed to a halt, a man got out of the passenger side, and the car slid away. It was too dark for me to make out the man's face, but Les recognized him. She sauntered right over to meet him, and they walked together onto the beach.

All I could see were their dark shapes outlined on the shore. From where I sat on the steps, they looked distorted. Their legs seemed stretched out, unusually long and expressive. Even without the difference in height, though, there was no doubt in my mind which were my sister's legs—the animated ones, the ones that moved with a lighter tread, the more flirtatious ones. First, they walked down to the water's edge where I lost their silhouettes for a minute against the gloomy darkness of the bay. Then they reappeared, moving toward one of the lifeguard stands. They leaned against the lifeguard stand, but I could still pick out their legs among the other silhouettes of the upright posts and crossbars. They must have talked standing there. They were there for a while. Les's legs were the ones that kept flickering, always moving from side to side. She moved away and then spun back around to face the stand. She stood with her hands on her hips, her head cocked to one side, and her weight on one leg. Then she slowly sauntered back toward the stand, twisting her heels in the sand. She stood in front of Pete's legs with one knee bent in toward him. It was a provocative pose, and I could see that Les had a very good figure. But when they moved together, I could no longer pick out legs from legs, just one dark blot against the sky.

six

After I left Aaron at the seaside bar in Omaha, I drove all night, dreaming about Leslie and the other women I've known. There's a children's song that advises us to count our blessings instead of sheep as a way to drop off, but I've always found that counting my blessings was a sure way to stay awake. I feel guilty about every one.

First, I felt guilty about Sara, small and sleek and sybaritic as a house cat. Sara and I shared the emotional conviction that pleasure is only enhanced by the knowledge of sin, and afterglow only deepened by remorse. Ours had been a torrid courtship, followed by a wedding in the Roman Catholic Church. The lack of sin was one of the great deficiencies of our married life. Suddenly we were sanctified, we were *supposed* to screw. It was "the married act," and lost a lot of its thrill. Most recently, Sara was my "estranged spouse," and I found that legal term perfectly apt. We'd been spouses who became estranged after three years of marriage, and it added a whole new dimension to our relationship. Sara, for instance, started to hate me. She'd never particularly liked me, but not liking someone is a pale emotion, compared to hate, which is bright and red. She threw things, she drew blood. Every week or so after our estrangement, Sara would call me up on the phone and announce her intention of coming by the apartment at such and such a time to pick up some clothes and the blender. Always the blender. And she was always late. We started screaming as soon as she got in the door, circling each other, alternating stances as victim and tormentor, moving closer and closer until we were brushing against each other on the turns. Then, when the screaming reached a certain prede- termined, instinctive pitch, we started tearing one another's clothes off and copulated like maddened animals on the hand-woven rug Sara's Aunt Weedie had given us. We always forgot the blender.

I also felt guilty about Hannah, although I might have been the only man who could. Hannah was a sexual comedienne. That was her métier. She didn't take any part of sex seriously, particularly not what she called its "romantic accoutrements," by which she meant "love and marriage and the baby carriage." Hannah never had less than two or three lovers, and though she allowed that, in a certain way, I was her favorite, I knew better than to drop by without calling first.

When Hannah offered to come with me to California, I thought she was joking. She offered all sorts of transcontinental delights. "I'll suck you off across the Great Divide! We can do it doggy-style on top of Mount Rushmore, looking down Lincoln's nose! Woof, woof! Come on, Jeremy. We'll go off together like Old Faithful, every hour on the hour, all the way across... Say yes, you'll take me with you. I'll be good, I promise."

Suddenly I realized that Hannah was being serious for once in her life and I'd have to tell her no. No, I wasn't driving across the country to have a good time. If anything, I was doing it to suffer, to purge myself of just such pleasures. Anyway, Hannah was crude. She was a notorious person. Emotionally, Hannah could be a snake, always seducing somebody's best friend or roommate or brother or sister or father or mother in order to get back at him or her, or for no reason at all. Jumping from Sara to a more permanent state of affairs with Hannah would have been hopping from the refrigerator into the fire, and I thought I might crack from the sudden change of temperature. I dropped her a month or so before I left.

And finally, unreasonably, I felt guilty about Lucy. Instead of asking her to some preppy party, I should have asked her to marry me. Lucy was desperate. She might have accepted. We could have eloped to U.Va., spent our honeymoon in freshman orientation. During fraternity rush, we could have gone as a couple and given a whole new meaning to pledge week. It wouldn't have mattered how long the marriage lasted or what I might have missed being hitched. The sacrifice alone would have redeemed me. I wondered, though, exactly what sort of sacrifice the practical-minded Lucy would have wanted out of me. She might have wanted me to go to business school, then put on a fedora and ride the train into New York. She might have wanted a mansion just like Malcolm's in Tory Hole. I could have offered her only romance and student housing, and Lucy was such a down-to-earth girl.

Western Nebraska wasn't flat as I expected, nor did it roll. Instead it rose and fell in long drawn-out swells like the breathing of someone sleeping deeply or the motion of the sea. I saw thunderstorms in the distance, three distinct spots where lightning was shooting up from the earth to meet the lightning forking down. Closer, they looked like spider webs, and as I drove right into the path of one storm, I wondered if my rubber tires would insulate me. Yes, I was sure they would, but in any case decided not to rest my arm on the metal of the door. The grain elevators on the horizon seemed to move in the flickering light. They looked like *War of the Worlds* creatures walking across the land.

I crossed the border into Wyoming just before daylight. The sunrise was pale and colorless. Wyoming is the first Western state, in my opinion, because water is a problem there. The little towns are rawboned and cheerless. If left unattended for a year or two, they look as though they might well blow away, all the way back to Nebraska. I drove on into Wyoming feeling hollow and dry, with a hard-on in my pants for Lucy Pardieu, now Trumbell, the girl who might have had my baby if not for the difference of a month or two.

I found the early morning sunlight harsh and irritating, offering no sense of new day, just a feeling of here-we-go-again. The sun came slanting in the passenger window, throwing me optically off balance, and my sunglasses didn't help. Of course, I was lucky that Lucy hadn't come to visit me in Virginia. I'd always been lucky, especially

in what I'd missed—menstruation, molestation, unwanted pregnancy, the kind of shame only a woman can feel in front of her
father. Some people have all the advantages. Some people get all
the breaks. No, it's not fair, I told myself. Some kids go to prep
schools and debutante balls, while others get bad grades or bad skin
or drunken fathers or no fathers at all and go west to places like
Gardiner, Montana, or Gardena, California.

Pete Pardieu had once lived in Gardiner. Les had lived in Gardena when she was married to Hank. Like millions of people before
them, she and Hank drove an old car west from the Oklahoma hills
to the desert of southern California. They settled in a suburb of L.A.
where the towns meld together along a six-lane boulevard punctuated
only by traffic lights and the occasional oil refinery. Here, the customary landmarks are the hamburger and taco franchises and the
chain restaurants, many of which derive their names from fairy tales
and children's lore. To get to Hank's and Les's place, you hung a
right at Long John Silver's, passed the Princess Slipper Motel and
one or two Jack-in-the-Boxes and a Captain Cook's Seafood, and
took the second legal left after the big yellow disk that stands on top
of a building and revolves and glows in the dark all night long,
denoting a restaurant by the name of Peter's Pan. Les's and Hank's
place was the first two-story building you came to after that, three
blocks down.

Hank and Les worked hard when they lived in Gardena. At first
Les took a job as an undercover agent, a kind of Pinkerton person,
investigating a large-scale theft ring among industrial employees.
She was a paid snitch and decided to go into another line of work
when a fellow employee offered to "kick the shit out of that stomach
of yorn." Les was six months pregnant with Barbara at the time.
After the baby was born, she started managing the apartment complex where they were living. Les changed faucet washers and fuses,
toting the baby around on her hip and shaming a few of the tenants
into performing some of their own minor repairs. Hank studied
accounting and worked in a factory on the evening shift making
tires, watching the years ahead roll by. One day, adding and subtracting, he discovered that his wife's little brother, whom she wouldn't

shut up about, was ten years younger than he was but would finish college first. No wonder Hank hated my guts; I was a walking kick in the teeth for him.

Bob the Blob and Maria moved out to California not long after Hank and Les. Soon Maria had a little baby, too. They named the child Nanette and liked to tell her no. Bob found a sedentary job as a postal clerk and settled down to put on some serious weight. In all fairness, it should be mentioned that Maria knew how to cook only pasta. It should also be mentioned that Maria always preferred Hank to Bob and married the latter only after Les had already scooped up the former. Still, no one thought Maria really minded. She and Les were best friends, and the two men were Marine Corps buddies after all. They'd looked very similar in their uniforms. Certainly, no one ever thought of Maria as the devious sort.

Who knows what might have been going on in her head? I doubt that anyone, even Les, gave Maria's circumstances a lot of thought. For five years, there was nary a peep out of her. Hank was working and studying and gobbling aspirins like M&Ms. Les was changing washers and managing the tenants' minor repairs and disputes, calling in a plumber only when the sewer snake wouldn't do the trick, calling in the police only when a gun was involved. Barbara grew but still liked to ride around on her mother's hip. Some people said they were "inseparable" as though that was a condition that ought to be corrected by surgery. Others noted that Les's hip was a good place for keeping an eye on the kid. Meanwhile, Bob was fattening on pasta and beer, and Maria seemed the same as ever: cute as a windup doll and approximately as independent of thought.

Then, one evening while Hank was at the factory, Les received a call from Pete Pardieu. She was icy to him, she said. She told him she was married and to leave her alone. Then she hung up the phone. The following evening when her best friend, Maria, was over, Les mentioned the call. She had not yet mentioned it to Hank, who still harbored a considerable amount of jealousy and random rage toward Pete Pardieu. Les wondered aloud whether she should say anything to Hank. He'd been unusually edgy lately, worrying about the financial burden of a second child. Maria said, "No. Better not tell him. He might not understand."

On her way home that evening, Maria stopped by the factory where Hank was at work.

What is known is that Hank Jakes regularly consumed large quantities of aspirin in his efforts to rid himself of the headaches which he claimed "darkened his sight"; that Hank Jakes had never been pleased about his wife's second pregnancy, which both termed "an accident"; that Hank Jakes did not return to the apartment he shared with Leslie Jakes on the night of January 29, or on any subsequent night, sleeping instead at Maria O'Neal's, Bob O'Neal having been relocated on the street; that Hank Jakes failed to deposit his paycheck of February 16 in the joint checking account he shared with Leslie Jakes and that furthermore he refused to pay any of the rent, thereby precipitating the notice of eviction proceedings delivered on March 1 to the premises now occupied solely by Leslie and Barbara Jakes; that when informed of the eviction notice, Hank Jakes accused his wife, Leslie, of "whoring" with Pete Pardieu; that Hank Jakes retained an attorney and filed for divorce; that Leslie Jakes was forced by eviction proceedings to quit said premises formerly shared with Hank Jakes; that on March 15, 1968, Leslie Jakes, at that time more than seven months pregnant and accompanied by her daughter, Barbara, age four, boarded Trans World Airlines Flight 703 bound from Los Angeles to New York.

What is not known is what Maria said to Hank on the night of January 29, or where Pete Pardieu was calling from, or what exactly Les said on the telephone to Pete, or whatever happened to Bob the Blob. After the separation and before her departure, Les might have met or spoken again to Pete Pardieu and neglected to mention that detail, even to her little brother and confidant. In any case, my sister asked for no money from Hank, so the court awarded her the minimum allowed by law, twenty-five dollars per month per child.

I decided to stop in Casper, Wyoming. The van wasn't overheating yet, but I figured it could use a siesta during the hottest part of the day. That was my excuse. The truth was I was feeling the effects of

the road myself. It wasn't that I was sleepy exactly (I had some pills
for that), just jumpy from fatigue.

I parked beside a municipal park with all the usual features—a
few trees, swings, a slide, and a sandbox. Along one edge of the
park was a riverbed, which turned out to be empty except for old
bedsprings, refrigerators, and sinks. Driving the interstates and sleeping in rest areas was no way to see the country, I decided, not the
real country of discarded bedsprings, refrigerators, and sinks. I lay
down to take a nap and stretched out under a tree a short distance
from the playground area, where I could watch the children and
their mothers before I fell asleep. They looked lean for mothers. I
wondered if they were happy in their lives, hanging out at a city
park, chatting about their kids. I wondered if they looked at me with
longing or interest—a random male, a stranger on the loose—or
whether they noticed me at all. It was impossible to tell at this
distance. The sun was hot, the heat was prickly. I peeled off my T-
shirt and lay back down. As I fell asleep, I wondered if any of them
would trade her life for Leslie's, driving cross-country with two children and three animals, along with all their accoutrements.

In my dream, I was driving. Sara was with me in the car. We
were searching for a camping place, someplace secret where we
wouldn't be found and prosecuted for trespassing or camping without
a license. Then suddenly we were in the middle of a campground.
It was very crowded with cars driving by and tents right next to us
and ropes stretched across the ground wherever we tried to walk.
The sun was blinding; I had to close my eyes. There were also lots
of trailers, the Airstream kind except they had big picture windows
and TV antennas that reached way up into the sky. Sara and I were
trying to find a spot for our tent. It was a pup tent, and, we found
as we put it up, transparent besides. Still, we had to make love. We
were burning with it, yanking on each other's zippers and pants.
Maybe no one will notice, we told ourselves. Sara was on top of
me. She was pushing, pushing, but she was too dry. My penis
wouldn't slip inside. Meanwhile, I was trying to cover her up. There
were men outside who'd see her bare backside. But whatever clothes
I draped across her immediately slipped off.

I woke with the T-shirt in my hands and didn't know whether to be relieved or more embarrassed that the playground was empty. All the mothers and children were gone. Could any of them been close enough to see the bulge in my pants? Had I been rolling around in the grass thrusting into empty air? I decided not to take any chances and hurried back to the van before the police came to arrest me for my crime.

Wyoming is a vast plateau, the continental roof, and it seems to get more wear and tear up there. Everywhere you look there's erosion—scars both man-made and natural, suggesting that God has been doing a little strip mining of His own. Mesas were melting down like heaps of ice cream. Just east of Laramie, I'd passed a sink in the ground with walls as steep and sheer as a toilet bowl. But if in the daylight the landscape seemed harsh and dry and interminably bleached-out and dreary, at night the colors were softened, the house trailers were obscured, and the effect was almost magical. Night encourages movement, and movement promises something of a vague and tantalizing sort—fantasies fulfilled under cover of darkness, then left behind; the perfect, impossible dream of a one-night stand. There's always the hint of some threat in the West—a stray bullet from a ranch war or a drunken Indian running you off the road in his battered pickup truck, but danger doesn't belie the beauty. If anything, it enchances it.

Wyoming's river names seemed to speak of a strictly functional relation to the world. In the town of Shoshoni, I drove along Bad-water Creek, crossing Poison Creek. To the south was Sweetwater River, along with Muddy, Bitter, and Alkali creeks. The highway sign read GAS DIESEL FOOD TOWING without either punctuation or a name. To the north, though, I could see the great black loomings of the Big Horn range, making the night sky blue, and I wondered about the people in those little towns with names like Lost Cabin, No Wood, Ten Sheep, East Thermopoli, and Tipperary. Were they any different than their flatland cousins? Did their lives live up to their expectations? Did the landscape satisfy them, or only inspire them to further discontent? Passing through such beautiful country, we may think how superficially we're experiencing the place, but people I've known who grew up in these gorgeous but isolated parts of the world always tell of the grinding boredom, the raw and petty lives of the people who live there, and the terrible itch to get away. The mountains of North Georgia, where I'd just been living, were one of the prettiest places I'd ever been, and yet the people there were the meanest I'd ever lived among. You'd think they had only to step out on their stoops and gaze at the mountain peaks to keep themselves from beating their dogs, lying to their parishioners, murdering the local newspaper publisher, or (for that matter) taking up with floozies and deserting their wives. Even in the loveliest places, many people seem to feel an aggravation, a maddening discontent. In fact, it may be stronger there. But is it enough to say that we lack a mythology of our own for our native land? Or that our visions and dreams are out of sync with what's good for us and what's likely to come to pass?

There were moments when I wondered if reckless driving wasn't the last outlet for the great American spirit that had tamed the West, shamed the Indians, and killed off all the buffalo. Again and again throughout the night, big cars and trucks swerved around me and roared off down the road, where I could still hear them a few minutes longer, gunning their engines, squealing around the curves. Whatever the reason for their wildness, the drivers in Wyoming and Montana were notoriously fast and reckless, and the highways only minimally patrolled. The daylight speed was unlimited, and at night there were no cops around.

I was moved by the spirit, and it was just as well that my old motor couldn't be coaxed to propel me faster than fifty-five without overheating, throwing a rod, gobbling a bearing, or otherwise crapping out on me. But if I could be moved by this reckless spirit, then surely Les could be, too. She'd be driving safely because the kids were with her in the car—of that I felt pretty sure—but she'd be straining at the throttle, chomping at the bit. She'd want to go faster, faster, whooshing down this curve and across the overpass. Les would be listening to the night sounds—the hoot of an owl, the longer hoot of the railroad, the sudden squeal of tires like a frightened animal, the mounting whine of a dragster winding out his motor as far as he dared.

I drove southwest along Muskrat Creek to Riverton, then turned north toward Tagwatee Pass, climbing a long dark river valley between walls of mountains, up the Wind.

I arrived in Grand Tetons National Park in the early morning and, first thing, spotted an elk beside the road. He ran off as soon as he saw me. I pulled over and stopped the car, then followed him on foot into the forest. Running through a gray mist that hung just over the ground, I came to a cascade of water down a granite face and below it a stream of harmonic pebbles glittering in the morning sun. I stood on a bluff overlooking the creek and listened. To my right stood the elk, overlooking me. His legs were so spindly and his massive trunk so far off the ground that I didn't recognize him at first. Then I realized my elk was a moose. Moose are mean. They charge trains. I walked backward all the way to the van.

I reached Yellowstone at midday and could almost smell Les around there somewhere, yesterday, today, tomorrow. Already the traffic was bumper-to-bumper, backed up five miles before Old Faithful. Many of the other vehicles were towing trailers or were themselves motorized trailers or different kinds of mobile homes. A few of these motorized mobile homes were in turn towing trailers, with motorcycles strapped onto their back ends. It seemed fantastic to have come these two thousand miles to the Rocky Mountain range, confronted a wild moose in the morning, and joined a traffic jam so close to the wilderness in the afternoon. The incongruity did not entirely surprise me, either. America, after all.

I was more concerned about my engine temperature. The little needle on my gauge rose up to the red line in the stop-and-go traffic, and it hung there, mile after mile, until the cars began to thin out on the other side of Geyser Central. I reached Gardiner, Montana, in the middle of the afternoon.

My first sensation was familiarity; my second, contempt. Gardiner couldn't have been a more ordinary western town—western in its total disregard for planning or design, ordinary in its ugliness. The town was divided into two parts, which might seem to suggest a design but actually defied one. There were a few structures clustered around the Cattleman Cafe and a somewhat greater concentration of life around the corner and down the road—by car fully a mile away. I drove to the farthest edge of town and parked, intending to sleep in the van for a few hours and then poke around some more. But the layout of Gardiner kept me awake, in that it made no sense at all. Here were half a dozen buildings, including a bank, a liquor store, a luncheonette, a laundromat, and "Feeds," all on a one-way street that was lined with slots for diagonal parking like so many cilia, those little directional hairs which help keep us from gagging on our food. Except this throat didn't lead anywhere, only out toward isolated ranches and farms. Behind me, at the mouth of town, were a grocery, another café for drinking beer, a gas station, and one frame house with upstairs dormers gaping out at me like two buckteeth. It didn't make any sense that the two halves were separated. What's more, this second group of buildings was clumped right at the base of a long and very steep hill, possibly the base of a mountain, a location that might appeal momentarily to the eye before the brain begins to wonder just who would want to slam on his brakes coming off that grade or choose to start climbing it from a dead stop. Between the halves of town was nothing, just vacant land in need of mowing. The weeds were much too high to walk through comfortably, especially if one were carrying groceries, especially if there were rattlesnakes. So instead of being able to walk the hypotenuse, cross-country as in any other rural town, people were forced to drive the outside legs of the triangle in order to get from gas or grocery to bank or Feeds. I wondered if maybe the setup of Gardiner made more apparent sense in winter when everything was covered by about four feet of snow, or in the nineteenth century when horses walked and people rode.

I woke up in the dark, shivering. The temperature had dropped. I pulled on a sweatshirt before I got out of the van. Everything looked different. I checked my watch—it read 8:15—but it felt as if months had gone by. The wind was raw even though it was only

September, less than a week past Labor Day, but it felt like April to me. Now I admit I'm the kind of person who can stir up memories with desires and come up with cruel concoctions at any time of the year, but I've always found April to be a month of heightened treachery. March may come in like a lion and go out like a lamb, but in April the lamb grows little pointed teeth like a weasel, turning on you viciously when you're least expecting it. And I don't mean only weather. I've always felt my most dangerous inclinations in the month of April. Sara and I had our worst fights every year in April, and when I finally turned on her, snapping and lashing out like a weasel myself, it was in April.

Papa also died in April, and that month was the worst of my life. Les and I weren't even speaking—it was our Black Saturday between Good Friday and the Resurrection, except it lasted all month. Sara and I were newlyweds then, and we fought continuously for days on end, stopping long enough only to get a few hours sleep and go to work, then picking up where we left off. We fought about Leslie. Leslie never liked Sara. She hadn't even come to the wedding. We shattered our china (the everyday set), screaming our throats raw over Leslie, fighting on even as we screwed. As Sara put it, "I want to make you come so hard you lose your mind!" and that was the danger all right. We coupled as adversaries, enemies even, grinning into each other's faces like two skeletons, riding, riding, each in pursuit of the other's madness.

My grandfather was the kindest man I'd ever known. When he died, the effect seemed supernatural—like Pandora's story played backward in the other hemisphere. Kindness became a pile of ashes in a crematorium box.

The same ill April wind seemed to be blowing that night in Gardiner. I hurried through the shut-up "downtown" section to the luncheonette on the corner, already on the other edge of town, and came to the realization that I should have driven. By the time I got there, I was in a foul mood. It would take everything I had to be civil, but I'd have to expend it. People in Montana carry guns. I was a stranger in a cow town, and it's hazardous for strangers to be rude in rural luncheonettes.

The waitress who came over wore her hair wrapped in a way which has often tempted me to look closer and be sure that something isn't crawling out from between the lacquered strands. "Whatter ya gonna have?" she asked. She wasn't chewing gum but looked as though I'd just caught her between sticks. I ordered chicken with whipped potatoes and Jell-O salad. She nodded her head approvingly.

The waitress left me alone to eat, coming over to jabber only when I was drinking my coffee after the meal. This I understood. I'd read that many primitive peoples regard eating as a private act and a vulnerable occasion. Dogs, too, like to eat in solitude. The waitress cleared my plate and offered me more coffee. She was in her early thirties, not much older than Les, I guessed, but what a difference.

The food might have appeased my immediate appetite and soddened my sharper memories—at least temporarily—but I still felt grouchy. Was this the way my father felt? This waitress wasn't the least bit pretty, but at a certain angle her face looked vulnerable in spite of her beehive and her makeup, her chafed hands and elbows, not to mention her voice. I wondered about the rest of her, her hipbones for instance, or her ass, whether they were as raw and chapped as some of her other protruding parts.

"You drivin' somewhere tonight?" she asked suddenly.

"Yeah. Idaho."

"Look fer snow 'bove six thousand."

I managed a smile. "Thanks, I will. Do you think I shouldn't go?"

She shrugged, making it a hard motion. "No skin off my butt what you do."

Encouraged by this interchange, I asked about the dude ranches in Gardiner. "*Dude* ranches?" She looked at me incredulously.

"Yes, that's right. I knew a guy who worked here once."

She turned and hollered toward the kitchen. "Mona, this guy wants to know if we got any *dude* ranches in this godforsaken burg!" Mona came out of the kitchen to see who'd asked such a question. She looked like a Mona, rotund and earthy with wide features, now arranged in an angry scowl, no doubt on account of the question.

Mona stood with her hands on her hips and stared at me. She didn't say anything at first. I figured I'd asked the wrong question, and was just wondering what they did to people who asked it when Mona said, "Shit, I don't know. I only been livin' here since July." I didn't bother asking about Pete Pardieu.

It was snowing when I got back to my turn-off. I'd already driven forty-four miles out of my way to see Gardiner, so I thought it wasn't unreasonable to drive a few more to admire Old Faithful, which I'd glimpsed earlier but not like this, steaming like a subway vent in the falling snow.

The snow had turned to sleet, then rain by the time I reached West Yellowstone and started climbing. I hit snow again at 6,100 feet. It was a blizzard before the road leveled out at Targhee Pass. I wondered if Les were driving through it.

She was, somewhere, I felt sure of it, although peering ahead into the thick cloud of flakes, I couldn't feel her near. Neither could I see any lights other than my own headlights, which reached only a few feet ahead. A dark shape loomed up on the right. It was a signpost, but I had to stop the car and get out to read the sign. The sign read, TARGHEE PASS, ELEVATION 7078. Driving on, I couldn't see the side of the road anymore. I could only see the white line running down the middle. I hugged the line. Later, I straddled it to maximize my margin for error, the distance between me and the precipice that was probably there. The road went up and down. The snow became heavier until it was all a single cloud. Sometimes I lost the line entirely for minutes at a time, moving the wheel instinctively. When the line appeared again, it was usually nearby, but more than once I saw the guard rail suddenly jump out of the cloud and I had to swerve back to keep from hitting it.

Outside it was a blizzard. Inside, the heater roared. I was encapsulated and nearly blind in my capsule, but felt sure that Les and the kids were somewhere out there in the same storm, inching their capsule along the same as mine and peering through the snow for the broken white line. Les would be silent, hunched over the wheel. She'd have put the kids to bed for the night. Mat might well be sleeping, but Barbara would be wide-eyed and terrified. The child had an aerial in her head. In fact, they might be Barbara's signals I was picking up instead of Les's. They weren't Les's, no. Suddenly I felt very cold. Les was lost to me. In that moment—at least in the present tense—I felt she was dead.

I switched on the radio and the static came in sweeps, approaching and receding. The music was some comfort, but when it ebbed again, I felt even more alone than I had before I heard it, as though the mortal world were moving away from me. In a news bulletin, I heard some mentions of chains. I turned off the radio. I had no chains, my tires were worn, it wouldn't help me to know now that chains were required for crossing the pass. I stopped to read another road sign, CONTINENTAL DIVIDE. Then another, TRUCKS USE LOW GEAR. I downshifted, pumping the brakes as the road began to descend.

seven

The last time I saw my grandfather he was standing in a hospital window four stories up. He'd gotten out of bed, which he wasn't supposed to do, to wave good-bye at my car as I drove out of the parking lot. That morning, I was taking the kids to visit Papa before driving south to continue my life as a newlywed in Virginia, where Sara and I had an A-frame cottage on a street with the idyllic name of Rose of Sharon Road. Papa had been in the hospital for only a short time, a series of tests. But he was eighty-two, and suddenly he looked his age, standing in his pajamas in a full-length window four stories up. Papa waved to us. Mat saw him first and screamed, "Stop!" I stopped the car and we all waved back at Papa. His pajamas bagged on him. They hung down his arms and bunched around his feet.

"Papa's going to die soon, isn't he?" Barbara asked.

"Papa's not gonna die!" Mat said.

"Never?"

A few days later, Papa came home from the hospital. All his tests had come back fine. Sunshine and Fog decided not to postpone their vacation after all. They took off for Honolulu. A week later, my grandfather was dead.

Les started apologizing as soon as she called. She was sorry for waking me, it was one A.M., and she didn't seem to hear me telling her that I'd been awake before she called. It was just that she had to talk to someone, she was so upset now that the kids were asleep, but she shouldn't have called in the middle of the night. I was married now.

"What difference does that make? What is it, Les?" I almost had to beg her to tell me. "Please. I can tell there's something very wrong..."

Only then did she say that Papa had died. "But don't come," she said. "There's nothing you can do here. Believe me. I don't want you to come. It's an eight-hour drive. I'm really all right now. It was just that I was alone here, with the kids, when it happened."

"When did it happen?"

"Last night, I guess, sometime. I found him this morning. His heart gave out. He died in his sleep. At least, I think he died in his sleep."

"Why didn't you call me earlier?"

"I had so many other calls..."

"You're alone there then?"

"Mother and Dad asked me to stay with Papa while they were away. You knew they were away? They went to Hawaii, first time they've been back in fourteen years. They told you that, didn't they? Anyway, there's nothing you can do here. Papa isn't here. I mean, his body isn't even here. And Mother and Dad won't be back for a week, so you won't be able to see them. I had Papa's body sent to California. They're going to stop there on their way home. There won't even be a funeral here..."

Sara and I left that night, arriving mid-morning at my parents' house in Tory Hole. My sister stood in the doorway, taking us both in. "You shouldn't have come. There's nothing for you to do here," she said, whether to Sara or both of us I was never sure.

Sara stepped forward and hugged her. She said, "I'm so sorry, Leslie," and I could tell she meant it. I could see Sara was crying by the way her shoulders shook. Then I looked at my sister's eyes, dry and furious. Les was the taller one, unwillingly stooped in this embrace. She'd always been very picky about when and whom she hugged.

"It's cold out here," I said to break them up. "Let's get inside."

Les wheeled away as soon as she was released. "I'll make some coffee. You can stay in Mother's and Dad's room. There are plenty of sheets, and they have the biggest bed. Maybe you'll want a nap? I left some towels on the bed. Barbara went to school today, and Mat's in daycare, so it should be quiet until they get home at three-fifteen."

"Why did you send the kids to school?" I asked in the same rapid tone.

"It's better to be busy at a time like this."

"How's Mat taking it?"

"He doesn't believe it yet."

"And Barbara?"

"Fine. She seemed to be expecting it."

"Yes," I said. "She asked me a couple of weeks ago if Papa was about to die. The kid's uncanny."

"You never mentioned that she'd asked you that."

"You never asked. She's your daughter, I thought you knew what went on in her mind."

"Do you both want coffee?" Les asked.

Sara must have felt left out by our quick-fire conversation; surprised, if not shocked, by the cool way we dispensed with death. Les and I hadn't even embraced, nor would we. Within a few minutes of our arrival, Sara softly announced that she would like to take a nap. "Will you show me which room, Jeremy?" she asked in a significant way.

Once inside my parents' bedroom, Sara locked the door. "Please hold me," she said. "I know everyone has their own way of dealing with these things, but you and your sister are so calm and so controlled that it scares me. Please, just lie down with me for a second and hold me."

For whatever reasons—because we were lying on my parents' bed, or because Sara was playing a little tug-of-war with Leslie, or because the proximity of death can engender desire (an affirmation of life, after all)—it wasn't long before our breathing came heavier and we started tugging off our clothes. We made love like children; our movements were heavy and textbook methodical, our cries soft

and light. It was two hours before I got back down to the kitchen
to finish my coffee, and by that time, Les had left the house. She
didn't return until she'd picked up the kids after school.

Sara napped until dinnertime. Neither of us had slept at all the
night before, but as Sara had said, everyone has his own way of
dealing with death, and mine wasn't sleeping. Instead, I walked
down to the pond to feed the ducks, just as Papa used to do every
afternoon. He always kept a sack of feed on the backseat of his car.

My grandfather rarely referred to things by their real names. He
called this feed sack "turtle food," he did bird calls for the family
cat, and he mooed like a cow when he wanted to attract the attention
of the ducks. Having lived for seventy-five years in apartments in
downtown Oakland and San Francisco, my grandfather called himself a country boy. He called Les "Lester," Barbara "Barbell," Mat
"Matterhorn," and me "Gerrymander"—for no reason at all.

The ducks didn't need to be called. They started charging out
onto the driveway as soon as I took the sack in hand. They gathered
at my feet, berating me like cats, until I spread the seed. I counted
thirty-four including yearlings. The first year Papa came there'd been
only six, but the gaggle grew as Papa fed them. Nature had intended
for these birds to fly south for the winter and not come back until
May or June, and they would have if my grandfather hadn't spoiled
them with the dole. "Turtle food," I said softly, but I couldn't bring
myself to moo at them. I wondered if Papa used to moo when no
one else could hear. Probably. He had a pure heart. I stood shivering
with my hands in my pockets, watching the ducks waddle and peck.
This weather was deceptive. I'd gone out without a jacket. Slowly
I climbed back up the stone steps to the house, then drank cold
coffee until Les came home with the kids.

I'd always gotten along with Barbara and Mat, if only because
I let them use me as a jungle gym and willingly dropped everything
to do my imitation of an ape afflicted with sneezing and a runny
nose, just like the Dristan ad. I was happy to play with the kids the
rest of the afternoon while Les puttered and made telephone calls,
then just sat and watched us from the other end of the room. Finally

she said, "I'm glad you're here, Jeremy. The hardest part is just being alone."

"What about us?" Mat said very earnestly. "We're here, aren't we?"

"Shut up, dunderhead," Barbara said and started tickling her brother. "We don't count." They fell to the floor squealing.

Les smiled like the Mona Lisa. I reached over and took her hand, which was as close as we'd come to a hug all visit. "Thanks," she said, blinking rapidly. "Will you keep an eye on me tonight?"

"Sure." I didn't know what she meant.

After dinner, Les announced that she was going to get a sitter, unless of course Sara and I wanted to watch the kids. Both of us said we did. Then Les said never mind, she was leaving late enough that the kids wouldn't need a sitter, they'd already be in bed. She'd just ask Shirlee, our next-door neighbor, to keep an eye out for fires, earthquakes, hurricanes. Jay had a big dart tournament in New York that night. She was going to meet him afterward. Maybe we'd like to come along?

Sara hesitated, but I remembered that Les had just asked me to keep an eye out for her. "Sure," I said a second time.

"You don't have to come if you don't want to," Les said to Sara. "Neither of you."

"No, I don't mind," Sara said. "I've had a good nap. I worry about Jeremy, though." She turned to me accusingly. "You haven't slept at all."

We all drove in to meet Jay at the Lion's Head, a bar epitomizing much of what I found frightening about New York. Standing at the bar when we walked in were what I took to be the serious poets. There were about twelve of them, all six- or seven-footers, two-hundred-pounders, with long red beards. Jay wasn't there yet. Les pointed us toward the back room. "The writers give this place atmosphere, but watch out for them, they're a bunch of lechers."

"Big ones," Sara said. "Do they also prophesy?"

"I'm sure they will for you..."

"No, no. I think I'll pass."

"Didn't Aaron used to live around here?" I asked.

"A few blocks," Les replied. "We used to come in here some-times."

"Doesn't coming back to a place make you nostalgic?" Sara asked.

My sister actually rolled her eyes. I tried to redirect the conversation, telling Sara about the plague of robberies that beset poor Aaron. "He was burglarized every month at the first of the month—in a very businesslike manner—until there wasn't anything left to steal except the food in the refrigerator. So they took the refrigerator. And then there was his car . . . a Karmann Ghia. But you can tell it better than I can, Les."

She shrugged. "His neighborhood was in transition."

Sara nodded knowingly. "I know just what you mean. The same thing is happening in Baltimore." Sara had grown up rich in Baltimore. Her family was Catholic provincial.

Les turned her lazy gaze on Sara. I could see her laying for her. "What exactly is happening in Baltimore?"

"Well frankly, the blacks started moving up, from the South I mean, and taking over."

"The *South?* Do you mean Washington, or the south side of Baltimore, or the Old Confederacy . . . ?"

Sara blanched. "All of them really. I'm sure you know the de-mographic trends. When the blacks move in—"

"Demo-graphic trends," she said slowly, swilling her drink, "are just a bunch of bullshit. We talkin' 'bout *people.* Black *people.* 'I too sing America.' Ever hear of Langston Hughes? Or don't they read him down in Balt-ee-more?"

Sara shook her head. "I don't believe this. You're as white as I am and no matter how many Black Panthers you go to bed with, you'll never change that."

"That nigger's on the inside, honey. You can't be fuckin' a man that's in jail."

"I don't have to put up with this . . . this, this *shit.* I didn't drive all the way up here to listen to a lot of Northern hypocrisy." Sara looked at me to come to her rescue. "Well, *excuse me,*" she said sliding out of the booth and stalking off toward the bathrooms.

"Lay off her, Les," I said quietly. "She's not a racist."

"I know. And I'm sorry. I'm just feeling a little out of control tonight."

"I understand."

"No, I don't think you do understand. I don't see how you can. But I'll apologize to your wife as soon as she gets back."

"What is it I don't understand, Les?"

"That I really *am* crazy tonight." Les turned her eyes on me like a flashlight, briefly, then dropped them again. "Can you keep a secret?" she asked in a younger voice.

"I always could."

"All right. Papa's death isn't the only thing that's happened to me this week. I also just had an abortion. And I'm not even sure who the father was, Jay or Dudley. Dudley was out on bail for a while pending his last appeal. So if I'd had the baby, I wouldn't have even know what *color* to expect..."

"Oh God, Les, I'm sorry." I reached for her hand, but she withdrew it.

"I might as well tell you everything at the same time. The other thing that's making me crazy is I'm not at all sure Papa died in his sleep. His eyes were open when I found him. He was looking right at me."

"Les," I said and moved around to her side of the booth. She started to cry and turned away from me. That was the way Sara found us when she came back to the booth.

"Jeremy, may I speak to you for a moment please?"

"Just a sec."

"*Now.*"

"Go ahead," Les said. "I'm all right now, really. Sara, I want to apologize for jumping all over you like that. I'm sorry. I don't know what came over me. I don't know what I'm even saying tonight. Forgive me, please."

"Jeremy?"

I let go of my sister's hand and followed Sara to an empty booth in the next room. "I won't put up with this," she said. "I simply won't. How could you just sit by and let her treat me that way? How *could* you, Jeremy? What your sister said to me was unforgivable. I want you to take me back right away. And I won't ride in the same car with that... person. I won't sleep in the same house with that ... person. How can you treat me this way? I'm your *wife*. I won't put up with it, Jeremy. I won't. I won't."

In a sense, Sara shot her bolt in the bar. She delivered all the lines and made all the pronouncements that she was to repeat throughout the night and the next day, the next week, throughout April and into May. We drove back to Tory Hole without ever meeting Jay. It wasn't clear whether Les had even reached him on the phone. Maybe she'd set everything up earlier in the day. Maybe she'd only left a message at the Brooklyn bar where his dart match was being held. Maybe she hadn't called at all. Sara and I stayed up arguing late into the night, then suddenly during one of our long bitter lulls, I realized that she'd fallen asleep. For a little while, I stared at her puffy cheeks and gloated about how ugly she looked. Then I got out of bed and went out into the hall.

Les was standing there in the dark. It was about three in the morning, but she was still fully dressed, just standing in the hall. "I'm sorry, Jeremy. It's horrible for you, isn't it?"

"I'm all right. You've got enough to worry about without concerning yourself with my marital discord."

"I know who you're fighting about. I could hear you all over the house."

"You only provided the occasion, not the cause."

"You don't really believe that, do you?"

"Yeah. But don't worry about it. We'll weather the storm."

Les reached out and touched my lips. "Will we?" She let her hand slip down and traced my chin with her finger. "You have a good chin."

"We have the same chin." I took her hand and our fingers intertwined. We smiled at each other, crookedly. The moment was charged, our fingers twisting, straining toward new combinations. I don't know which of us broke it off or how long we stood like that. I've never analyzed the incident. I try not to think at all about that night.

• • •

Les and I didn't talk for four months after that, but our meeting in the hall was not the reason. Les had already gone to work when Sara and I got up the next morning. We left to drive back down to Virginia without seeing her or the kids, and I didn't see any of them again until August of the summer when they moved into the house with so many doors and broken windows that Les called it the House of Doors on Hoyt Street—as opposed to the House of Doors in Half Moon Bay. Visiting my parents for a few weeks, I helped her fix it up. Sara was on the Maryland shore, also taking a break from our arguing. All of Les's floors had to be waxed and buffed, all the walls had to be painted, all the doors had to be sanded and restained and some of them replaced entirely. The house had been vacant for a while, and the neighborhood boys had been practicing their stone-throwing on its windows. I was over there every day for two weeks, but even so, Les and I didn't talk much. Maybe we were shy with each other. More likely, it was hard for Les to confess that her last confession to me had been pure fabrication.

I was changing a lock when she walked up beside me and leaned against the wall. "Tired?" I asked her.

"Exhausted. Always. I'm the saint of perpetual exhaustion." She smiled. "You remember that abortion I told you about after Papa died?"

"Of course I remember. Is anything the matter? Are you all right?"

"Relax, I'm fine. I just wanted you to know that I never had the abortion. I wasn't pregnant. I lied."

"I don't understand. Why would you lie about that?"

She giggled, looking off down the hall. "I don't know, I didn't know how else to express it, how upset I really was after Papa died."

"That's all right," I said, although I was shocked, more shocked than I'd been before.

"Of course it's *all right*, but I wanted you to know. It had something to do with the way Papa's eyes were looking at me. I felt unclean, ashamed, as though I *had* just had an abortion."

eight

Fog died almost a year to the day after Papa. It was Indian summer in April when he died.

My father had a heart attack on a hot day in Brasilia. We had to have the funeral without him. It took two weeks to fly his body back home.

My father died of a heart attack in the other hemisphere, but as far as I'm concerned, he's still living in Brasilia, a city without a past or much reason to exist at all, except as a place for Fog now that I can't see him anymore.

nine

The snow slacked off on the west slope of the Rockies, but the road was even slipperier. At least it seemed slipperier since I was driving downhill and had to use the brakes, making the back tires fishtail. The snow changed to sleet at four thousand feet, then rain.

Suddenly I was exhausted. The road was safer now, but my eyes were so tired I could barely focus through the storm. I thought I could feel Les's presence, somewhere near me on the road. Other moments, though, I could feel her in my chest, expanding. I realized I wasn't safe to drive.

I started looking for a place to stop and sleep as soon as I got down the mountain, and the first sign I saw read HENRYS LAKE RECREATIONAL AREA. It included a line drawing of a tent, but the tent just looked like geometry to me, and I drove on by. It was five A.M. when I pulled into Henrietta's Campground, found an empty slot, flopped down in the back of the van, and fell into a dead sleep.

I awoke what seemed like a few minutes later to the noise of someone pounding on the door and screaming, "Open up! Open up in there!" It was a woman's voice: Henrietta, I supposed. I had my wallet out when I opened the door, and Henrietta seemed to take that as a sign of good faith. Her voice softened. "You just come down from the pass last night?" Henrietta was short and stocky. She wore overalls and exuded an acrid no-nonsense air, but with the gray light of a rainy dawn at her back, she looked ethereal to me. It wasn't easy to accept this incident as reality once I'd closed the door and lain back down.

I dropped right into a dream about Leslie. She was wearing a short dress and sitting on a kitchen counter with her legs crossed provocatively. This was a party. There were others in the kitchen— tall swarthy men with chest hair curling out of their open shirts. I was trying not to look at their chest hair, or at my sister's legs. "Yes, that's right," she was saying to me. "That's what I asked you to do." Then the room changed shape, elongating into a corridor. Les was still sitting on the counter, but at the other end of the corridor. I tried to move toward her, but my legs were weighted and I could manage only the smallest steps. Les was still looking at me, but she was fading into a blaze of white light. I couldn't look at her. My eyes stung. I strained to see her through the gathering glare. Then she was gone, and I woke up with the sun in my eyes. It was a gorgeous day, newly washed like mornings in May.

I showered and changed my clothes. That afternoon, I drove downhill, southwest along the Henrys Fork of the Snake toward Idaho Falls, sweeping around the highbanked curves and admiring the tall beauty around me. Fog's in his heaven, all's right with the world.

It's not that I didn't love my father. As a boy, I worshiped him and hung on his every word, depending on him more than most sons depend on their fathers if only because I saw less of him than most. Even later, as a teenager and afterward, I tried hard to learn the grammar of my father's languages—accounting, Keynesian economics, and golf—while struggling to write my emotional needs into the budget proposals he had me prepare for every term at Deerfield and every semester at U.Va. I never got enough of my father; maybe no child ever does. But when I heard the news that he'd died in South America, what I felt first was sad for Les.

I may not have gotten all I wanted, but I'd already gotten what I needed from Fog. I was the boy. I was tall, taller than my father before I was seventeen. I played sports. Several times in similar contexts, he'd told me I had "brains." ("You got the brains, why don't you *use* them for crying out loud!?") So I knew my father loved me, approved of me, even allowed me a measure of respect. Les never knew these things, never had these certainties for herself, and now she never would. Many times I'd told her to pay a visit to Fog in his early-morning lair. This was his best time of the day, the two hours before Sunshine got up, and he always appreciated the company. By six or six-thirty, he'd fixed the coffee and parked himself beside the transistor radio where (forsaking the expensive stereo console) he liked to listen to the news and weather. Fog knew a station that played only news and weather. Sipping black coffee and smoking his unfiltered cigarettes, he tuned one ear to the radio while his eyes scanned the newspaper, which he always read from back to front, sneaking up on the headlines inductively, as though to minimize their shock. Every other hour of the day, Fog would be inaccessible—either at the office or on weekends playing golf, or in the evenings asleep by eight o'clock, but early in the morning, my father was always in the kitchen, generous with his opinions and his cigarettes, open to new ideas and changes in my college major, or any new proposal as long as it was well thought out. We talked about politics and presidents and South American land reform. Or if the political issues were too charged, as they tended to be in the late sixties, we could always talk about sports. My father and I shared a love of baseball lore—his intrinsic, mine acquired so that he'd like me more. More than anything, we shared a love of each other, and we had only to find a topic oblique enough to express it.

But when I suggested to Les that she get up a little earlier to visit with Fog, I might as well have been recommending Little League baseball as a way for her to make new friends. "You've got to be kidding. I'm tired in the mornings, and I'm in a hurry if I'm going to work. And weekends I like to sleep in. Let him make time for me, if he wants to talk to me so much."

The drive down through Idaho was lovely and peaceful. The air was cool, so the van didn't threaten to overheat, but the sun was warm slanting in through the windows. It felt like spring. I watched vast panoramas of spanking new land moving by. The Snake River was emerald with the turbulence, running full from the storm. I too felt the turbulence, relieved to be down the mountain and across the Continental Divide, where the rivers flowed west, gushing. I was in the home stretch now. Suddenly, I wasn't worried anymore. Les and the kids were around here somewhere, down the mountain, safe and sound. I stopped for a late lunch in Sugar City, reaching Utah early in the evening.

Around dinnertime, I passed through a succession of Utah towns with white boys' names—Ogden, Layton, Perry Willard. I was hungry by the time I reached the city of Bountiful, but drove on in prejudice against the name. The landscape had changed for the worse, I thought. These might as well have been the valley towns between Bakersfield and L.A.; they were all fast food and subdivisions like the crosshatchings of God's grid laid upon the land. The road swept down from Brigham City toward the seat of the Mormon Empire, Salt Lake City.

I wondered what Les would have to say about the lay of this particular land. She liked Mormons no more than I, referring to them as "Aryans" whenever she saw them prowling around on their ten-speed bicycles with their white shirts, black ties, blond hair, and blue eyes, scanning the streets for the weak and the sick and the spiritually vulnerable.

I reached Salt Lake before midnight and didn't stop to eat. I was fasting to regain my lyrical edge. When I hit I-80, I hung a right for Magna, Utah; Wendover, Nevada; and points west, meaning the Promised Land. The road ran straight and wide, a pathway to the moon. This was the country that the movie crews prowled: The American West, A Mythical Extravaganza. Mesas, canyons, cracked earth crying out for a cup of fresh water. Even to me, western Utah looked like lunar landscape. I felt a free-floating pity. Let America be the place it used to be, could still be, has always tried to be. Let a thousand rifles bloom. Near the little town of Low, I watched the moon rise over the mesas. Then I broke my fast.

I stopped at a truck stop and had an American feast: two cheeseburgers with everything on them, plus fries, vanilla milkshake, coffee, and peach pie à la mode. Why not? This was my country, I was entitled. Here I was—free, white, and over twenty-one, male and middle-class, equally at home on the West Coast and the East, descended from a whole range of standard Americans—Puritans, pioneers, and potato-famine refugees, not to mention the Polack on my father's side. So why did I leave the truck stop thinking, "America never was America to me"? And why did I feel so dizzy?

Just west of Low, I passed a marker put up to attract motorists' attention and give them something to yap about in the car. The marker read DONNER TRAIL. Certain lurid stories have the power to capture the American imagination, at least collectively, more strongly than our myths or our monuments or any part of our native land-scape. The Rosenbergs, for instance, those dirty commies who stole the secret of the atom bomb. Charles Lindbergh, less for his heroic flight than for his kidnapped baby. Manson and his merry band of sex-and-drug-crazed hippies slicing up a starlet and smearing her blood all over the walls. Also the Donner-Read Party, bound from Illinois to cannibalism in 1846.

Taking the wrong turn west of the Great Salt Lake, the Donner-Read Party arrived late at the pass over the Sierra and found them-selves snowbound from October on. Forty people died. Forty-seven survived by building crude shelters and eating mice, their own an-imals, their shoes, and finally their dead, including their leader, George Donner. When the snow melted in the spring, the trees near their camp were seen to have been hacked off at the ten-foot mark, which was the level of the winter snow. Donner Pass is now a national historical landmark, great interest having been aroused by the tale. The area is known today as a "year-round resort." (People ski in the wintertime.) My family used to spend summer vacations at Donner Lake.

But if only forty people died, what's been all the fuss these hundred-odd years? Larger parties of pioneers were massacred by Indians. Ships routinely went down with all hands aboard. Hundreds of people died in the Chicago Fire, thousands in San Francisco in 1906. Tens of thousands of Americans perished in 1919 just from coming down with a bad case of the flu. More recently, a planeload of soccer players got away with eating their teammates without nearly the infamy that the Donners have had to put up with all these years. Of course, those were South American soccer players, and we don't expect as much of people who speak foreign languages. It could also be that in this century we're so jaded by such things as death camps that we no longer fully appreciate the finer horror of eating one's family members. But in the nineteenth century, it was considered more than just good form to bury your dead. The bone that must have stuck in everyone's craw wasn't so much the dying, but the price people were willing to pay to survive.

Of course, people today derive some consolation from donating their bodily organs to science, offering their hearts and livers and kidneys for transplant operations. For the Donners, too, it might have even been easier to die knowing that they'd go to feed the ones they loved.

"I'm a-gonna die now, 'Liza."

"You mustn't say that, Mama!"

"I gotta. I know there ain't much meat left on these bones a mine, but I want you and Sissy to have what there is a it. Don't give none ta them Reads, neither. They didn't give us a hair a Emmy Lou. 'Member? 'Liza, you gotta promise me, you gonna eat me when I'm gone."

"Oh, Mama! I couldn't do that hardly!"

The real sacrifice was on the part of the living, not the dead. I drove on into Nevada through a glorious sunrise of orange and rose that I could either watch in my rearview mirror or see reflected in the desert in front of me. "Here's to the living," I said to myself, but I wondered if I'd be willing to eat my parents to survive or whether I'd be one of those who preferred to die. Les would have the courage to do it; I doubted that I would.

I rolled down the windows to get some fresh air. Surprisingly, I felt neither guilty nor sickened by my gruesome predawn reverie. If anything, I felt liberated and decided to spend the day in a cheap motel—my first of the trip. It would be too hot on the desert to sleep in the van, and I wanted another shower before my last lap. I didn't want to arrive at Stanford with three days of road grime impacted on my skin. And the thought of a bed was pure fantasy.

I ate breakfast and found an eight-dollar room in Deeth, Nevada. The desk clerk was a girl of about eighteen, probably the daughter of the people who owned the place. She was pale with long, limp hair, but attractive, even sexy, in that she looked so bored. Stripping off my sweaty clothes and crawling into bed, I wondered if she might come tapping at my door with fresh towels or linens. I'd be naked between the sheets. Would she be startled? Or would she say, "I don't care, have your way with me"?

What an arrogant male thought, I thought. I should be ashamed, I told myself, but I was asleep by then.

I dreamed of the Old Grimm Place, the first house we lived in in Tory Hole. I was standing in the dining room, which was lit only by the blue light of the television and the yellow streaks that filtered in at the window shades. The room was dingy, as though the Grimms had never left. Les was there. She and Mother sat facing the television set. They were older, quite a bit older than when we'd lived there, but I knew in the dream that we'd always been living in that house, that none of us—not even Les—had ever escaped. "Where's Pa?" I asked. My mother turned and glared at me. Her expression was furious, her eyes were red. Les slowly turned her head toward the kitchen. I followed her gaze. Then suddenly I understood everything, or what seemed like everything in the dream—why my mother was so mad at me, what was cooking in the kitchen, and where my father was. I woke up with that knowledge, translated into the kind of wisdom that can be had from a Chinese fortune cookie: The father must die for the son to be finally free. Funny that fortune cookies never mention what the daughter needs.

Deeth was black when I left it, surrounded by low, dark hills. There was no light from the land, or very little. The sky was lighter, flashing yellow in the distance from the lightning, but still this place looked like a caldron viewed from the inside. I drove over Golgonda Summit that evening. All around me were peaks—Mount Tobin, Ruby Dome, Adam Peak, Matterhorn—but I couldn't see them except when the lightning flashed. I reached Winnemucca around midnight, turned off the highway, and homed in on a casino. I had twenty dollars to blow and no father to tell me not to. If I marshaled my money, I could spend a few hours here with no consequences. No one would ever have to know. I ordered an Irish coffee and approached the blackjack table. Blackjack was the only game I knew how to play. Fog had taught me.

Two players were already seated at the table, a man and a woman, both beefy and in their sixties. "Pull up a pew," the man said. "Pee-yew!" the woman said, then laughed. I would have placed her behind a plastic TV tray, not at a blackjack table. "Just kidding, hon. You sit yourself down. We could use another hand."

"You can say that again. Maybe he'll change our luck before this gal takes us for our britches," the man said, indicating the dealer, a lovely young woman who looked to be part Chinese. I sat down and handed the dealer my money, which she changed into silver dollars and a five-dollar marker with a series of machine movements. The older couple continued to grin at me. "Name's Roy. This is Muriel. Call her Tonto," the man said, thrusting out his hand, which felt as broad as the prairie and as rough as a burro's hide.

"Jeremy Morgan," I said and shook hands with both of them while the dealer shuffled. She was totally expressionless. Her eyes were as lifeless and dull as a doll's.

For the first half hour, I bet timidly and lost two dollars in all that time. Gambling was starting to seem like work, so I resolved to loosen up and play until I'd either lost my other eighteen dollars or gotten the dealer to show emotion, whichever came first. I ordered drinks all around and bet the whole eighteen. When I won, Tonto winked at me and Roy said, "Tip the dealer a penny. Luck is like love. It needs to be fed."

I gave the dealer a silver dollar and smiled at her flirtatiously. She took my money, tapped it twice on the table, and added it to her stack without betraying the least expression and without saying a word. Again, I bet all I had, thirty-six dollars. "That's the spirit!" Roy said. Tonto winked again—because it was lucky, I supposed.

I won again. I tipped the dealer two dollars this time. She repeated the thank-you procedure. On the next hand, I bet fifty dollars, the table limit, and won again. This was starting to be fun. Tonto reached across the table to fondle my hand. "Let me touch you, baby! It might be contagious! Maybe a little'll rub off!"

The dealer looked me squarely in the eye and blinked.

If Buddha had been a gambler, he couldn't have had a poker face any more inscrutable than my lovely Winnemucca blackjack dealer who, I decided, would have a name like Jasmine or Lotus Flower or Rosebud. In the next four hours I went from rags to riches and back to rags four or five times. Roy and Tonto stayed as long as they could—and I could see they hated to go—but then they couldn't stay awake any longer. Once, when I was way ahead, I said to the dealer, "If you crack a smile, I'll quit." She dropped her eyes. She wouldn't look at me at all after I said that.

When the dealer took her breaks, I played the slot machines or just sat at the bar rather than play with the replacement dealer. I'd been up as much as five hundred dollars and down as low as two, and I'd been that low three times. I loved the thrill of winning, also the powerlessness of losing, but it was the woman who kept me on there through the night. She was every woman I'd ever loved, plus all the ones I'd never have, never even meet. How many angels on a silver dollar? I saw them all projected in her eyes.

She was Sara with her long sleek fur, Hannah in the evasive flick of her eyes, Lucy in her mysteriousness and deep practicality. She was my mother when she looked at me so coolly, Leslie in the shape of her chin and the delicate line of her jaw, which meant she looked a bit like me. She was Les in her remoteness, Les in her withdrawal and mechanical efficiency. I knew what she'd say if I tried to touch her. "We're not demonstrative," she'd say. "It's in our code. It's in the contract we sign."

She left by a back door. The barman came over and told me that the blackjack dealer had finished her shift and gone. I walked out of the casino with no more nor less in my pocket than I'd had when I went in—how many hours before? It would be getting light soon. I could wait for her in the parking lot—maybe she hadn't really gone. Or I could drive around and look for her in her car. There couldn't be many people stirring so early in this town. I stared out my windshield and considered, strong in the steel of my van. After a while the sun came up in the east. Then I drove on.

• • •

The road roller-coastered across the rest of Nevada. From Winnemucca it ran downhill to Lovelock at 3,900 feet, then up again. I
passed Ragged Top Mountain (elevation 6,333) in the Humboldt
range, then rolled down again, reaching Reno at mid-morning and
Donner Lake a little before noon. Seen from the highway, the lake
looks like glass inlaid in rock and pine, and its color is cobalt blue.
I drove down to the lake, then all the way around it, checking the
campgrounds and parking lots for a late-model VW bus with Connecticut plates. My timing might be off by two or three days, but I
was sure Les would stop at Donner Lake. There was the beach where
we'd gone swimming, the spot where Sunshine like to spread her
Indian blanket, and Fog taught me to play blackjack using stones
instead of chips. I saw the mountainside where we used to ride
burros, and later horses, and the "tree line," which I'd thought was
a concept like the equator or the international date line. Vacation
homes now rimmed the lake, where once there'd been only cabins
and tents. Donner had grown up, but who was I to mind? Across
the lake I saw a crew of carpenters working shirtless in down vests,
thrusting up a frame of white pine against the deep blue sky, and
envied them the beauty of their work. The ring of their hammer
blows and their movements were out of synchrony—familiar phys-
ics. I drove on.

The western slope of the Sierra seemed surprisingly hot and
forested, both beautiful and a little dangerous in combinations pe-
culiar to California. A truck cab passed me without its trailer; it
looked like a modern-day version of the headless horseman—a severed head on wheels. I'd come home! I kept the excitement a low
fire, though, tamped well back in the stove. The road descended in
wide, banked curves beside canyons with names like Emigrant Gap,
where some poor emigrant's car could easily careen off the shoulder
and into a bottomless ditch. I felt off-balance, as though I might
fall in myself.

But there was no stopping me now. I reached Sacramento by
mid-afternoon. What about Leslie? a small voice inside me chirped
as the traffic intensified and the tract housing flashed by faster and

faster on either side. Where would she live? Where would she find a job? The sign said SAN FRANCISCO 38 MILES.

By the time I reached the Carquines Bridge at the outer rim of the Bay Area suburbs, traffic was nearly bumper-to-bumper but still moving along at fifty-five. Of course, if anyone slammed on his brakes, there'd be a pile-up of two or three hundred cars. I crossed the Bay Bridge from Oakland to San Francisco against the rush-hour mob, then joined the traffic jam myself downtown. After crossing the country, I didn't have to arrive at rush hour. Of course, I could still pull off the freeway and stop for a beer in a San Francisco bar. *If* I could find a place to park. Would there be room for us in California? The van was starting to overheat. Les! I hadn't thought enough about Leslie, and I'd had three thousand miles. I'd just whiled them away, vainly singing of myself.

Part Two

ten

The fog had already started to roll in by the time I escaped the traffic snarl heading out of San Francisco. It was cool in the city, cooler still in Millbrae and San Bruno where I could see the fog blowing across the hills, destination—Candlestick Park. Here, baseball fans had to wrap up in blankets for the night games in July, sometimes even in September, the "fair-weather month." Driving south on the Bayshore Freeway, I noticed that the circle was unbroken. Sprawl was now continuous around the bay. The peninsula had really grown up in the last fifteen years. Along the freeway were billboards, tract housing, and industrial shells where once there had been only baylands, a couple of airports for Piper Cubs, and that perfect habitat for seagulls, garbage dumps. Houses cut into the hills where there had once been only snakes, madrone, and poison oak. I'd expected no less and didn't really mind the changes. California wasn't my sacred turf, or at least not mine alone, but a wet dream for millions. L.A. might be our bastard child, but it was ours nonetheless. I felt it was wrong to pick and choose what I liked of California, pretending that the rest was no part of me. We'd Californicate this place together, in more or less equal shares, the other immigrants and I.

New houses and buildings obscured my view of memorable sites, but I could still glimpse them, in my mind's eye pick them out. The rusting corrugated walls of the older, shanty warehouses. The redwood enclave which was Clyde Divine Swim Center. That gave me a tingle, but it was the sight of the fog that held me.

Toward Belmont the fog receded as it always did, and I could see its line of gray as a cresting wave all along the ridge above the reservoir. Here was my source of expectation, the promise perpetually given that would never be fulfilled, the font of all my longings and midnight trips to the kitchen cupboards to rummage for what I knew I'd never find. Or so I liked to think. Imagine a great wave that rises up every evening and subsides every morning but never curls into a breaker, just hangs over the hills brimming with anticipation, wisps of fog feathering off its crest. To watch the fog is to be left suspended, never satisfied, never quenched. Already the lights of the houses on the hillside were beginning to blink on. A line of taillights ran up into the hills from my old hometown of Belmont. That would be Cañada Road, beyond it the way to Half Moon Bay. Deep in these hills I knew were lovely tiered houses in the wide California mode with patios and buena vistas and swimming pools and hot tubs and sleek Jaguars in the drive. Something was promised me—as a native, as one who carried that cresting wave around with him in his head— and it was all I could do to convince myself that cars, villas, and vistas were not it, not what I wanted, or at least not all.

In those lovely houses or those cars might be beautiful women, blond matrons tanned from toe to crown, or gorgeous girls of eighteen or twenty in strapless evening gowns. I might go driving through the hills with one of them, sweeping around the high-banked curves. We'd stir up the scents of acacia, mimosa, laurel, and thyme. The women would drive. I imagined them all fitted out in pedal pushers, fifties garb, and T-Birds of the same era. We'd sit in silence as we drove, only the tires would whisper. Our chrome would flash in the moonlight twisting out of the curves, but in the lee of the redwoods, we'd see only the silver beams of our headlights and feel only the rich red glow of the dash bathing our skins with light. We'd sit apart in each other's presence, calm and contemplative (that is, vacant), absorbed in ourselves, while outside the car heaved and roared. The car whined anticipation in low gear. The car throbbed with mechanical passion and life. Wasn't it the car that promised satisfaction,

that we were going somewhere and the somewhere we were going
was worth the trip? We'd have to make love with the engine running.
It was the car as much as the woman that I wanted in my dream.

Maybe high in the hills in Woodside or La Honda, Les and I
could ride to the shore. The sun would be warm on our backs, and
the hooves of the horses would raise puffs of dust. We'd wear crumpled old cowboy hats made from straw and listen to the slow creakings
of our saddles, smelling the sage for hours on end, traveling over
these hills as they were traveled in the century before. It might take
us all afternoon to get across, but we wouldn't mind. We'd have
years.

And then what? A Lone Star beer in a cowboy bar and a CW
polka, holding the chafed skin of a cowgirl in my hands? I couldn't
take the horse to bed with me any more than I could the car. What
was it that I wanted? Maybe the sexy hills themselves with their hips
and great languorous thighs? I could only gaze at them, I could
never stick one in my mouth and suck. No, if I was in love with
the Coast Range, then that was a love I could never consummate.
There would be no crescendo (not unless you figured on an earthquake). The wave would never break for me. I drove on in quiet
desperation, afraid I might miss it, if I could ever figure out what
"it" might be.

In Palo Alto, I felt the tug of other falls. It was time to get ready
for school. Soon I'd have to transform myself, first find a place to
cocoon, then emerge as something I didn't know how to be—a
graduate student in modern thought and lit. My fellow first-year
students would be butterflies, I felt sure, still fluttering from the
senior theses they'd written on the "Relative Uses of the Nose" in
Proust and Gogol, comparing the pizza parlors and the secondhand
bookstores in "Cambridge," "New Haven," and most euphemistic
of all, "Poughkeepsie." I was a mere moth, the graduate of a state
university. I knew I should be nervous, but all I felt was political
loathing for the Miami opulence of the palm trees and the perfect
lawns, the uniformity of tile roofs, and the well-endowed Catholicism of the fresco on the chapel wall. Wasn't this just the kind of
place where Bebe Rebozo would be rumored to be?

The department was closed by the time I arrived, but Stanford University, in its largesse, had provided me with the temporary use of a dorm room at the nominal fee of fifteen dollars a night. I could see that the institution was going to make life easier for me, at least as long as my fellowship money held out. In the morning, I could consult the Stanford Housing Office, secure in the knowledge that their listings were the best around since most people would rather rent their apartments to a graduate student at Stanford than any other form of refugee. And in the meantime, I had a bed for the night. I had clean sheets. On the pillow it said STANFORD UNIVERSITY.

I wondered where Leslie and the kids would sleep. If they drove high enough into the hills, they might find a tourist cabin. Or they might be camping out somewhere. Knowing Leslie, I figured she'd seek out the places where the Mexican farm workers stayed. Of course, they might still be driving, across the salt flats of Utah, the higher deserts of Nevada, down from Donner Pass. Our rendezvous was still five days off. We'd arranged to meet at ten A.M. on September sixteenth in front of the last house we'd lived in in Belmont. In the meantime, I could scour the campgrounds of Santa Cruz, La Honda, Pescadero, and Half Moon Bay. Or I could try not to worry. I could be sensible and look for apartments, return to this dorm room at night and observe my fellow students twirling their tennis rackets and tossing their frisbees, coming and going from their sporting events. These would be my fellow Californians, their hair short or blond or tousled, pick any two out of three. Watching them, I imagined they'd want to be MBAs, make millions and move to Atherton, the exclusive 'burb Gum's kin aspired to (and never achieved), where all the houses featured electronic gates and drive-ways flanked by statues that had been manufactured without heads. Who needs one in Atherton? Watching these kids, I could feel my prejudices rising in my throat. What was the matter with me?

Later on, I picked out a more interesting pair just going out for the evening. The woman wore a gauzy wrap-around skirt and a tube top. She was bohemian and undeniably voluptuous in her clothes which wrapped and clung rather than just hung. I could see the line of her panties from ten yards away. Close up, I could even make out a word stitched onto their side. The word was Monday. This was Wednesday. I was intrigued. The guy with her had curly red hair and a beard to match. He wore his guitar slung upside-down over his shoulder like Dylan used to when he was still singing "Subterranean Homesick Blues." I figured that I might find a place to fit in after all; I was still singing that song too.

The first day of apartment hunting, I found myself a boarding-house room on the Alameda de las Pulgas, the Way of the Fleas. My landlady was a Steinbeck character. She called herself Tangerine. When she asked me where "my people" came from, I mentioned a lot of places including San Jose, and right then she took my hand. "Then you're a prune picker! Glad to meet 'cha! I'm a prune picker too!" She held my hand so long I started to wonder if she were checking for calluses. But I didn't mind Tangerine. The rent was cheap, and I didn't have to put down a deposit. Best of all, I could live like a migrant worker, paying by the week, and I knew that Leslie would approve. Tangerine even had a place for her to look at, "an awful nice cottage" over in South Palo Alto.

I arrived in Belmont half an hour early for my rendezvous with Les. Her car wasn't there yet, and I started wondering if she'd be coming at all. Had something happened to her? Had I gotten the day wrong? the month? the year? This was definitely the right split-level. I'd know that garage door anywhere. I could have found it in the rubble after the earthquake. But believing that I was really here and that any minute now Les was going to pull up in her VW bus covered with dust and stuffed with the kids and animals was another matter entirely. I started up my engine and let it idle for a minute. Then I decided to drive around.

I passed White Oaks, my old elementary school. A moody child, I'd spent my first few years daydreaming during class, dawdling on my way home from school, and fawning over little girls. My most serious crush was on Francine Corbette, whose hair was as yellow as the Crayola and whose name reminded me of sports cars. In fact, that was nearly the sum of what Francine meant to me—fast cars and yellow Crayolas—although I gave her a ring, a sunburst of rhinestones in a simple plastic setting. In the second grade, we were "going steady." We ate paste (which tasted like poi) off each other's fingers and during recess wandered hand-in-hand through the playgrounds until a third-grader called me a sissy and shoved me into the thornbush. That night I asked my sister what to do. "Scalp him! Stomp the kid!" Les told me, picking the thorns out of my skin. "You gotta pound him! You gotta rub his face in the dirt until he takes it back!" What's in a name? I wondered, but Les was my big sister and I did whatever she told me. Forsaking Francine during recess, I lurked beside the thornbush until the third-grader came along, then I called him a dumb-ass and shoved him in. We wrestled, got into trouble, had to stay after school. Afterward I was offered membership in the school gang, which rumbled intramurally.

It was still only quarter of. I drove very slowly back toward Diamond Drive. The neighborhood was smaller. My van filled the little streets. I felt as though I were driving a tank or a semi. The curbs looked like wrinkles in the pavement; I could run right over them with my tractor treads. This was the route I'd walked as a child, hurrying to school, dawdling home again. But it's difficult to dawdle in a car when you have only three blocks to travel and nowhere to stop along the way. I wondered what had happened to Francine Corbette. Had she grown up into a "good girl" or a "bad girl"? A "fox" or a "dog"? She was probably married by now. If she had children, did that make her a "cow"?

Turning the corner, I saw that Les was already parked in front of our old house on Diamond Drive. I looked at my watch. I was late. It was ten after already. Barbara and Matt started cheering as soon as they saw me. Then the dog joined in, barking. I heard myself barking back. Three narrow streets converged in front of the house—not quite as I remembered. Two streets went up, one went down. Les had parked in the only full-sized spot, and I drove around the circle where the roads came together without seeing any place large enough to fit my van. The kids continued to cheer, so I circled around once more before coming to a stop right in the center of the intersection and jumping out to greet them. Leslie and I didn't hug or kiss (we didn't do that), but I mauled her children in her stead.

Then I hopped back in the van. "Clown," I heard her say somewhere behind my back.

I parked up the hill half a block away and ran back down. Everything looked miniature to me of course, the split-level we'd once lived in and the converging streets and curbs, but what I wasn't prepared for was the steepness of the grade. I almost lost my balance running down and couldn't stop until I grabbed onto Leslie's VW bus. The kids interpreted this as antics and cheered all the louder while I tried to catch my breath. "I must have gotten top-heavy. In my old age," I gasped.

"Clown," Les said, more sharply this time.

I probably looked stricken. I felt as though I'd been slapped.

"I was only *kidding*. You don't have to *cry* about it, Jeremy."

"I'm not..."

"Why're you so sensitive all of a sudden?"

"I don't know what you're talking about..."

"All right, I'm sorry. I didn't mean to hurt your feelings. It's just that we've been waiting—"

"How long? Five minutes? I got here half an hour ago, and I've been driving around." Suddenly I was aware of Barbara and Mat, watching us. "Hey, what's going on? I feel like I've just stepped into the middle of a play, and we both know our lines. Are we reenacting something?" The kids had gotten back in the cab of the bus and sat huddled together in the passenger seat like Okie children in a modern-day Walker Evans shot. Les stood apart. I stepped as casually as I could toward the bus and wrapped an arm around Barbara, who immediately hugged me back. Mat jumped down and started shinnying up my leg. "Have the natives been restless?" I asked.

Les shrugged. "I guess I'm a little strung out. I was worried, that you wouldn't show up."

"I *am* a native," Barbara said with wonder.

"Me too," said Mat.

"No you're not," she corrected her brother. "You were born in Connecticut, which means you're a Yankee, not a Californian like Mommy and Jeremy and me."

"Tell her I'm a native, Mommy!"

"You're a native," Les said dully.

"See!"

"She doesn't mean it," Barbara said. "She's just trying to get you to shut up."

"Mommy! Tell her, Mommy!" Mat was pulling at her jeans, yanking on her pockets and her blouse.

Les was slow to wake up. It struck me how tired she must be from the drive. "You're a native American, Chico, one of the aboriginal peoples. Will that do?"

"See!"

"See said the blind man," Barbara mocked her brother. "You're still a Yankee."

"No I'm not! I'm a redskin!" he protested.

"Connecticut Yankee from King Arthur's Court!"

Mat was on the verge of tears. "I don't have to go to court," he said, and I wondered where he'd learned the word. "I didn't get a ticket. I wasn't doing nothing wrong. Tell her, Mom!"

"Come on, you two," Les said briskly. "Poncho! Chico! Both of you shut up now. We're going to walk the dog." At the sound of the word "walk" Blazes came to life and started throwing himself against the inside of the bus with deep, resounding thuds. Les reached in and grabbed him, snapping on his leash in one smooth motion. Then she released his collar, and Blazes took off, dragging Leslie behind him like a rag. She looked even skinnier than I remembered.

The rest of us had to run to catch up. Blazes and Les were already halfway down Emerald toward Pearl by the time we reached them, and before we knew it the five of us were rounding the corner onto Sapphire. "These blocks have either shrunk, or we've sped up," I said, trying to remember the sequence of streets below Sapphire: Ruby, Garnet, Agate, Opal, Amethyst, with Topaz almost downtown.

"Shrunk," Les said. "Listen, I'm sorry if I'm weird. I feel like I'm in a time warp, or one of those dreams in which you're thrown back into the past, trapped in a high-school class, forced to take an exam as a twenty-five- or thirty-year-old, except no one can tell that you're twenty-five or thirty, they think you're just the same old kid.

You think, I've asked for this every time I wished if only I could go back there with what I know now, and then there you are and you hate it. You open your mouth to scream and nothing comes out. You pinch yourself, but it doesn't work. Your eyes are closing, your legs are so heavy you can hardly drag them along..."

"Quite a nightmare. Sounds like somebody's vision of hell," I offered.

"I thought *I* was the one who went to parochial schools... To me it just sounds like fear of paralysis."

"I thought that was *my* fear..."

Les suddenly lurched ahead at the end of her leash. "No, mine."

I had to hustle to keep up with her. We were practically running down the street, the kids strung out behind us. "I keep expecting to turn the next corner and see the ghost of Fog," I said. "He'll be holding a paint brush. He'll be painting the garage."

Les finally smiled. "No, he won't. He'll be waving a broom, running down the street pursued by a black widow spider."

We laughed, trotting along. "You know, I looked for you all across the country. I even thought I saw your taillights now and then, but of course I was wrong. When did you get here?"

"Three days ago."

"Four," Barbara corrected her, calling out from behind. I was surprised she'd even heard us.

Les ignored her. "Mat thought he saw your van in Illinois, but when we caught up, it turned out to be a *moving* van. Didn't look a bit like yours."

"How was it for you, cooped up in the bus with seven creatures?"

"Six. Either Hortense or Calisher died." She shrugged. "For me, the trip was a little like steerage, except I had to drive."

"You didn't happen to cross the Rockies in that blizzard, did you? West Yellowstone and Targhee Pass?"

Leslie stopped, yanking Blazes to a halt. "Were *you* there?"

The kids caught up and crowded around us. Blazes was straining against the bit, starting to gag. "Yeah. I crossed just after midnight. It took me the rest of the night to get down."

"We were a few hours ahead of you then. But it must have been the same night. How many summer blizzards could they have?"

I giggled. "I don't know. It didn't seem like summer anymore."

"I know what you mean," Les said, her eyes perfect circles, they were open so wide. "Did you sense anything? My presence?" she asked.

I was embarrassed. "More Barbara's, actually."

"Oh. Well, she was awake all night. Weren't you, Poncho? You didn't close your eyes all night."

Barbara didn't say anything. "You know," I said to her, "I was picking up your radio signals crossing the Rockies in that storm..."

"Well, I was sending them all right. They spelled SOS."

eleven

*L*eslie had driven across by way of Mount Rushmore and Wounded Knee, hitting as many of the Indian reservations as she could—Crow Creek, Pine Ridge, Fort Hall, the Northern Cheyenne Reservation, and the Little Big Horn—because Barbara and Mat were one-eighth Cherokee on their father's side and fascinated with their Indian roots. They had spent a night in Livingston, Montana (one-time residence of that Connecticut Indian, Pete Pardieu), dropping down into Yellowstone from the north. They hadn't stopped to see Aaron. Les said she didn't even know his new address. Les and the kids had been two days ahead of me out of Chicago, but only three or four hours crossing the Rockies at Targhee Pass. That night they'd slept at Henrietta's Campground just as I had, but left early in the morning, about the time Henrietta was rousting me out of my sleeping bag by beating on the side of my van. I must have passed them again in Utah when they detoured for Fort Hall. Then they must have passed me back in eastern Nevada on the night of my gambling spree. They hadn't camped at Donner Lake as I'd expected, but had driven straight through, arriving a full day before me. For the last four nights they'd been camping somewhere on the coast, near Half Moon Bay, near Pescadero. Leslie was vague about that. She didn't seem surprised that we'd leapfrogged across Utah and Nevada, and the vast stretches of highway collapsed as we talked about them. Our relative routes across the country,

139

which had seemed to me so crucial as I drove, lost significance in the face of the most remarkable thing of all—that we were together in California again.

Leslie stood at the center of our little reunion: the eye of the storm. Barbara and I were exuberant, laughing and grinning and touching each other's shoulders and waists, but Mat was getting out of control. He was shinnying up my legs and giggling wildly, yanking at my neck to get high enough to kick his sister in the head. "That's enough, Mat," I said, grabbing his legs to restrain them, but he only giggled and squirmed all the harder. Meanwhile Blazes was leaping around and straining against his leash until he gagged. Les was unperturbed. She seemed pleased that I'd found a place for her to look at in Palo Alto, even if the landlady was named Tangerine. She said she'd rather live in the Haight or the Panhandle sections of San Francisco, but the schools there were dismal. ("Hideous" was the word she used, and I wondered if she'd heard something about them or just driven in and made an aesthetic call.) The Palo Alto schools were very clean and orderly—"like West Germany," she said—but she hadn't been able to find a thing to rent there herself. "No kids, no dogs. *Verboten.* Just like Tory Hole." In spite of the commotion, Les and I talked easily about the past, the present, and the immediate future. The shock of first seeing her wore off. We sat on the curb. The only thing that continued to astound me was our setting here in Belmont, in the neighborhood of the precious and the semiprecious stones, and how impalpable this homecoming was turning out to be. The streets were entirely deserted. We heard no other voices but our own. It wasn't that I'd expected a brass band and all our childhood friends gathered around to greet us, but neither had I imagined that this place would be quite so dead. I felt as though we weren't really here so much as in a Disney movie, floating an inch or two above the sidewalk, about to be whisked off to some new locale.

"Let's drop in on Dr. Miller," Les suggested out of the blue. Dr. Miller was our old pediatrician and the man Sunshine credited with saving her life.

"Is someone sick?" I asked, looking instinctively toward Mat.

"Yeah, sick in the head," Barbara snickered, but Mat was too far gone to hear her. He was trying to climb up on Blazes, who was in turn twisting this way and that and barking out his objection to being mounted like a horse.

"No," Les said. "We're all fine. I just want to see him again."

So we climbed back into our cars and drove down the hill, tandem this time since I didn't remember where Dr. Miller's office was. "Neither do I," Les said, "but we'll find it. The pathway is ingrained. We'll just follow our noses and the smell of alcohol." Les drove ahead, Barbara and Mat waving out the back window and making faces at me behind. I waved back and grinned and frowned. I did my gorilla routine and managed to keep it up for five minutes in spite of the traffic all around. Then I pretended to be a haughty stranger who refused even to notice that the kids were stretching out their mouths and nostrils with their fingers and beating their heads against the glass. We were still only halfway down the hill, and the kids showed no signs of tiring. This was going to be a long ride. I tried to take an interest in the scenery—the stucco houses and the terraced gardens giving way to apartment blocks, shopping centers, then gas stations and fast-food eateries like International Pancakes and The House of Pies. This was the landscape of reality? But the kids just thought my gazing was part of the game and mimicked me, rolling their heads around. We passed Leslie's old school, the Convent of the Purple Heart, but when I pointed it out Barbara only imitated me and Mat only imitated her.

Then a funny thing happened. Mat disappeared. He must have suddenly jumped over the seat when I was looking at the scenery. Barbara was still there, though. She smiled at me, I smiled back. It was as though we were watching each other on closed-circuit television screens. Then she stopped smiling and just stared.

As soon as we crossed into San Mateo, Leslie veered into a filling station and pulled up near the rest rooms. I figured I knew why Mat had suddenly disappeared from the back window. He'd been voicing an urgent need for a bathroom. I felt even more sure of my conclusion when Les jumped out of the driver's seat and started rummaging in the back for some clothes. But then she came up with clothes not only for Mat but also Barbara and apparently for herself. The whole family disappeared into the women's room.

They emerged ten minutes later all neatly dressed and combed, looking as though they were off to church. "Dr. Miller's a father figure for me," Les explained.

When we reached the office, Les scrutinized the list of names, then heaved a sigh of relief. "I was terrified on the way over here," she said. "It's been fifteen years, you know. Doctors don't ordinarily live to be so old."

"Old pediatricians never die. They're preserved in formaldehyde."

"Jeremy!"

"Pediatricians are immortal. Dr. Miller most of all. Anyway, Sunshine would have told us. She called him when she was out here after Fog died, and that was only a year and a half ago."

"I guess you're right," she said, already more concerned with tucking in her son's shirt and straightening her daughter's part. "I'm getting nervous. Why am I getting nervous? I've known him all my life."

"That's why you're getting nervous, because you've known him all your life."

"You're quite the philosopher today. Have you started your modern thought classes or is this just an aftereffect of your cross-country drive?"

I smiled. "The drive."

The waiting room was crowded. I gave my name to the receptionist since mine was the name that had remained the same. We only had to wait a few minutes before Dr. Miller came to the door. "It's true!" he said, holding out his arms. "I couldn't believe it. I had to see for myself." Leslie kissed him on the cheek while I shook his hand. He looked diminished, shrunken from the man who'd towered over my measles and my chicken pox. "How did you know I'd be in today? Did you set this up with Betty as a little surprise? I'm 'semi-retired,' you know, meaning my partners are trying to put me out to pasture, ease me out the door..."

"Now, Dr. Miller, you know that just isn't so," the receptionist protested squeakily from behind the frosted glass.

"We didn't know whether you'd be here or not. We're just lucky," I said.

"May you always be," Dr. Miller said solemnly. Then he announced to the patients assembled around us in the waiting room: "Old patients never die! But they grow to be six feet three!"

"Unless you preserve them in formaldehyde," Barbara said in a low voice.

"I heard that!" Dr. Miller said, wheeling around to face her and finally smiling. "And I know where you got your sense of humor..." He ushered us into his office, then shook hands with each of the kids in turn, calling Mat Matthew and pronouncing all three syllables in Barbara's name. "And your husband? Where is he?" he asked Leslie.

"I'm divorced."

"A shame," he said with more accusation than sympathy in his voice. "You young people, you don't know how to stick it out anymore. You reach for your parachute at the first sign of rain..." (Bumbershoot, I said to myself.) "How long were your parents married? Thirty years?"

"Thirty-two," Les said.

"Thirty-two. You see what I mean. You ever heard the phrase 'Till death do us part'? Those words ring any bells for you?"

Les shrugged and looked away from him. I thought she might start to cry. "I'm getting divorced too," I said.

"So, it's a movement. Or maybe you're just a copycat, taking after your sister?" He shook his head, disgusted. "You've both made a mess of things. I expected more. Given your genes, I would have expected more. What do *you* think? Don't you think so?" he suddenly asked Barbara, who was sitting very properly in the corner, where she could be seen, but only if you looked for her. "Don't you think they could have stuck it out?"

"You haven't met my father. Or my Aunt Sara," she said softly.

"Speak up, dear. We can't hear you."

Barbara straightened. "I said, you haven't met my father or my Aunt Sara. So I don't see how you can act so sure."

"Aha!" Dr. Miller laughed. "She's part of each of you, the little judge and the gangster girl, all rolled into one. I like your spunk, young lady. Well—maybe you haven't made such a mess of things after all," he said to Leslie. Then he turned to me. "How about you? Any kids."

"No kids."

"What's the matter? You weren't so sure the marriage would last?"

"Something like that."

"Always the prudent one," he said to Leslie, poking his thumb at me. "That's another judicial trait. You're going to law school, I suppose?"

"English."

"*English?* What, English school? You don't speak it well enough already?" He paused for me to answer, but I didn't oblige. "Well? Cat got your tongue? There's no telling if *you* won't say. What can you do with English? Graduate school?"

I nodded.

"What school?"

"Stanford."

"Fancy, fancy. But an excellent university. Who's footing the bill? Your poor mother? A widow paying tuition for such a fancy school . . ."

"I've got a fellowship, as far as that's concerned."

"Well, congratulations, as far as that's concerned. He says, Mind your own business, as far as that's concerned. Why's this brother of yours so closed-mouthed?" he asked Leslie. "Why not just come right out with the information? It's good news. Why keep me guessing? It makes people nervous to be guessing. They worry, they might be wrong. Always I could see you thinking, thinking, judging, never telling. It made me nervous. You were always such a moralistic child . . ."

"I'm sorry that you felt that way."

"So judgmental, so serious, staring, never smiling . . ." He pursed his lips and squinted at me, his narrow accusations cutting through my dignified veneer.

"I never judged *you*, Doctor. If anything, I thought you were

God." I smiled, floundering for a way to overcome the barriers of disapproval and pride. "I was just thinking, I've never thanked you for helping Mother when she had polio. I was pretty young, but anyway . . . She always said you saved her life."

"Saved her life? That's ridiculous. Your mother saved her own life. She doesn't know what she's talking about anyway, she was delirious at the time. There's no one to thank, believe me, unless you want to go to church and thank your God. Better yet, just thank your mother. She's the one who had the guts to persevere." Dr. Miller waved his hand to dismiss the thought, then turned to the kids. "When he was your age, your Uncle Jeremy was a little judge, always talking right and wrong, always deciding fair and not fair. I asked him, 'Whoever told you life was supposed to be fair?' And he just glared at me. Somebody had told him, that's for sure. For him, it was a premise, you understand? It was self-evident, as in 'We hold these truths to be self-evident.' Maybe you've heard the phrase? *He* had anyway. So that's your uncle. That's how he looked at the world. But your mother here, was she a different story! She was a terrorist! A one-woman PLO! All my nurses were afraid of her. *I* was afraid of her! She was a howler and a screamer, a kicker and a biter! You should have seen her! Oh, you should have seen her." He smiled, and Barbara and Mat grinned back at him. "A holy terror like your mother doesn't deserve such wonderful kids . . ."

twelve

eslie moved into Tangerine's cottage on Thursday. She enrolled the kids in Palo Alto schools the next morning, then drove up to San Francisco to show them the Steinhart Aquarium in Golden Gate Park. I had to register for classes, so I drove up separately and met them at the Cliff House after lunch.

The Cliff House was where the family used to gather when we lived in California. It was Gum's idea. Of course, she would always be the first to point out what a shabby substitute this new Cliff House really was. The old place had been a Victorian palace. It even looked like Queen Victoria—a great squat structure with a crown of gables and spires and below clapboard skirts that concealed just how heavily it sat on the rocks. That was the old San Francisco, where ladies wore white gloves when they went shopping even though they took the bus, even though they were immigrant stock, and Gum's vast clan used to gather at the Cliff House for Sunday lunch. The original Cliff House burned in 1907, but that didn't stop tradition. We still met there after mass on Sundays— Gum and Papa, Sunshine and Fog, Les and I, and always a few odds and ends of Gum's Irish relations—although as Gum constantly reminded us the new Cliff House was no more than a pale imitation, a mere remnant of the glory of the past, a kind of duplex of two mediocre restaurants where once there'd been one that was grand. ("How old was Gum when it burned?" I asked as a child, but no one answered me.) What we were left with in the fifties was a big block structure, its front designed to look like the entrance to a dry cleaner's and on the side its concrete skirts laid bare for what they were—retaining wall.

Yet it was the old Cliff House that Les and I expected, and like Gum this was the one we described to the kids as we sat in one of the touristy restaurants sipping our Irish coffees with fake whipped cream. "Did you see the ruins of the Sutro Baths?" I asked Leslie.

She nodded. "Gone."

"The seals don't even look the same."

"Yeah, they've gotten gray and fat," she agreed.

Barbara looked at us as though we were crazy. "When did you say this place burned down?"

"Nineteen oh-seven," Les said in a theatrically offhand way.

Barbara hesitated for a moment, subtracting. "That's before you were born, isn't it?"

Les nodded. "Thirty or forty years," she said.

"That's even before *Grandma* was born!"

"Easily."

Barbara looked from one of us to the other. "You're loony-tunes, both of you, you know that."

Mat came running back from the picture window looking out on Seal Rock. "Where are the seals?" he whined. "I don't see any."

"There aren't any," Barbara said. "People just pretend they exist. For the tourists, and the rock's good name."

"You have to look carefully," I said. "The seals are the gray things. They look like rocks except they swim and crawl. When they crawl, they look like beetles."

"That's what they really are, Mat, water beetles," Barbara said. "The seals all died a long time ago, in nineteen fifty-nine, if they ever existed at all."

Mat looked confused and as though he might start to cry. "You said there'd be seals here, Mommy!"

"And so there are, Chico. You just have to use your imagination is all."

"That's what they tell you about everything," Barbara went on. "You remember what they said at Wounded Knee, don't you? And at the Little Big Horn?"

Mat threw himself into Les's lap. I signaled for the check. (She let me pay without a protest.) Then we gulped the rest of our drinks and left.

Outside I fed quarters into the binocular machine and held Mat up long enough so that he could see the seals and settle down. He was on the verge of tears, and it took a long time to get them in focus. Afterward we drove in tandem south along the coast road, Highway 1, through Pacifica and Devil's Slide. Mat rode with me. As we followed Les and Barbara down the coast, he asked me question after question about his newfound seals: where they slept at night (on Seal Rock), what they ate (fish and chips), what ate them (sharks and Eskimos), whether the sharks might not mistake the surfers in their black wet suits for seals (maybe, since sharks can't see very well and never wear their specs), and why I didn't grow a mustache or a beard like Jay and Sultan (I didn't want to cover up my pretty face).

Mat asked intelligent questions, and I liked answering him. It made me feel closer to Fog and Papa in an inverse way, although I noticed that Mat drew no real satisfaction from my answers, nor did he seem to hope for any. His eyes followed the cliff edge, then darted back ahead to the road to make sure that his mother's car was still in sight, sweeping like the beam of a lighthouse, repeating like an automated machine. Except his eyes seemed anxious, maybe more so because he didn't feel he knew me very well. I felt I knew *him* very well since I'd changed a few of his diapers, helped teach him how to swim, served as his jungle gym and pet gorilla ever since he'd learned how to climb, and held him once or twice when big dogs came around sticking their aggressive snouts between his legs and sniffing, but he probably didn't remember these occasions or recognize my claim to any intimacy beyond the usual grown-up's role.

On the other hand, Mat might have seemed nervous with me on account of the breakup with Sara. Kids take a dim view of divorce, and he had liked Sara, taking a sexual interest in her in his five-year-old way. Maybe he felt oedipal for lusting after his uncle's wife. Mat had been especially intrigued by Sara's breasts. She never discouraged him. She thought it was healthy, she said he was cute. When we came to visit, Mat liked to wake us up in the mornings. If we'd remembered to lock the door, we'd wake to find him peering at us from the space beneath the door where Fog had cut it off about four inches too short. Once, I woke up to see him standing over the bed and staring at Sara as at a sleeping goddess. The sheet had slipped off her, and she was bare from the waist up. Matthew was staring at her breasts rising and falling as she slept. He'd synchronized his breathing, or so it seemed to me. When he looked up finally and saw me watching him, he didn't return my smile but ran from the room. That afternoon he crawled into Sara's lap and confided to her, "Mommy's boobies are bigger than Grandma's, but yours are the biggest of all." Sara never tired of retelling that.

After the flurry of questions, Mat and I drove in silence. I could have reversed the situation and asked him questions—about camping across the country or whether he was scared to be starting a new school or how he liked Mount Rushmore, whether Teddy Roosevelt was carrying a big stick or it was true that George Washington's teeth were made of wood. But Mat hadn't reached the age of irony, and questions might have only made the poor kid jitterier.

Just south of Devil's Slide, a section of twisting highway and sheer cliff where the hillside was trying to slip into the ocean and take the road with it, Leslie suddenly pulled into a turnout and stopped her car. I pulled in behind her. She was already out of the car and walking toward the remains of a large familiar house set out on an eroding promontory. "Will you look at it?" Les said. I did. The house looked to be bombed out. There was very little of it to be seen. Only three of the walls were still standing. The fourth had already fallen into the sea, which was a few hundred feet straight down. The house had obviously been abandoned, and the reason was also obvious. The land it stood on had been shearing away until all that remained were the house itself, or most of it, and a narrow land bridge out to the road. Soon the house would go, too. Any minute now, the land bridge.

"It must have been a beautiful place. Can you imagine waking up to that ocean every morning, and hearing that surf come crashing down?"

"I think I remember it. How do we get in?" Les asked me.

Between the house and the roadway was a wire-mesh fence topped with barbed wire tilted toward us. This was the kind of fence only an expert could climb, and it was posted with the full array of hysterical no-trespassing signs. "Not over the top, that's for sure. Evel Knievel couldn't scale that. Maybe we cold swing out around one of the ends, though..." I started toward one of the ends. Les hurried to catch up. The kids hung back. They both looked nervous now.

"What do you think?" Les asked, her hands on her hips like a construction worker. "Think we can handle it?"

Mat started screaming before I could reply. "Don't do it, Mommy!" he was yelling over and over again. "Don't do it, Mommy!" After a moment, Barbara joined in. They hollered in unison, "Don't do it, Mommy! Don't do it, Mommy! You'll fall into the ocean!"

At first I thought this was some kind of joke. Les and I hadn't been contemplating anything dangerous, and if it had turned out to be risky to half-scramble half-swing around the end of the fence, we wouldn't have done it. Obviously. We were grown-ups, after all. "They sound like a weird chorus," I said before I saw from the sudden sag in Les's face that her children weren't teasing, they were genuinely afraid.

In Pescadero we stopped again and walked along the beach. There were no cliffs here, no condemned houses slowly tumbling into the sea. The beach was studded with ragged outcroppings of red rock, pocked by erosion. The ocean was a pale blue, whitened by the turbulence, and the surf seemed untamed, the waves coming in irregularly, crashing and roiling around the rocks. It was a pretty day, at least for Pescadero. The fog had lifted, but the wind was stiff and cold.

We came to a small stand of rocks like a climbing toy, set out a few yards into the surf where at the farthest ebb between waves you could walk out and touch the rocks without getting more than the soles of your feet wet. Les and I stopped and watched the cycles of the surf around the rock. There were only a few seconds between the waves, then the surf swept back in, sometimes crashing up to the top of the rock and filling the wind with spray. "What do you say? Are you game?" Les asked me.

I knew what she meant. In that sense, we'd been here before. Les slipped off her sandals, approached the water, waited for a long ebb, then neatly dashed out, tagged the rock, and ran back in just ahead of the incoming wave. The kids gathered around her, awed but uncertain, touching their mother as though inspecting her for damage. Les brushed off their hands and stepped away from them. "Your turn," she challenged me.

My timing was less perfect. An incoming wave was almost upon me by the time I tagged, so instead of racing back to the beach and losing the race, I hopped up onto the rock like a monkey and scurried to the top. The water splashed up only to my ankles, but I feigned panic, hamming for the kids.

Mat looked even more worried than before, but Barbara knew I was clowning and pulled out her Instamatic. Then Les dashed out again to join me, and together we posed for pictures, miming terror, then nonchalance with the breakers arching at our backs. The next waves broke higher, and then even higher than that. Our rock was getting slippery, the water splashing up around our waists. "Put your arms around each other!" Barbara called, and this once we did. First we wrapped our arms around each other's shoulders, then we leaned into it, posing cheek-to-cheek. I felt giddy—whether from the contact or the fear of slipping, I wasn't sure. By the time Barbara was satisfied with her snapshots, both Les and I were drenched and shivering. But we couldn't stop giggling. We called to the kids to come join us on the rock. Barbara smiled and shook her head, but Mat was visibly bothered by the suggestion. He ran away.

As we drove, I wondered if the children of adventurous parents turn out more fearful and instinctively cautious than those reared in more traditional households. Leslie and I grew up in a world where nothing bad or unhygienic or particularly interesting was likely to happen to us, at least as kids. And as a result, we grew into adults more childishly fearless (and foolish) than most children, certainly more than these kids, Barbara and Mat. Maybe children need a context of overprotectiveness to rebel against, to venture out from, to leap from into thinner air, to serve as their standard of what's too safe and secure—a little silly, a little suffocating, a little boring—the touchstone that having known in childhood we can safely abandon as adults.

Les's kids were never in any danger of being bored. They may have felt at times that their world was built on sand, but they were always entertained. Leslie's friends were an interesting lot—photographers, conceptual artists, and investment brokers who liked to get out to "the country" every once in a while, musicians, Black Panthers, and psychiatrists into transcendental meditation and hallucinogenic drugs.

The family pets alone were enough to keep the kids occupied. The turtles were escape artists, ingenious also in where they chose to hide. One of the cats was autistic and stimulated himself by the hour; the other was not only a mouser but a semiprofessional killer, a hitcat, dragging in moles, squirrels, birds, small rabbits, and even rats when she could find them in genteel Tory Hole. Flower was her name. She was mainly Barbara's cat, and out of loyalty she always carried her kills up the stairs to Barbara's room and consumed them underneath her bed. Flower was also the finest jumping cat I'd ever seen, able to leap tall furniture at a single bound and, when pursued by Blazes, to stay aloft (or at least appear to) for minutes at a time. As for the dog, Blazes Boylan, he combined all the traditional traits of both the Irish and the setter, except he didn't drink whiskey, only beer. He was brawling, loutish, disobedient, destructive, wild, and rebellious, but Les was convinced that his soul was poetic, and even after he'd started to bite people she wouldn't give him up.

Add two children with conventional tendencies and put them all in an old frame house (previously vacant and used as a target range for the local vandals), and that was my sister's family life before moving back to California. It may have been a full life, even a happy one, but it wasn't secure. Les was always feuding with her landlords. She had an acute sense of tenants' rights, perhaps from her days as an apartment manager, and she was quick to withhold the rent until repairs were made. My sister was expert in setting up escrow accounts, and Barbara also became adept at fending off the creditors and irate landlords who'd call up on the phone. The only trouble was the family was always on the verge of being tossed out on the street.

The last house, which we'd spent a month resurrecting without a dime of the landlord's dough, turned out to be the worst hole of all. The vandals weren't about to stop chucking rocks just because some woman moved in with her two little kids. Why should they? The lady wasn't even there in the daytime. We'd replaced all the broken panes when we'd repainted, resanded, revarnished, and waxed, and then Les had hired a carpenter to replace the first few broken windows in the fall. But that winter was the first of the fuel crunch. Prices for heating oil soared. By January, Les's oil bills had risen higher than her rent, and she couldn't keep up. Hers was a three-story house without storm windows or insulation. She plugged the drafts as best she could with cardboard and Visqueen, but there was nothing she could do about the ancient furnace that both guzzled and leaked. The landlord would make no repairs until that summer when the lease was up. Then he planned to raise the rent, in light of the recent renovation. When Les and the kids left for California, she was hundreds of dollars in arrears to Home Heating Oil, and the IRS was also dunning her for back taxes because they'd discovered that her ex-husband, who'd never paid more than fifty dollars a month in child support and that only rarely, was also claiming the children as dependents, and everybody knows you can't claim the same dependents twice.

Sometimes we forget the full extent to which children are dependent on their parents to set the boundaries of their worlds. It must be said that my sister wasn't always reliable (she wasn't always around), but she tried to compensate for her deficiencies by making her children laugh. Leslie was a closet comic. She impersonated animals or spiders or monsters on command once her kids were tucked in bed. Her stage was the upstairs hall where Barbara and Mat could look out and watch her from their darkened rooms. If they turned on their lights, she wouldn't perform. Her favorite character was "Renault Dough-Fiend," which was the name that fifties' teenagers assigned to the humpbacked French car of the time but became in Leslie's comic theater a kind of cookie monster whose particular obsessions were French bread and croissants. Les growled or howled or roared or whinnied (depending on the role), screwing up her face and clamoring on the floor. She was good at the voices and the sound effects, but the real secret of her success was her relentlessness. Les never broke out of character, no matter what, until her children were holding their stomachs, begging her to stop, falling out of their beds and rolling on the floor. Then she swore them to absolute secrecy. They had to swear never to tell anybody—not Grandma, not even Jeremy— about Renault Dough-Fiend and the lizard-who-loved-to-dance and their mother who acted like an idiot.

But although Leslie might send her children off to bed laughing every night, laughter can slip into more maudlin emotion once the light has been snapped off in the hall and the child hears in the darkened theater the whining of the wind through the masking tape around the cardboard windowpane. Leslie might be downstairs, out of earshot, or she might not be at home at all. The children must have asked themselves why they lived that way. Their friends didn't live that way, their grandparents didn't live that way. Not even Jeremy lived that way. Why us? they must have wondered as they sailed off to sleep.

That spring the telephone would ring late at night. Leslie ran to answer it. She didn't want its insistent alarm to wake the kids. The calls began in February, coming at first only in the late afternoon just when she got home from work, then in the evenings too. At first Les heard only silence on the other end of the line, then vague angry words: "Bitch, dyke, stupid broad..." The voice, when there was one, was male. Les filed a complaint with the police and changed to an unlisted phone number, but she had to give the new number to some people—her doctor, her boss, her mechanic, her children's schools. Maybe she wasn't careful enough. After a short interval, the calls started coming again, even later this time, and this time they were threatening.

At her mechanic's, there had been a man who'd asked her out for a drink and then gotten angry, throwing tools around, when she'd refused. That was in the winter sometime, when she wasn't sure, and she wasn't even sure he was still working there. Also in the winter, Les had had to fire her afternoon baby-sitter, a girl of about sixteen, because small items were turning up missing—record albums, cosmetics, costume jewelry, beers. She'd hired the girl on the recommendation of the nuns at Mat's parochial kindergarten, so it was hard to believe she was involved in obscene phone calls. On the other hand, it was true that the girl had a delinquent boyfriend and that she helped out from time to time in the office at Mat's school.

Les must have felt trapped. Her kids were helpless and afraid, and she was helpless to stop the ringing of the telephone. The police said there was nothing they could do, not without a suspect, not without a name. Sometimes Barbara took the calls. She just screamed back and slammed down the phone. The bigger problem was Mat. He started having nightmares and waking up shrieking in the night. He saw devils in the grain of the woodwork and apemen in the shadows on the floor. He was even afraid of Renault Dough-Fiend. Once he woke everyone up with his screaming because he saw a pool of blood on the floor, and the floor really was wet where he pointed, but it turned out to be only a puddle of pee where Blazes had lost control.

For a few minutes every night, Leslie became the Friendly

Monster-Who-Lives-Under-the-Bed, invisible when you looked for
him but when you needed him, always there. "But Mommy," Barbara said in exasperation. "There's no *room* under our beds. We
sleep on mattresses on the floor."

"Literal child!" Leslie growled. "Don't you realize we monsters
have our magical ways?"

Barbara never did.

We drove back from Pescadero by the most roundabout, tortuous,
winding route—Alpine Road to Page Mill Road. Leslie drove ahead
with Mat. Barbara rode with me. Les's VW cornered much better
than my van with its aging shocks, so I had to push it to keep up.
I concentrated on the road and drove well, accelerating in the curves
so that we rounded them under power and therefore under complete
control. From time to time, my worn tires complained a little against
the pavement, but mostly I took the curves just under squealing
speed.

Barbara was green by the time we reached the summit and
started back down the inland side. She gazed out the side window
into the middle distance rather than looking at the road. I let off
on the accelerator. The road curved into deep hollows where the
hillside sprouted ferns and seemed to ooze groundwater like an
oversaturated sponge. Then it twisted out to the edge of a canyon,
and we found ourselves driving at treetop height through a grove
of redwoods, their trunks descending like deep-sea pilings from the
level of the road.

Barbara was still trying to ignore the view. "How're you doing?"
I asked her.

"Okay," she said without looking at me.

"You know, I can't tell if you're green when your face is turned
away..."

"I'm all right. Really I am."

"Honestly?"

Barbara hesitated. I knew she didn't like to lie. "No. Honestly,
I'm terrified."

"Because of my driving?"

"No! I mean, it's not that I don't trust you or anything. It's just that . . . it's out of my control. And it's such a long way down."

"I'll slow up."

"No, don't. We'll lose them. Let's just get it over with, all right? I'd rather. Really." She turned to smile at me, even if it was only weakly. "Please don't be insulted or anything. I feel the same when Mommy's driving . . . worse."

"When you were crossing the Rockies for instance?"

"Yeah, but more than that, Big Sur."

"When were you *there?*" This was the first I'd heard of the kids being in Big Sur.

"Last week, just before we met you. I guess you weren't supposed to know yet. Sometimes I forget what I'm not supposed to tell."

That night I stayed for dinner, and as soon as we'd put the kids to bed, I asked Les, "How did you like Big Sur?"

"So you heard about that." Les moved around the room gathering clothes and toys and sticky bowls, avoiding my eyes. "Barbara?" she asked. I didn't answer. "It's not a matter of liking or disliking Big Sur," she went on. "It's a very powerful place."

"It's dramatic . . ."

"It's more than that. Like another glass of wine?"

"Sure. Do you mean magical? Or *cosmic?* Something like Taos, New Mexico?"

"No, not like Taos. At least I don't think so. I don't really know the Big Sur lore." Les poured us each another glass of chablis from a half-gallon jug, then sat down and finally faced me across the dining-room table. "You're too skeptical, Jeremy. Maybe that's why I didn't mention it, that we'd gone there, before."

"*Another* time?"

Leslie hesitated. "No. That's why I didn't *tell* you before."

"Well, tell me about it now. I have a sympathetic ear." I tugged my earlobe. "Don't I have a sympathetic ear?"

She looked up at me and smiled. "You're cute, Jeremy, and just dripping with sympathy, I can tell. Your capacity for sympathy is like mine, pathological. If a Martian were to land in this apartment and start describing his planet in terms of its big red oceans and continents made from fire, either one of us would be fully capable of jumping up and saying to him, 'Yes! Yes! I know exactly what you mean!'"

I laughed. We dropped our eyes and sipped our wine. "So tell me about it," I said after a while. "The big red oceans and the canyons and the continents made of fire. I won't be cynical this time."

Les shrugged, a little helplessly. "The wind blows all the time, like the flat parts of Wyoming, except it's the furthest thing in the world from flat. While you're driving, you don't notice the wind so much, except when you're coming out from a protected place into the open, or onto an exposed point of land. Without the wind, it just looks pretty. Like a postcard. Like you said, dramatic. It's exciting landscape, but also innocent in much the same way as a beautiful dream, and you have to keep reminding yourself that this is real and you're not dreaming and if you don't pay attention to what you're doing, you're liable to drive right off of that cliff . . . two thousand feet, into the ocean."

"Didn't Barbara help you keep your mind on the road?"

Les smiled for a second and nodded. "That's the first chill, the danger, which you never quite forget about, which is just as well since people *do* drive right off the road and fall into the ocean. But driving off cliffs isn't unique to Big Sur, I don't suppose, or even to California. They do it in Greece, and Switzerland. They do it in the mountains everywhere—"

"What's the second chill?"

Les nodded. "The wind. It's so cold. It blows down the coast, out of the north—"

"Northwest."

"The same as it does at Stinson or San Francisco or Half Moon Bay. Except in Big Sur the wind seems stronger, more *willful*. It really seems to have a life of its own. Do you know how the wind can blow so hard that it blows away all your thoughts and empties your mind?"

"Yes." I nodded, no longer certain whether I'd known it before.

"So that is just takes over everything? And nothing else seems to matter anymore—not the sound of the cars whizzing by behind you on the road or whether you're parked illegally or Nixon is still president or where the hell you're going to find a job and a place to live, or even yourself, or even your kids?"

I didn't know, but I tried to imagine. "You're standing at the cliff edge, on sandy soil. You can't hear anything. You can't even hear the kids calling your name. The wind is pushing you, nudging you from the side..."

Les looked up and smiled at me. "Yes, that's right. When were you there?"

"What I felt," Les continued on our next family outing, which was across the hills again, this time to Half Moon Bay. "What I felt wasn't the temptation to jump exactly, but a desire to let myself be swept away."

"To fall?"

"Only if that's the direction I was blown," she said complacently.

We were driving up another steep and narrow road, Old La Honda Road, passing through some of the last stands of first-growth redwoods still remaining in these hills. Les was driving. Barbara and Mat were playing gin rummy in the back. It was moist and cool under the ancient trees. The light came down in shafts, flickering through the bus as we moved through patches of bright sun and shade. Les drove slowly. The only anxious note was the engine's high-pitched whine, straining in second gear. We'd seen no other cars on Old La Honda even though this was Sunday, the most popular day of the week for motorists to take to the hills.

I said, "I never thought of you as passive. I don't think I know that part of you—the submissive Leslie, the Leslie who was married to Hank, silent partner to a frightening act."

"That's because you've never been my lover."

I was shocked, but tried not to show it. "Then's it a sexual submission?"

"What else? Oh, come on, you know what I mean, Jeremy. Don't play dumb with me. I've seen you and Sara together. Don't tell me you weren't taking a plunge when you married *her*."

"Look who's talking. We're not discussing suicide then?"

"Of course not. I said I was never tempted to jump, didn't I?"

"Not jump, no. Not as long as 'jump' is carefully defined..."

thirteen

*L*ife started getting busy after the trip to Half Moon Bay, and we didn't have much time for our Sunday outings anymore. Within a period of a week, I'd started classes, moved into a "shared house" with a man and a woman whose relationship I didn't understand, and gone to bed with two different women I hardly knew but who were now calling me up on the phone. I was getting jumpy, even before my past—in the person of the henna-haired Hannah—showed up at my door.

Les was busy too. She'd settled the kids in school and found herself a job as lab secretary for the endocrinology department at Stanford Hospital. And since the job didn't start right away, she was attending every garage sale in the area in an effort to furnish her place. On top of all that, she'd twice had to bail Blazes out of the pound on charges of disorderly conduct, biting an animal-control officer, assault, assault with intent to bite, and resisting arrest. The dog already had a rap sheet as long as his leg. But if Les left him alone in the apartment, he "acted out," as she put it. If the windows were up, he burst through the screens and scrambled across the porch roof to a low spot where he could leap to the ground. If she closed the windows, then the best she could expect returning home would be a ransacked apartment; the worst, shattered window panes. In his frustrations, Blazes had also taken to chewing up books. He was indiscriminate—fiction, poetry, potboilers, cookbooks, it didn't matter to him. Sometimes he even ate the pages, leaving just the bindings like husks on the living room floor.

"What am I going to say to the public library?" Les asked me en route to the flea market in San Jose.

"Tell them anything. Tell them you were burglarized. Tell them that you were bringing the books back to the library when your car slid into the bay and you're terribly sorry but their books went down with the ship. They don't care what you tell them, they're just going to charge you for the books no matter what..."

"All right. Maybe I could make something up then. But not that my dog ate fourteen library books. I couldn't tell them that. It might be a record. They might call somebody, like the *National Enquirer*. 'Welfare Mother Feeds Library Books to Starving Dog.' 'Trapped Canine Forced to Survive on Books Weeks Overdue at the Public Library!'"

"You never told me these were *overdue* books."

Les slipped into her thug voice. She sounded like Brando in *On the Waterfront*. "I guess I was hidin' it from ya. 'Cause you're my little brudder an' ya kinda look up ta me and everythin'... I was ashamed."

"Oh, sis, sis. Maybe if you'd come to me sooner..."

"Whaddya think? Is it curtains for me then?"

"No, bars."

"You mean...?"

"That's right, sis. The Elbow Room, the Hideaway, the Barrel & Stave, Dinah's Shack. Unless of course you want to turn state's evidence and give us the lowdown on the bow-wow there..."

"I'm no canary!"

"Maybe not, but he's no prince..."

Les made a face at me. "I never said he was."

"Oh. I thought maybe you considered him enchanted..."

Les smiled. "I know better than that," she said, leaning over and giving Blazes a kiss on his wet floppy lip. "Anyway, I've had enough of princes. Haven't I, lover? I'm into other things now. Like Catherine the Great..."

"What are you into?"

Les gave me a sideways look. "Wouldn't you like to know..."

We drove in silence for a while letting our mutual embarrassment subside. Passing out of the hard little kernel that was downtown San Jose, the traffic quickened, the buildings flattened, and the hamburger joints and taco stands proliferated. "We're getting close. I can smell it," Leslie said.

"What do you smell? That's cheap ground beef."

"Uh-uh. I know that smell. I'm a native Californian. That's the smell of fleas at public auction."

"What do they smell like? Shetland ponies?"

"Wet dog."

Suddenly her mood seemed different. I wondered if the landscape might be affecting her. The road ran straight as a plumb line, just barely descending toward Salinas and the farm towns on the way. First the hamburger joints gave way to car dealers, like regimental headquarters with their ranks of shiny automobiles baking in the sun and their lines of bright flags hanging disconsolately. Then, very quickly, the car dealers disappeared too, to be replaced by two long stucco walls, as high as the Alamo's, to keep out the road noise and the riffraff. I knew that behind each wall would be a subdivision compound.

"I guess the term 'flea market' has special significance in San Jose," I said. "Speaking of which, has Tangerine started to fumigate yet?"

"Fumigate?" Les was startled.

"Just kidding. You know, Alameda de las Pulgas, the Way of the Fleas."

"We're on it right now. This is the same road, continued..."

"I know. I'm a prune-picker, too, you know." Houses started appearing around us. Then they dropped a story and started moving further apart. Each had a yard, which was overgrown. Many of them also featured a chained dog. They looked poor and inhospitable. Water seemed to be in short supply. "Why don't you bring Blazes over to my place on Saturday?" I offered. "Give him a chance to run around."

"Your roommate wouldn't like it."

"Which roommate?"

Les slowed the car, peering around for a street sign. "The cuter one, of course."

"Jacques? I don't care whether he likes it or not."

"I'm warning you, he won't like it. He's very sensitive about those chickens of his . . ."

"Well, that's just too damn bad. I'm living there too now. Fuck Jacques anyway," I said, annoyed.

"Hm. I wouldn't mind, but your other roommate is already doing that."

"No, no, you're wrong about that. Margaret is much too serious about the house. Anyway, Jacques already has a girlfriend, in Berkeley, and she's as jealous as they come."

Les gave me a second sidelong look. "I don't care what she is. I'm *never* wrong about that."

With Les's words in mind, I tried to see my household through new eyes. My room was located at the forecastle of the house, separated by a living room, a dining room, a long kitchen, and a hall from my two housemates' more stately bedrooms. It was true that they shared a bathroom and their own little hall. I didn't know for sure what went on in there when the kitchen light was turned off, and sometimes in the mornings I did find the door closed to their hall. On the other hand, they couldn't stand one another. They feuded over dirty dishes. They squabbled about the household bills whenever we happened to sit down to a meal at the same time. Even when they'd interviewed me for housematehood, they'd done so in separate rooms.

I'd met Jacques first, since he'd been the one to answer the door. He was making plum wine in the kitchen, trying to decant from one great chemical jug into another by means of a siphon fifty or sixty feet long. His lab wouldn't let him cut it, it seemed. Jacques was a biochemist with a postdoctoral fellowship to do research at the medical school. The kitchen smelled like salad dressing, but since Jacques was first a scientist and second a Frenchman, I figured he might resent a first-year student in American lit telling him he'd made vinegar instead of wine. So I kept my mouth shut, tilting jugs and elevating the hose. Jacques hardly said anything either: "*Attendez... Non, non, ici...*" But apparently I made a good impression. After ten minutes of silent toil, he said, "I think Margaret would like to make your acquaintance also. *Là-bas.*"

I knocked on the door, and the voice of Marlene Dietrich told me to come in. Margaret was smoking a clove cigarette and writing a letter in bed. She was wearing a crepe de chine robe. Her room was teeming with pillows, cushions, quilts, and bric-a-brac. It felt European. Margaret stuck the cigarette between her teeth to shake my hand. Then I sat down at her bedside. I felt as if I'd slipped into the world of *The Magic Mountain*, but before I could ask Margaret if she'd been ill, she started talking of her own accord: "I don't really use the house. I don't even know why I'm living here. The chickens, the garden, the goats—I never even notice these things. As you can see, I live in my room primarily. But there's one thing I do insist upon... You've met Jacques. I know he's in there dribbling vinegar all over the kitchen floor, and you can bet he won't clean up after himself when he's through. All right. I've shared houses with men before, and I know their strengths and weaknesses. But the one thing I can't abide is a dirty kitchen, and one slob is more than enough ... Do I make my position clear?"

"Perfectly, but I don't do windows."

She didn't seem to hear me. "I'm just grateful that you'll have your own bathroom..."

Margaret's eyebrows were as dark and dense as a Rorschach test, yet each moved independently, arching and stretching as she spoke. She wasn't unattractive. Her looks were dark and sultry. Her voice was even lower than mine. Margaret had a certain sexual allure, something smoldering (was it clove?). But she was a no-nonsense woman, and I couldn't imagine her putting up with Jacques's nonsense in her bed, much less his. Jacques rarely even changed his sheets. His undershirts were stained. They hung from his shoulders like cobwebs, they were so stretched out. No, it was impossible. I didn't even think that Margaret liked men.

Anyway, as I'd told Leslie, Jacques had a girlfriend of long standing in Berkeley. Her name was Frankie, and she'd been a graduate student in anthropology for years and years. Frankie was a hard-faced woman. She looked like Zelda Fitzgerald in her asylum days, except Frankie was younger, thirty or so, Les's age. Every weekend Frankie came down, ostensibly to visit, although she spent most of her time sniffing around, the rest of it screaming at Jacques. I'd heard her opening and shutting Jacques' bureau drawers when he was out with the chickens, and twice I caught her going through the medicine cabinets. She wasn't the least embarrassed. "Can I help you?" I asked when I discovered her in mine. I was expecting her to say "You got a Band-Aid?" or maybe "Where do you keep the drugs around this place?" But she didn't say anything at all. She just twisted her head around and fixed me with her red-rimmed eyes. I thought the next thing I'd hear would be the voice of Satan telling me my mother was a whore, but she just went back to rifling my small assortment of tablets and ointments and creams. No, Margaret wouldn't be fool enough to take a chance on Frankie. One false move—a sock left under Jacques's bed, a vibrator under his pillow—and that would be it: lye in your cold cream, razor blades hidden in your Aspergum, ground glass imbedded in your diaphragm.

"She thinks she's doing research," Jacques said when I asked if his girlfriend always went through people's medicine cabinets.

"She takes her work to heart."

Jacques shrugged. "Anthropologists," he said. "They have no theory, only method."

"What's Frankie's method?"

He shrugged again, gallically. "Primitive."

It was always interesting to me which women Leslie would like and which she'd despise. Sara she could never abide. She also loathed Frankie on first sight, but she and Margaret hit it off immediately in spite of the fact that Barbara and Mat were having a water fight in the kitchen when they met. Les and I were in the living room, waiting for the giggling to die down before we went in to quell the disturbance, when I heard the back door slam and then a long pause before Margaret slowly intoned, "Hello there."

"Oh, no," I said.

"What's the matter?"

"Margaret..."

Les rushed in. "Don't worry, we'll clean everything up," she said.

"I'm not worried. Water's good for the floor. It might loosen up a few of the wine stains." Then she introduced herself to Barbara and Mat, shaking hands with each of them. "Speaking of which, where is the little old winemaker?"

"Berkeley," I said.

"Ah, hiding out at his moll's?"

"What's he hiding out from?" I asked. Margaret and Les smiled at each other, and from then on they were friends.

There was no accounting for my sister's taste. Men she usually liked, but she liked the strong, silent brutal type most of all. As for women, Les was more particular. She considered Sara a stuck-up priss. "Sugar and spice and everything nice, that's what Sara was made of," she said after we broke up. "What that girl needs is a good dose of crabs." Nor did she like Hannah. A bit of a buffalo gal herself, you'd think Les would like the rough-and-tumble type, but no, at least not for her little brother.

Hannah even looked like Leslie. Both were long and lean and shaggy-haired (although Les's hair was not at the moment red). Both were rebels who thought of themselves as "bad girls" and had paid dearly for their pasts. But Les was against her from the first time I mentioned her name.

Not that I was ever *for* her. After all, hadn't I left her behind in Georgia, where I'd expected her to remain? Hannah would only embarrass me at Stanford, asking guys to join her in the bathroom, eating cake out of strange men's hands (wasn't that how I'd first met her at the faculty reception at Frankincense?). But Les disliked her for all the wrong reasons. She called her a "trollop" and a "tramp." And she said these things without ever having met her, strictly in the abstract sense.

I don't know how Hannah found me, or managed to catch me

at home in the middle of the afternoon, but there she was when I answered the door, dressed in cutoffs and a tank top, her standard garb. I had to laugh, just from the shock of seeing her. "What are *you* doing here?"

"Avon calling," she said. "I was in the neighborhood, so I thought I'd drop by." Then she kissed me and, octopus-style, walked me backward toward the couch. "Speak now if we're not alone in the house, or forever hold your peace."

"How do you spell that?"

"*P-I-E-C-E. C'est moi, monsieur.*"

Later, as we lay on our backs, head-to-foot, plucking dust and lint off our sweaty bodies, I said, "You know, this is the way the Boy Scout manuals taught us to stretch out our sleeping bags, so that we wouldn't be tempted to touch each others' private parts..."

"Didn't those Boy Scout manuals tell you to vacuum once in a while?"

"I wasn't expecting to use the rug today. Anyway, I just moved in, it's not my dust."

"So much the worse. Whose is it?"

"It could be anyone's. I share this house with a motorcycle gang."

"Oh yeah? Will you introduce me?"

"You still haven't told me what you're doing here, Hannah. Aren't you supposed to be in school at Georgia, locked away in some sorority?"

"They kicked me out of Phi Delts. First they took me out in the quad and stoned me, then they snubbed me socially."

"What for? Your outfits?"

"Sugar, you don't want to know."

"Sure I do. I'm dying to know. This is starting to sound interesting."

"Anyway, I transferred. To Berkeley. Remember I told you I've got a brother who's an admissions officer there?"

"No, you never mentioned it. But that still doesn't explain why you had to leave Georgia."

"I broke up with my boyfriend."

"I never knew you had a boyfriend."

"Well, you're the one who had a *wife!*"

"But you knew all about her..."

"All the more boring for me."

"Touché, touchy. Why are you being so combative, Hannah? Why don't you just tell me why you left?"

She didn't answer, preferring to focus all her attention on her lovely linty backside instead.

"Hannah? Why did you break up with your boyfriend?"

"I didn't. He broke up with me. He found out that I'd gone to bed with his roommate. You satisfied?"

I shrugged noncommittally. Hannah pretended to be more concerned with her lint-plucking than with her confession, but I could see her scrutinizing me on the sly, gauging my reaction. "But that's not what really did it, made him break up with me. What really did the trick was when I told him I'd fucked three others of his friends..."

"One at a time, I hope."

"Together."

"Come on, Hannah, you're just making this up to get me hard again."

"It's not doing a lot of good, I see... Anyway, Larry was out of town. He was in Taos. I wanted to go, but he didn't ask me. So maybe I was pissed. Or maybe I was horny. I don't really know why I did it. Perversity?"

"Redundancy."

"You do love it, don't you? I can see that I'm starting to get through to you..." Hannah started to reach up my leg, but I bent my knee to block her. We stared at each other down the length of our bodies, all covered with cat hair and lint.

Then I climbed to my feet. "Care to join me in a shower?"

Hannah looked up at me resentfully. "You always take a shower. Who do you think you are, anyway, Lady Macbeth?"

"It's not guilt that motivates me."

'What is it then? Godliness?"

"Perversity?"

She smiled. "Redundancy," she said.

• • •

We're all of us redundant, I philosophized in bed, where I made it a point to lie awake alone, at least for the week after Hannah's sudden visitation. We're all creatures of habit, I said to myself before I recognized the thought as a cliché and then started doubting the sentiment itself. We have conversations, we say things, we don't know if we mean the same things or not. Hannah once told me, "Screwing is habit-forming." In what context I couldn't remember. Who knows what she meant by that? Surely screwing was a lot more than addictive, even for those who practiced it casually.

Hannah was a PK (preacher's kid), so sex for her had probably begun as a way of rebelling against her father, the president of Frankincense College, a Baptist minister and well-known hypocrite besides. Of course, once a teenage girl starts screwing, the boys come very quickly to expect it of her, and the act becomes something akin to habitual—one way of getting people to like her, a kind of social grace like shaking hands or dancing cheek-to-cheek. But beyond that initial stage and after she'd begun to enjoy it, I felt certain that screwing became something else for Hannah. A self-assertion, a pagan sacrament perhaps. You bring the blanket and the bourbon and the condom; I supply the lips, breasts, and honeypot. By the time I met her, Hannah approached sex with a sense of comic abandon, a kind of practiced roll-me-over, as well as a childish delight so smooth and polished that it had survived the years of males' contempt.

We'd met at a party in the presidential mansion. I was eating cake off bone china, and Hannah walked up and stole a bite. Then she stepped back and grinned at me. She had chocolate icing all over her teeth, one of which was chipped. I took a retaliatory stab at her coconut cream and dropped a forkful on the carpet. People started to gape at us. "Daddy," the college president, turned and scowled at us from the other end of the room, but I didn't care anymore since I already knew I'd be leaving. During the course of the party, Hannah and I exchanged bites and lascivious glances. By the time it was over, we were feeding each other with our fingers, Hannah had twice suggested that we duck into one of the upstairs bathrooms, and Sara had stormed home to start packing her bags. I never could have managed it without Hannah.

Her favorite place to screw was the woods. I remembered how she liked to strip and get me to chase her through the woods, and then afterward we'd have to try to retrace our hurried steps and find our clothes. One time Hannah convinced me to make love to her in a brown muddy pond that was warmer than the air even though the air was hot—this was Georgia in July. Only later did she mention the water moccasins living in that pond. It was Hannah who tried to seduce me in a mountain stream so icy that my testicles withdrew into the trunk whence they'd descended when I was fourteen, and no amount of enticement would coax them out again. Hannah's impulses were so natural and healthy and fine, so different from her father's and everyone else's at that college, that I had to respond in spite of myself. When I was sweaty, as I tended to be that summer in Georgia, she liked to lick my skin, beginning at the neck and continuing, pulling off my clothes as she went along. She called me her "salt lick." I called her my "buffalo gal."

Hannah and I had some good times together, but we never had a chance for more. I was still married to Sara for one thing, and, even if I wasn't living with her, I was hardly a free man. I admired Hannah and I learned from her. I was grateful. She helped me through a very tough time. But I was never in love with her. That I could never let myself be. She reminded me too much of Leslie.

I felt sorry for poor Hannah, gauging the degrees of shock on my face as she confessed her betrayals, fueling my fantasies with her pain. I felt sorry for Leslie, leaving two or maybe three boyfriends behind in Connecticut while bringing along a dog which embodied all the worst masculine traits. Sinking deeper into maudlin emotions, I felt sorry for myself, putting three thousand miles and any number of cardinal sins between me and Sara just to be absolutely sure that my bridges were well burnt behind me.

In my self-pity I lay awake wondering if we aren't always redundant, repeating our errors again and again and again with different faces, different bodies, different genders and species in different places, outfits, styles of hair. Everyone comes to California expecting a fresh start, whether they admit it or not. Yet all of us come with our baggage in tow—our bad habits, address books, old photograph albums, and unruly dogs. Also our predilection for the wrong kinds of mates. As Hannah (my font of wisdom apparently) had told me, "The easiest people to fall into bed with are always your old lovers, because you know it won't work out with them, except in bed." And I had to admit that the woman I wanted was Sara, who as it turned out was suing me for divorce.

I checked the time to see if it was late enough in the night to call her and catch her in the morning before work. It was still too early, so I climbed out of bed and started a letter. I wrote about Leslie and Blazes Boylan—the scourge of the bookshelves, the masculine stereotype, the symbol of everything wrong with my sister's men, the dog. By the time I'd written the letter, I knew that the sun would be up in the eastern United States, and Sara always rose with the sun. But I didn't call her, and I didn't address the envelope. I'd meant the letter to be funny and oblique but meaningful, and I knew it was only oblique. So I went back to bed and masturbated, falling asleep as the shadows brightened into gray shapes in my room.

Leslie appeared with dog and children the following Saturday. I was in the shower when they arrived, and I saw them drinking apple juice and coffee with Margaret on the patio when I got out. Still dripping wet, I called out the bathroom window, "I'm sorry, I thought for sure you'd be late!"

"When am I ever late?"

"Always! At least till now. Are you turning over a new leaf?"

Les turned halfway around in her chair. "What kind of leaf did you have in mind?"

Barbara and Mat had already run off to the backyard by the time I'd dressed and emerged. I could hear Blazes whining and rattling his chains just beyond the patio wall. Only Les and Margaret were still sitting at the patio table. "Blazes isn't chained, is he?" I asked.

"Oh yes he is," Leslie said.

"But the whole point, I thought . . . I wanted him to be able to run free for a change."

"Blazes has been naughty," Margaret explained.

"Blazes has been a real asshole," Les corrected her. "He tried to bite Jacques."

I tried not to smile. "What did Jacques do? Bite him first?"

"Kicked him," Margaret said, returning my faint smile.

"Which came first?"

"We'll never know. There were no witnesses to the crime itself, except for the victim and the perpetrator, whichever they may be. They're really two of a kind, you know," Margaret announced pleasantly. "Blazes and Jacques, I mean. Lazy, wanton, good-for-nothing, mean-tempered, self-centered, self-pitying, self-satisfied sons-of-bitches..." She and Leslie exchanged a smile. "However *he* is a beautiful animal."

"Yours too," Les said.

"Thank you, but he's not really mine. I just kind of borrow him from time to time, and only on weekdays of course. However I have my tai chi on Tuesdays and Thursdays, so if you'd like to take him out for a spin..."

"Thank you, no," Les said. "I'm on sabbatical from men."

Margaret and Leslie exchanged another knowing smile, and I began to feel left out. "I know the feeling," I said and went off to check on the kids.

I found them in the chicken coop where Jacques kept an ancient hen and an ancient rooster, along with a self-feeding trough and a spigot set to drip water at a constant rate. As I entered, ducking in under the five-foot doorway and the cobwebs, Jacques was explaining the beauty of this entirely automated, minimum-care facility. Apparently the stroke of genius behind the water-dripper was removing its washer. Now the chickens could go for months without seeing another living creature except each other, and the occasional spider of course.

For a few moments all of us gazed with wonder at the two geriatric chickens, huddling in the corner farthest away from us. The hen was as round as a softball with legs. The rooster looked like a chain smoker. Alternately he eyed us fiercely, one eye at a time, and pecked at his mate's feathers. I noticed that the hen's tail had been plucked clean. She looked like a baboon from behind.

While Jacques rambled on about the care and feeding of chickens, I poked around the shed. The corners and walls were entirely hung with cobwebs. The floor was carpeted with equal portions of spilled feed and excrement. In the laying box, I found a golfball—perhaps as a model for what an egg should aspire to, or as a reminder to the hen to try laying, something she hadn't done in years. When I approached the old couple, the volume and pitch of their cackling rose sharply to the level of insane babble. They started to shriek as I drew even nearer. The rooster flew up onto the shoulders of the hen, placing one gnarled claw right over her head. "Leave them. They are no good for the pot," Jacques said. The thought of eating them had never occurred to me.

Barbara and Margaret spent the afternoon hemming curtains. Barbara was teaching her how to sew. "You must think I'm a failure as a grown-up, but when I was little and people used to ask me what I wanted to be when I grew up, I told them a boy," Margaret explained. "My mother always said I threaded a needle like Huckleberry Finn, and I knew exactly what she meant since that was my favorite book. I hated dolls and everything they stood for— ribbons, bows, pink dresses. Where did you learn how to sew? Your grandmother teach you?"

"I taught myself," Barbara said simply.

Meanwhile Mat was hunting lizards out near where the goats were kept. Les and I sat in the sun and talked, and every now and then Mat reported back to us on how many lizards he'd almost caught. Finally he came running up with the tail a lizard had dropped in order to get away. Then, since Mat was obviously hunting around under rocks and woodpiles, I decided to warn him about black widow spiders. I'd never actually seen any around the yard, but we had a number of likely spots. Naturally Mat ran right off to look for some.

Blazes Boylan slipped his chain late in the afternoon while

the rest of us were clustered in the front yard, otherwise engaged. Les was holding her six-year-old son by the shoulders, as though restraining him from a brawl, which wasn't far from the truth. Jacques and I were bent over Mat's opponent—a small wooden box set into the ground and containing three sprinkler valves in addition to a nest of black widow spiders. "Watch out! They can jump!" Mat warned us, repeating the very words I'd said to him not more than an hour before. "The bad ones have red spots. Those are the females. Can you see any red spots?"

"Like polka dots?" Les asked.

"This isn't funny, Mommy."

Jacques and I didn't say anything since neither of us was willing to get close enough to look for spots. I was busy mashing spiders one by one with the narrow handle of a hoe, while Jacques stood by holding a bottle of DDT (the household size). The spiders were hopping around inside the box and trying to climb up the handle of my hoe. They were gorgeous, their forelegs long and shapely, making them look like dancing girls in black leotards. It seemed a crime to kill them. Jacques was transfixed, his lips pulled back in a grimace, baring his teeth. "These are *deadly* spiders?" he asked.

"No, not unless you're a six-year-old," I said. I rattled the hoe against the side of the box, trying to flush the last, largest spider out of hiding. "That's everyone except for Mama Bear. I think she's hiding under the bed."

"The *mother*..." Mat said dramatically, twisting toward Leslie, who played her part by crossing her eyes, baring her teeth, and clawing the air with her hands. "Mommy, this is *serious!*"

Jacques poured the rest of the bottle of DDT into the box. Mat squirmed free to take a last look before I closed the lid. "That should hold them for a few hundred years," Jacques was saying when we heard the first bark. The barking continued—a raucous, fun-loving sound, really more like a dog-cheer than a normal bark. All of us turned in the direction of the sound, which was the backyard near the chicken coop rather than the side yard where Blazes had been chained.

"Oh, lord, no, not the chickens," Les said.

"*Les poulets!*" Jacques screamed and was off and running before I'd even had a chance to translate.

I took off after him, reaching the shed just after he did. Blazes was still outside, barking in at the chickens through a wide crack between the boards, and Jacques was kicking the dog in the hind-quarters, the end where he had no teeth. "What do you think you're doing?" I said and reached for Jacques's arm. He shook me off and continued to stomp the dog with his foot, his lips drawn back in the same ugly grimace I'd seen on his face at the black widow box.

Blazes turned on him suddenly and seized him by the pantleg before he could jump away. Jacques was left standing on one leg. For a moment they seemed to be playing a snarling game of tug of war with Jacques's leg the object being tugged. Then Jacques went down. The pants tore with a squealing sound, and Blazes yanked the last few threads loose to get himself a mouthful of corduroy, which he held down with his paw and started tearing with his teeth.

It seemed to me that Jacques was getting just what he deserved, and I was enjoying the show. But then he began to howl—Jacques, I mean—and I realized that he was terrified. I reached out and grabbed Blazes by the collar. In reflex the dog snarled and sunk his teeth into my arm.

Fortunately his mouth was still sheathed in corduroy, so only his uppers actually punctured my skin. Blazes looked sorry as soon as the damage was done. He let go of my arm, sheepishly lay down, and started spitting out the cloth, working his tongue to find the last threads. Maybe he hoped I'd kick him to make him feel better, but I didn't do that. I just said, "Oh, Blazes," and cradled my arm.

I knew from the dog's eyes when Leslie arrived on the scene. Blazes looked right past me. His eyes seemed to focus on his fate in the middle distance, not far away. He whimpered once, then dropped his eyes and head and stretched out in the dirt. "Blazes!" Les commanded and slapped her thigh sharply. He slunk obediently

toward her, his head down, tail between his legs. Leslie snapped
the leash onto his collar and led him away.

Jacques didn't thank me, then or later, for restraining the dog
when he was down. Nor did he express regret for having kicked
him. When Les came back from locking Blazes up in the bus,
she followed Jacques inside and offered to pay for his torn pants.

"I could sew them," Barbara said, but nobody paid any attention
to her.

"The dog is *vicious*," Jacques said with a lift to his chin. "He
should be put away."

"He's just a little high-strung," I said to Leslie. "Has anybody
got a Valium?"

Nobody paid any attention to me either. "I'm really very sorry.
I apologize to everyone," Les went on, unable to look anyone in
the eyes. "All I can say is this won't happen again." To Mat and
Barbara she said, "Get your things together. Where are your shoes,
Mat? Find your shoes. We have to go now."

Mat crawled under a chair to look for his shoes. Jacques turned
on his heel and left the room. "Listen, why don't you stay for dinner?"
Margaret asked, looking first to Leslie, then to the kids.

"A great idea," I agreed, even though I had a date with Hannah.

"Thank you, no," Les said, still not looking at anyone.

"Why not?" Margaret asked. "Do you have other plans?"

Les didn't answer. I could see that she was teetering.

"Can't we, Mommy?" Barbara asked gently.

"Can't we, Mommy?" Mat echoed in a louder tone of voice.

Margaret smiled. "Jacques will be leaving for Berkeley as soon
as he changes his pants..."

"Please, Mommy! Please say yes!"

"Come on, Les..."

She smiled slightly, beginning to crack. When she finally nodded
assent, Mat cheered and threw his shoes back under the furniture.
"All right, I'll just go to the store and pick up some ground beef and
hot dogs," Les said, explaining, "My son eats nothing else."

"I'll start the charcoal," I offered. "Actually, I have to go to
Berkeley too, but not till later on."

Leslie froze, then slowly turned toward me, her smile twisted into a quizzical expression. "You're leaving?"

"I have a date with Hannah," I confessed.

"*Hannah?*"

"You remember, of the henna hair. It's not really a date though. She just asked me to help her move some furniture."

"Some furniture. I can imagine. She needs some help making her bed go up and down."

I had to smile. "I guess I don't *have* to go. I could call and put her off, except she doesn't have a phone..."

"Forget it. Matthew, what did you do with your shoes? You just *had* them a second ago."

"*I'm* not going anywhere tonight," Margaret said in her deep, resonant voice. "And I'm the one who asked you, after all."

Leslie hesitated, then suddenly sat down. "All right," she said to Margaret although she was looking at me. "*Let* them go to Berkeley. Let the boys run off to see their girls. We'll sit home with the kids. Sew, darn. You got any ironing?"

I felt as though I'd been pickled, canned, and labeled for what I was and would always be. "I don't have to go, I guess."

"Go, go! Good riddance. But someday you can explain to me why you can't leave the bad girls alone."

fourteen

*L*eslie dropped out of sight for more than a week after that discomfiting day with Blazes and the black widow spiders. She didn't call as she usually did two or three mornings a week, and when I finally tried to reach her one evening, she wasn't at home. I had to talk to Barbara instead.

"I'm not sure where Mommy is, but she'll be back any minute now. Do you want me to have her call you when she comes in?"

"Sure, if you think of it. How are you doing, Poncho?"

"Fine."

"How do you like your new school?"

"It's all right, I guess."

"Is everything all right? Is there anything wrong there?"

"No. No, we're all fine. Do you want me to leave a message for Mommy?"

"No, it's nothing important. I just wanted to chat. If you're still up, you can just tell her I called."

"Okay."

"How's Mat doing?"

"Oh, he's fine. We're watching a monster movie."

"Then you got the TV fixed?"

"Well, no, not exactly. It couldn't be fixed. We had to get a new one."

"At least this one will last for a while."

"Yeah. It's not really new, though. I mean, not *brand* new. It's new for us, but it's a used television set."

"I see."

"We got it at a garage sale. Maybe Mommy should explain..."

"No, I understand. I'll let you go now. Good night, Poncho. You can tickle Matthew once for me. And tell your mother I called."

She didn't call me back, though, and another weekend went by. I tried again to reach her on Saturday afternoon, but there was no one home. Then I got busy myself, with Hannah, with school. I felt guilty, of course, felt that Les's trouble, whatever it was, was my fault. The fact that Leslie was making no effort to get back in touch with me had nothing to do with the point. (The point, increasingly, was my guilt.) That day with Blazes and Jacques hadn't seemed so bad at the time—not at least until I was on my way up to Berkeley— but it loomed more worrisome as time went by.

Finally, I dropped by Les's office at the endocrinology lab. I didn't call first, I just decided to veer off at the last moment toward the hospital and cut my eleven-o'clock class. Les was glad to see me. She introduced me to two of the residents who worked in the lab—Dr. Chandi, who was tall and gracious, and Dr. Gold, who was brusque. Then, since it was already late in the morning, Les suggested that I meet her for lunch. "That is, if you don't have to move any furniture or anything... I know that van of yours is in great demand."

In fact, I did have a noon seminar that I hated to miss. "No, no other plans. Shall I meet you in the lunchroom, then, at twelve?"

"Quarter of. Beat the rush of relatives who just hang out here between visiting hours."

That meant I had half an hour to kill. I found the lunchroom, but the plate glass doors were closed, and the workers inside were still wiping down the tabletops, dumping silverware into bins, and clattering the dishes on the cafeteria line. I tried the door— it wasn't locked—but suddenly a hesitancy overcame me, and I didn't want to go in. This cafeteria was intended for hospital personnel—doctors, nurses, lab technicians, who had important jobs here, trying to save lives—and the food service workers were busy getting ready for them. What right did I have to bother them now?

I crossed over into the reception area of the hospital and found the gift shop. Here at least I had a purpose: I could browse. The gift shop stocked the usual assortment of flowers, plants, boxes of candy, and greeting cards. Mixed in with the get-well cards, I found a small section of condolence cards discreetly tucked away at the bottom of the rack where they wouldn't catch anyone's but a child's eye. Some of the cards featured black borders, others a single rose. Some had both, black borders and a single rose in various colors— red, yellow, black. *Red?* What did red stand for? I wondered, and started sorting through for other variations on the theme. Death, of course, was never mentioned, nor were any of its usual euphemisms: passed away, met one's maker, joined the choir invisible, given up the ghost or bought the farm. Instead the messages relied on symbolism and elliptical references, to "your time of trial," "your tragic hour," and several segments of the Ecclesiastes lines popularized by the Byrds: "To everything there is a season, a time to sow and a time to reap . . . a time to gather stones together."

"May I help you find something?" the saleslady asked, startling me.

"Oh, no thanks. I'm just browsing."

She hesitated. Then she said coolly, "Well, you just take your time then." I waited for her to move away before continuing to rifle the cards, but she took a long time doing so. First she had to adjust the placement of some potted plants, then straighten the cards on the rack just above my head. I waited her out, though, crouching in front of the condolence cards. What did she think I was, a shoplifter? Then I remembered something Les used to say. "Petty crime will set you free." She'd say that when we ran the tolls on the turnpike, leaving the bells ringing behind us as we roared away like Bonnie and Clyde. I unbuttoned my shirt just above my belt and slipped in the card with the black border and the red red rose, thanking the saleslady on my way out the door. She just stared at me.

When I got back to the cafeteria, the doors were still closed, but I could see Leslie sitting inside. There was a clock on the wall above her head. It was still only twenty of. I saw that Les had gotten her hair cut. Why hadn't I noticed that before? It twirled up in peaks and soft curls, looking like Margaret's hair, like a lot of people's hair. Les looked nice sitting there, patient, attentive, both special and ordinary. She looked pretty; I could see that. She also looked like me. The tabletops were an orange Formica, the walls behind her green. The early lunch crowd moved around her, as if she weren't there. It frightened me to see Les sitting alone.

I stood on the outside for some minutes watching my sister here among her co-workers, one bright spot of importance in an otherwise anonymous room. It was a minor leap of faith just to believe that she belonged here any more than I did. Leslie looked so vulnerable, so nearly forlorn. She might have been my lover, not my sister. In a certain way, she might have been me.

The spell was broken by a voice at my back, a woman clearing her throat with practiced authority. "Excuse me," she said. I turned, half expecting to see the gift shop lady backed up by a SWAT team, but she was only a nurse pushing past me to get in the door. When I looked back up at the clock, it was quarter of.

"Am I late? I was over in the gift shop, brushing up on my petty crime."

"I snuck away a little early," Les said, brightening into a smile. "Have you been waiting long?"

"No, I literally just walked in a second ago."

I looked at her but didn't say anything. Then I pulled the card out of my shirt. "Look what I just stole."

"I thought you were kidding. Why did you steal that?"

"It didn't seem right to pay for it."

"Why would you want it? Did somebody die?"

"No. I don't know, I was just shocked by the symbolism. I thought it was perverse."

"You're becoming a graduate student. What have they been making you read? Maybe we'd better get in line before the noon rush."

In the food line, Les turned maternal, warning me against the Jell-O, advising me to take some salad, acting like an older woman friend. I couldn't help worrying about the card which I'd left in plain sight on the table—stolen merchandise, after all. Returning with our trays, I asked, "Do you eat here every day?"

"I've only been working here two weeks, Jeremy."

"That's right. Les, I'm sorry about last Saturday . . . Saturday before last, I mean."

"What for? What did you do except get bitten by a mad dog?"

"That's something of what I mean. It was really all Jacques's fault."

Les waved the issue away with her fork. "I don't want to talk about that. Let's just forget about it, please. You haven't said anything about my hair. Is that because you hate it, or you didn't notice? Tell me the truth. You hate it, don't you?"

I had to smile. "No, I think it looks very nice."

"Nice. I know, it's just like Margaret's, but she won't mind. Jeremy, I want you to tell me, do you think I'll ever learn to stop fooling around with my hair?"

I shook my head gravely. "But why should you? At least you didn't color it this time."

"You should have seen me, eyeing those bottles of tints and dyes like an alcoholic in a bar. I almost . . ."

"Oh, Leslie."

"Oh, Jeremy! We all have our foibles, you know. Speaking of which, guess who's coming out for a visit at Christmas . . ."

"Mother?"

Les stuffed her mouth with lettuce leaves. She nodded by way of reply.

"She didn't tell *me*," I said.

"She didn't tell me either. I'd just stepped out when she called. But she told the kids, then *they* told me, and now I'm telling you. Isn't it fun being part of a family network?"

"I'll have to clean up the house," I said bleakly, defeated by the mere prospect of chasing down the dust bunnies and wiping up my housemates' bathroom hairs.

"Your figurative house as well. You don't fool me, little brother. I know you lead an untidy life."

"It's neater than you think."

"Oh yeah? What about Little Miss Hannah-of-the-flaming-hair? Speaking of rinses and dyes, I mean..."

"I broke it off."

"When was this?"

I shrugged. "A few days ago."

"What happened?" Les was suddenly serious, in my opinion more than she needed to be.

"Nothing. I just told her I didn't want to see her anymore."

"That's *all*?"

"What else is there to say? That I'm a bastard and a prick and a typical male and I don't like being pursued across the continental United States... I didn't think you liked her anyway."

Les shrugged. "I never even met her. What about the other ones?"

"What other ones?" I stuffed my own mouth to try to hide my smile.

"Oh, this one and that one. You needn't act so coy. Margaret told me..."

"What does Margaret know?"

"She has eyes."

"Suspicious eyes. She's moving out, you know."

"I'm not surprised."

"Actually, Margaret and Jacques have been getting along better."

"That's because she's interested in someone else now..."

"Who's that?" Les didn't answer. She only cocked an eyebrow. "Oh, no. Please, not more of your intuitions."

"This is more in the line of a suggestion. You should consider it. She's a devoted friend. She's deeply sensual. A wonderful hostess. She'd make the perfect professor's wife."

"Uh-huh. Looking like a guy in drag?"

"Jeremy! I'm surprised at you. Didn't you know that half the models on the covers of *Cosmopolitan* are really men in drag?"

I laughed. "No, I didn't realize that. But under the circumstances, I'm not surprised."

Les made a face at her sandwich and pushed the plate away. "What circumstances? What are you talking about?"

"I'm not sure anymore. Boys in bondage? Dogs in drag?" She didn't respond to the subject, so I went on. "How about you? Anything new on love's horizon? You haven't been easy to raise on the phone . . . ."

"Me? No, no, all quiet on the amorous front. I'm a nun for all practical purposes, although Jay keeps threatening to fly out."

"For a visit, you mean?"

"Of course for a visit, and a brief one at that. Jay thinks he's a bird, and that every woman he meets wants to capture him and stick him in a cage and make him a parakeet. That's why he likes to keep things fleeting . . ." Les fluttered her hand, letting it fly off over our heads.

"Sara's thinking of coming out, too."

Les made four or five faces in rapid succession: horror, disgust, terror, conceit, the pretense of surprise. Then she let her hand crash into her potato chips.

"You should have been a clown."

"You *are* a clown if you let yourself get sucked back into that one."

"You mean my marriage?"

"Yes," she hissed. "Of course I mean your marriage. And don't give me that coy little smile you use on the coeds. This is serious. This is your *life*."

I smiled in spite of myself, then took a bite of Salisbury steak to avoid any further expressions or replies. The truth was tricky, and I didn't really want to confess that I was the one who'd asked Sara to come out for a Christmas visit and I was just waiting for her reply. Sara had told me that she had to check with her psychiatrist first. That was more than a week ago. But I didn't want to explain all that to Leslie. "How's Blazes?" I asked, to change the subject.

"Don't ask." I looked up expecting to hear a joke or an anecdote about the dog's latest misbehavior, but Les wasn't joking. She looked stricken. "I've . . . decided that I've got to get rid of him. You know what he does to the furniture and the books. He's just not an apartment dog. But I think I may have found a farmer who'll take him . . . ."

"That's what Sunshine always told us she'd done with Classy. I suppose it's the same farm?"

I regretted the question as soon as I'd asked it. Les reached for her purse and started to rummage. She nodded. She was starting to cry.

"Oh, I'm sorry, Les. That was lousy of me to say that. I don't know why I did. You love the dog. You've done everything for him. Everyone knows that." The tears streaked down her cheeks, trailing black mascara. I hadn't noticed before that she was wearing makeup. "Please don't cry. Maybe we can talk about this. Maybe I could take him for a while..."

People moved around our table, but no one paid any attention to Les's crying. I guessed it was commonplace here. "It's no use," she said. "He's already gone. He *bit* someone, someone else, I mean. Not badly. He didn't even break the skin. But this time it was a little girl..."

"What did she do?"

"Hit him over the head with a toy truck, but that's not the point."

"Oh, no? Then what is the point?"

"They offered me a choice. Either I'd have to go to court and probably pay some damages, or I could sign a paper allowing them to put him down... I can't afford to be sued for dog bites and take off work to go to animal court. I can't even pay the bills I've got now..."

"If you're short, I can help you there."

"No. That's sweet of you, but no, thank you. You'll need it for school."

"Not all of it. Not till spring at least."

"No, Jeremy. You don't understand. It's the oil company, those villains. Simon Legree Heating Oil. I owe them *hundreds* from last winter in Connecticut, and I was going to start paying them as soon as I got a little ahead. Except they found me first somehow, and now they want the whole amount. Legal threats. They say they're going to 'garnish' my wages. I always thought that meant throw a little parsley around. But no... they've sicced a collection agency on me. I get telephone calls at work. Dunning letters every other day."

"Why didn't you tell me? Oh, Les, I feel horrible..."

"That's why I didn't tell you."

"But I've got my student loan, a thousand dollars just sitting in the bank waiting for me to spend them. Can you imagine the temptation? Please, split it with me. You'd be doing me a favor. Otherwise I might blow it all on Hannah or Sara or some other woman you can't stand... Come on, Les. You can pay me back in the spring, when I'll need it..."

Les looked even sicker than before. "I wish I hadn't told you anything. I just... don't want to borrow any more."

"Why not? Because I'm your little brother and you're supposed to take care of me? Surely you can swallow that much pride."

Les didn't say anything, which I took to be a good sign. I took out my checkbook and started writing a check for five hundred. "No, four hundred," she said, touching my hand. I stopped writing, letting her hand rest on mine.

fifteen

Sunshine didn't come for the holidays, but she sent a crate full of presents in her stead. Barbara and Mat were only mildly disappointed. They got sweaters and jackets, swim fins and snorkels, books, watercolors, watches, and a fire truck capable of extinguishing a kitchen fire. And on Christmas day, Mother called ship-to-shore by way of Bimini. We didn't even know she was on a cruise.

"She's got a boyfriend," Les declared, picking up wrapping paper while the kids took their turns on the phone.

"What's wrong with that?"

"Nothing."

"You didn't really want her to come anyway. She'd just feel compelled to do her parent-as-cop routine. Ask a lot of questions, sniff around. This way, we don't have to worry about her. She's . . . otherwise engaged."

"You don't understand. She didn't come because she feels guilty."

"Why? Because she didn't come?"

"No. Not everyone's as convoluted as you are, Jeremy." Les started arranging toys in lines and circles. "You realize she's never visited Fog's grave? Not since the funeral, I mean."

"Well, he's buried in Oakland. That's not exactly convenient to Tory Hole."

"That's not the reason. The reason is she's scared."

"What's there to be scared of? This is California, not New England. There aren't any ghosts around here."

"Nevertheless, she's scared."

I didn't know whether Les was right or wrong, but suspected that at the very least she was overdramatizing. She liked to do that. She liked gothic plots. In fact, Sunshine hadn't had much reason to come until Les and I and the kids moved back to California. Her relatives were mostly dead or living in rehab centers. What was she supposed to do, fly across the country just to lay flowers on Fog's crypt? It was true, though, that she kept putting off her visit. First she was going to come for New Year's, then later on in January, then to catch the early spring. Les and I didn't mind. It was comfortable and somehow fitting to feel entirely on our own, like teenagers staying alone in the house while their parents are away, except our "house" in this case was a whole state.

There are really only two seasons in California, dry and wet. You know it's winter when the hills start turning green, spring when they look like Ireland, summer when they lighten to a shade of split pea on their way to becoming an inflammable blond again. Fall is characterized by the ever-increasing danger of fire, easing only when the rains begin. Except the rains were late in coming that year, the first of a three-year drought. The hills didn't turn green until the end of January, and as they darkened to emerald I was going up again regularly to Hannah's in Berkeley, even though Sara was the one I longed to see. I didn't mention either of them to Leslie.

We drove up to the delta over Washington's Birthday, Les and the kids and I, I mean. Her boss had a cabin in Walnut Grove, near Locke, the only rural Chinese settlement in the United States. That's what interested Leslie. Mat was interested in the crayfish. Barbara was interested in keeping an eye on everyone. And I came along for the ride. I hadn't been to the delta since I was a kid myself and mad to fish, and then the only places Fog would take me were trout farms where they grew the fish and stocked them in square pools that looked like sewage plants. I'd heard there were big catfish in the rivers and sloughs and sturgeons the size of sharks. Walnut Grove wasn't much, but Locke looked like an Old West town with saloons and wooden sidewalks and balconies leaning out over the dusty streets. This was the façade, of course, but it was an old façade. Locke wasn't a tourist town, at least not yet. The saloons and the restaurant were set up to serve the locals and the fishermen who cruised through the waterways, and behind the scenes were the old folks living in their little huts, hoeing their tiny plots, speaking Cantonese. We fished and put out crayfish pots without success, but mostly we just wandered around peeking at the Chinese and hiking out along the cottonwoods beside the sloughs. In the evenings we ate hamburgers because Mat and Barbara couldn't agree on anything else. Then when the kids were in bed, Les and I sat up with a bottle of rosé.

"Do you think Mat needs a father?" she asked me.

"He could use one. Of course."

"Barbara I don't worry about. We're a lot alike. *She* worries, but I can always reach her."

"She takes a lot on herself, though . . ."

"How did Mat seem to you today?"

"Fine. He's excitable, but then he's a kid. He really liked the crayfish. He thinks of them as some kind of aquatic lizard, I guess."

Les hardly heard me. "He likes lizards."

"Maybe he'll grow up to be a herpetologist."

"Snakes?"

"Among others, yes. It's the study of reptiles and amphibians."

"He was just asking about two-headed snakes when I put him to bed . . ."

"I was telling him about them today. You remember the one in the snake pit at Golden Gate Park?"

"Oh, right. I'm glad it's only that. I was afraid he was getting Freudian on me."

"So what if he does? Relax, Les. He's just a little boy."

"Barbara's sensible. She can take care of herself. But Mat . . . He likes everything creepy. Lizards, two-headed snakes, black widow spiders—"

"Snips and snails and puppy dogs' tails?"

"Is that all it is?"

"I don't know, Les. But I remember you used to chase tarantulas and keep a black widow in a jar. I had a hard time being as boyish as my big sister had been..."

Les nodded gravely.

"More wine?" I asked.

She nodded again. "Do you think I'm drinking too much, Jeremy?"

"You're just full of anxieties tonight, aren't you? How much are you drinking?"

"I drink a glass like this every night when I get home from work."

"Of wine?" Another nod. "That's nothing to worry about."

"I worry about Fog. He never drank so much. It was just steady, three or four a night, year after year..."

"That was Scotch, not wine."

She was silent for a while, twirling her glass. "I miss him."

"I thought you hated him."

"No, I loved him. We just never got along."

"I know. When I look at those photographs of you and Fog on the beach together, I could almost cry."

Les looked up vaguely. "What photographs do you mean?"

"You know, in the islands. They're *your* photographs, not mine."

"Oh, those. I couldn't have been more than three years old."

"What's the matter, Les? What's really bothering you?"

"Nothing," she said, staring deeper into her wineglass. Then she smiled, coquettishly I thought. "Jay's coming out. Did I tell you that?"

"No, but you said he was threatening. When's he coming?"

"March."

"Sara may be coming then, too. Maybe they could get together and cancel each other out."

"Maybe. But where would that leave us?"

"Alone together?"

Les didn't react for a moment, then she patted my hand and smiled. "Little brothers aren't enough. Anyway, you've got Hannah,

Margaret, and probably some others I don't know about. And I've never been attracted to younger men."

Jay's and Sara's visits did overlap. It might have been just a coincidence, but I didn't think so at the time. Sara's flight had been booked three weeks ahead of time, and I'd told Les what the date was when she'd asked. But she'd never tell me when Jay was coming. "Soon," she'd say. "Later on this month, maybe." I was beginning to wonder if he was coming at all when Les called up and asked me to meet her for a beer. "Can it wait an hour?" I asked. "I'm in my demonic house-cleaning mode." This was the night before Sara was due to arrive.

"No, come now. There's someone here who wants to see you."

Jay bobbed up from the table as soon as I entered the bar. I thought he looked jolly and buoyant as he shook my hand. "I'm glad you could finally make it out here," I said.

"What are you talking about? I've been trying to wrangle a solid invite for three months!" Leslie glared at him, narrowing her eyes. "Did I say something wrong again? The fact is, I've been sick, sicker than a dog. Lovesick," he added, turning to Leslie, who only scowled. "Can I get you a beer? Or a drink?" he asked.

"Whatever's dark on draft."

"How 'bout you, sug? You ready for another yet?"

"No. *Yes,*" she snapped. Jay bolted for the bar.

Les and I sat in silence for a minute or two. I finally asked, "Well, how's the visit going so far?"

She shrugged, not even looking at me. "He drinks too much," she said.

"Only beer..."

"You haven't seen him, eyeing the bottle on the shelf. He's practically an alcoholic, if you want to know the truth. He must drink twelve cans of beer a day."

"Quite a bladder," I said, but Les wouldn't even crack a smile. I didn't stay at the bar for long.

When Sara arrived, she seemed no less combative than my sister the night before. First she turned away when I tried to kiss her.

Then she said, "My bag is a blue soft-sided one. You won't recognize it because it's new. And I should tell you, the only reason I've come is because Brian thinks I have some unresolved feelings to work out with you."

"Brian?"

"Dr. Feckless to you."

"Oh, him. He's just plain Feckless to me."

Sara pulled out a cigarette. "You can laugh all you want, Jeremy, but we're engaged to be married."

"We're already married."

"Don't try to avoid the issue. You know who I mean."

I nodded, looking around at the crowd of potential witnesses. Of course I knew whom she meant. Brian Feckless was Sara's psychiatrist. Also her lover, apparently. She was rummaging for matches, but I ignored her even though I was holding a lighter in my fist. "Are you suing me for divorce then? When did all this occur?"

"Last night. Have you got a light?"

I handed her the lighter and went off to look for a suitcase that I wouldn't recognize.

We drove back from the airport by the scenic route, down through the hills. The sun was shining, the hills were a vivid green. "They are pretty," Sara said, as though she'd had her doubts.

"What do you mean, 'pretty'? They're sparkling! They're absolutely gorgeous! They're as green as Galway, only here the sun shines!"

Sara shrugged and rooted in her pocketbook for another cigarette. Physical terrain did not concern her so much as the emotional lay of the land. "Have you been seeing anyone?" she asked.

"I told you. I told you everything that night on the phone."

Sara looked out the window, disgusted. "I *mean*, have you been seeing a psychiatrist? Are you in therapy of any kind?"

"There was one. A transpersonal psychologist. I met her in a bar. Her name was Marsha, I think. But it didn't work out. She wasn't transpersonal enough for me..."

"It's all very well to be flippant, Jeremy, but you're really a very sick man. You've got some serious emotional adjustment problems. You need professional help."

"Is that what Brian said?"

Sara didn't answer.

"I've never even *met* the man."

"Maybe not, but that doesn't mean he doesn't know *you* inside and out."

We continued in that vein for the first three days of her visit, seeing no one and nothing of the area, just "working out our feelings" from dawn until dusk. After dark Sara sometimes turned tender. She made me dinner. She played some of her favorite albums. I wanted in the worst way to make love to her (though I might have chosen a cruder verb), but Sara insisted that we sleep separately, meaning that I sleep on the couch. Twice she came out in her nightgown after I'd turned out the lights. She sat on the edge of the couch and stroked my hair back at the temples. "I'm sorry to be doing this to you," she said both times. "I know it's hard for a man. It's hard for me too. But I have to. I just can't trust our feelings. I can't risk... that way we did it last summer. I can't risk having that happen again. You do understand?"

All marriages have their shorthand. I did understand. Sara planned to stay a week, and I was toying with the idea of asking her to try to book an earlier flight when Leslie called and suggested that we all meet for drinks. It turned out that Jay had an old friend from Tory Hole who ran a cowboy bar up in La Honda on Skyline Drive. The name of the place was Boots and Saddles. ("Puss and Boots," Jay said in the background.) "Come on, it'll be good for you," Les coaxed, from the sound of her voice her old self again.

"I don't know. We're kind of a social contagion right now—"

"Plague, you mean," Sara said in my other ear.

"We'll risk it," Leslie said. "Come on, it sounds like you two could use a night out."

"Well, maybe," I said. "I've just got to check with my better half."

"Sure. Why not?" Sara said before I'd even begun to explain.

• • •

Jay's friend, the proprietor of the cowboy bar, was a short, stocky man with stubby arms jutting out from his body and house-counting eyes. He sat with us for a minute or two with one of his arms stretched up and around Jay's shoulders, but he couldn't keep his eyes on us or his mind on the conversation. Shortly, he excused himself, then seemed to leap away, pouncing into a gaggle of people at the bar. Looking after him, Jay said, "There's a man who seems peculiarly suited for his work. Big hands for backslapping. Short arms for punching. A natural bouncer. Low center of gravity. Quick on his feet. And those eyes..."

"You mean he looks you square in the cocktail glass?" Les asked.

Sara and I laughed, but Les didn't seem to have caught her own joke. "I wonder what kind of tail he would have," she said vaguely. This was one of our childhood games, a kind of pin-the-tail figuratively.

"Rabbit's tail," I said quickly. "His secret self."

"Jackrabbit or cottontail?"

"Cottontail of course. Isn't he from Tory Hole?"

Les nodded approvingly. "Right."

"What *is* this, some kind of code?" Jay asked.

"They're showing off their siblinghood," Sara explained, leaning a little closer toward Jay than she really needed to to be heard.

But Les didn't seem to notice Sara wagging her figurative tail. "You have to guess the *inner* tail," she went on, developing the philosophy of the game as she explained it. "The tail is an invisible projection of the essential self. However, it's not necessarily the tail you'd prefer to have..."

"Sounds pretty Freudian to me," Sara said.

"More Jungian really." Les turned to Jay. "Your friend, for instance, has an inner cottontail, even though he'd rather have a panther's tail. He might even think he *does* have a panther's tail, in which case he'd be deluding himself. His eyes are what give him away. Those are the eyes of the hunted, not the hunter."

"Reincarnation?" Sara asked. She was interested.

Les shrugged. "I just thought archetypal."

"What's mine?" Jay asked.

"You're easy, since your nickname is so appropriate," Leslie said. "You have a bluejay's tail, and secretly you preen it, plucking out all the fleas."

"I've been exposed! I'm so embarrassed!" Jay said, covering his eyes with his arm.

I found myself staring at his handlebar mustache, which covered most of the rest of his face, and feeling sure that this man would never have the tail of a bird. "Jay would have a monkey's tail," I said.

Les looked at me sharply, then she continued in a serious tone. "We'll do Jeremy next. Now, you have to answer immediately. Everybody ready? All right. What kind of tail would Jeremy have? Don't think. React."

Sara and Jay both hesitated, probably balancing the degree of insult against the truth. I'd long ago accepted that I'd inherited my father's camel's tail. Even before Dr. Miller told me, I'd recognized that inwardly I scowled down at the world. I wasn't about to give myself away, though. "No premeditated tails," I reminded them. "You have to answer quickly or it doesn't count."

"A cow's," Sara said.

Jay said, "Possum's."

"Thank you, Jay." I bowed my head in his direction. "Now at least I can hang out at night..."

Jay groaned. "One more pun and I'll switch your tail."

"What about Leslie's guess?" Sara asked peevishly.

"She's disqualified for knowing me too well."

"And I suppose I don't?"

"Apparently not. A cow tail indeed. Moo-oo," I said to her. "Now we'll do Les and Sara last. Quickly now, what would be Leslie's inner tail?"

"Seal," Jay said.

Sara drawled, "I think maybe a cat tail."

"What kind of cat?" I asked. The answer Les and I had arrived at fifteen or twenty years before was a lion's tail, but I didn't expect either of them to guess.

Sara shrugged. "A lion, I guess. Isn't that her sign?"

It was. She was right on both counts, but none of us had the good manners to tell her so. Instead, Les said dramatically, "The correct answer is . . . an Irish setter's." We were all silent in response. I remembered that I'd never asked about the fate of Blazes Boylan. I'd promised not to. Was I now supposed to ask?

Jay harrumphed, pretending to clear his throat.

"Yes, Sara's turn," I said. "My guess is she has the inner tail of a mink."

"You know me too well," she purred.

"No, a sable," Les corrected me.

"You know me even better."

We all looked at Jay, who savored the attention for a moment, then shook his head. "I'm sorry, sugar," he said with a syrupy accent, "but I just don't feel I know you well enough yet."

It was true. Sara and Jay had only just met. This was the foursome that had not gotten together at the Lion's Head after Papa's death, when we had that horrible fight. Only Jay seemed unaware of what had happened and what might have happened if he'd shown up that night. "Well, who's ready for another?" he asked, twirling his mustache in his comical way.

Les looked at him sharply. At first I didn't know what Jay was talking about, I was so far from the here and now, and I wondered if Les wasn't similarly elsewhere. "Nobody drinking? No takers?" Jay asked again.

Sara accepted. I declined. "No," Leslie said. "*I've* had enough. Somebody has to drive."

While Jay was maneuvering his way up to the bar, I slouched back in the booth, giving Leslie some room to cool off. She was peevish about something, obviously. Sara didn't seem to notice though. She leaned forward toward Leslie in the other corner, stretching diagonally across the booth. She was eager to say something. My sister looked at her coolly. Sara hesitated, gathering her words. "What kinds of tails would you give your children?" she earnestly asked.

I expected an explosion, or at least some small sharp sound, a contemptuous snort. But Les treated the question seriously, as it had been asked. "It's not up to me," she said simply.

"But if it were . . . ?"

Les shrugged. I realized I hadn't read her as well as I thought I did. "Mat would like a dragon's tail. Something fanciful, magical, reptilian, and large. I'd give it to him if I could. Barbara I'm not so sure about. She thinks she'd like a tail like yours, long and sleek and gorgeous in a Park Avenue way. Universally accepted. Popular." Les looked at Jay over at the bar. "But if I had a choice, I think I'd give her a dragon's tail, too. I think she'll need it every bit as much as Mat." She smiled at Sara. "No offense intended."

"None taken."

Jay returned from the bar, and Sara leaned back again in the booth as he distributed the drinks. "Let's see," he said. "Beer for the bluejay, nothing for the seal. The possum is all set, hanging upside-down from his tree, and one vodka gimlet for the lady with the silky tail of a mink."

"Sable," Sara corrected him, flirtatiously. "It's so much more elegant, don't you think?"

"Oh, indubitably. Only the best for you, peach."

After that, Sara flirted openly with Jay, which worried me since my sister could be as jealous as a cat. But Les was deep in her own thoughts, leaning back in her corner of the booth. From time to time, she spoke simply and pleasantly, her voice coming from a long way off.

We left after midnight. Coming out of the raucous noise and country music into the quiet of the parking lot, shaded even from the moon by the redwood trees, it seemed suddenly cold and dark and a little sad to be breaking up the party, getting into our separate cars and driving away. I knew that we were getting out amicably while the getting was good, but still I hated to see the foursome split up. I'd felt a freshness, and a thrill, from the flirtations between Sara and Jay. Watching them, Les and I seemed to be relating by extension. Now they were saying good night and good-bye. Sara gave Les a quick and girlish hug, then hesitated before Jay. "Is it all right?" he asked, then went ahead and pecked her on the cheek. For a moment, Sara stood with her palms flat on his chest, and Les and I looked past them into each other's eyes. We could have been anywhere in that moment, sitting on opposite sides of a bed in which our surrogates performed or in the bed ourselves.

Then Jay stepped back, and they were gone. Sara and I watched their silhouettes cross the parking lot and called good night one more time, then got into our separate box ourselves. We rode in silence down the twisting roads. It wasn't any great distance, but a slow drive. I was spinning the wheel back and forth and thinking, trying to hold the scene in my mind. After a while, Sara said, "I liked him."

"Yes, I could see that you did."

"That's *not* what I mean. I liked her too."

"I'm glad. I always wanted you two to get along."

Sara didn't say anything more. The road straightened, and I leaned back from my cornering position hunched over the wheel. I felt dreamy. The van seemed to be floating downhill of its own accord. I might have been steering it, yes, but in a certain way I felt like I was only acting, simulating a drive. Someone else was directing this picture, and if things went wrong, it was his fault, not ours. Yes! I thought. There was somebody tracking us, filming all the time. That's the magic ingredient of California Life: "Candid Camera" lives. Our lives count, they're *seen*. Now, if only we could hear the sound track. If only we could be edited as we go along...

"You prick," Sara said—like a bolt from the blue, I thought. "You complete *bastard*. You won't even talk to me, you're so mad..."

"I'm not mad. If anything, I was feeling—"

"You *know* what this does to me. It just rips me up inside. You *know* silence is the one thing I can't stand."

"Like kryptonite? No, no. I'm sorry. I'm just quiet tonight."

"You're jealous, aren't you? What right do you have to be jealous of *me?*"

"I'm not jealous. I was just thinking..." I turned to smile at her, but she didn't see me. "Maybe I wasn't thinking of you at all."

"Uh-huh. Sure. You were just contemplating art and literature, I suppose. You were meditating..."

"I was considering the metaphysical applications of film, actually..."

"You're so full of shit I can't stand it. It's coming out your nose."

"My nose? Come on, Sara. Aren't you getting your idiom wrong?"

"My idiom? Don't talk to me about idioms. Just because you're a fucking *grad* student doesn't make you any less of a *turd*."

"And just because you were coming on to my sister's boyfriend doesn't make me any more of one."

"See! You are jealous."

"Well, so what if I am?"

That night, Sara and I made love for the first time in seven months. (Or at least we would have if I hadn't been impotent.) Maybe it was the liquor that helped her relent. Or maybe it was the flirtation with my sister's beau, renewing Sara's sense of possibilities. I didn't know, but I knew better than to look the gift horse in the mouth. For the rest of her visit, we were screwing all the time—in the mornings, in the evenings, ain't we got fun. Sara did seem like a sable, all animated pelt.

I found her sunbathing in the nude on the patio when I got home from classes on the afternoon of her flight. I'd looked first in my room, then peeked into Jacques's room, before I tried the kitchen and spied her sleek brown body through the screen. "Aren't you afraid of being ravished by a Fuller Brush man?" I called out the door.

"What do you think we Easterners come out to California for? Oranges and avocados?" she called back without opening her eyes or turning her face from the sun.

"What if Jacques had come home unexpectedly?"

"How do you know he hasn't already come and gone?"

That stopped me, for a moment. "Is this the same girl I married?"

"Nope." Then she added, "My friends will be disappointed if I come back from California without a tan."

"All over? What friends are those?"

"Wouldn't you like to know?" she said as she rolled toward me and smiled. I started unbuttoning my shirt. "When's my flight again?" she asked as I stepped outside. I licked the salt off her belly, then her thighs. She lay back and closed her eyes, and she didn't open them while I undressed, even though she must have heard the rustling and the sound of my pants falling on the flagstones. I cupped her ass in my hands and lifted her to my mouth like a gourd. She didn't even open her eyes when I entered her. Neither did she call out my name.

We were still making love an hour before her flight, and it didn't seem possible that we could make it to the airport on time. But we tried. On the way, I asked her, "Do you want to miss your plane?"

"Do you want me to?" she countered.

I drove sixty-five, and when we got to the airport, Sara ran for the gate. She made her flight and was gone.

sixteen

Over the next week, Sara and I fought the gallant losing battle on the long-distance telephone line. We could afford to, since we'd lost the marriage when she caught her plane. Every day we spoke at least once and sometimes two or three times, our conversations running on and on, twenty or thirty dollars' worth of anguish to enjoy, occasionally thirty-five. (Sometimes I said it, sometimes Sara did: "Psychiatrists cost fifty-five.") Failing marriages are all alike, and fortunately only the fact of this one's failure really pertains here. Each of us had a part to play; we played them. Sara went on and on about Brian and the differences between us. I talked about the hills' shade of green, quickly paling from emerald to pea. Each topic was a shorthand, a kind of short circuit, enabling us to emote. We addressed the real issue only once. After one of our poignant silences, Sara said, "You should never have let me catch that plane."

"You're the one who made the mad dash for the gate."

"What else could I do after you'd gotten me to the airport in time?"

"Dawdle."

"You're the dawdler, hon, not me."

Then we lapsed into silence again. Our silences were long and wistful as we listened to the static slosh between us like the tide. Sometimes we cried together, listening to the echoes of our own

sobs. We weren't just a continent apart, we were continents ourselves, adrift in geologic time. Where once we'd been contiguous,
now we were separated and every day floating further apart. I may
have even uttered that line, I was so perfectly self-absorbed.

On the seventh day, I had a telephone date with Sara for four
P.M., and Hannah called at three forty-five. "I have to see you!" she
said breathlessly, as though she'd run for the phone.

I was calm, unflappable. Hannah lived in Berkeley after all. "All
right. Anytime tonight. Anytime after five."

"I'll be right over."

"Where are you now?"

"Right around the corner. Just a block or so—"

"No, don't come now. I was just about to get in the shower,
then Sara's going to call."

"I don't care! I'll wait for you, I'll wait in the garden! I have to
see you right now!"

"I'm sorry, but you'll have to wait till five . . . Hannah? Hannah?"

I'd no sooner hung up than Sara called. We talked no longer
than usual, forty-five minutes or so. I heard Hannah drive up to
the house in mid-conversation. She waited on the patio for a few
minutes, scraping her chair, then moved into the kitchen where she
could overhear me talking on the living-room phone. I didn't bother
to shut the door. When I got off I poured her some wine and asked
her to be patient for a few minutes more. I noticed that she was
wearing heavy makeup and she'd put on several pounds. "I can't
talk here!" she said with a dramatic toss of her newly frizzled hair.
She'd had a permanent. And her hair was black. It wasn't hennaed
anymore. She looked like she'd just escaped from the set of a Fellini
film.

"That's all right, Hannah. I'll just hop in the shower, then we'll
go out to whatever trattoria you desire."

I'd been in the shower only five or ten minutes when the door
burst open, banging against the wall. The bathroom was filled with
steam, which wasn't clearing, which meant the door must have
closed again. I squinted, peering over the shower door. All I saw
was a looming shape. "Hannah?"

"No. Not Hannah," Les said. Then I saw her, all enameled in pastel shades, emerging through the steam. "Jeremy, you just can't go around treating people this way!" She was yelling to be heard over the sound of the shower. "I *know* how long you've been on the phone—a whole hour!—because I was trying to call you myself. And I know *whom* you've been blabbering away to because I just spoke to Hannah in the hall!"

"So you finally met." I shut off the water. "Then you know everything. The jig's up, I guess."

"Is that all you've got to say for yourself? Don't you think women have feelings too? You know what you're being—an insensitive, egotistical bastard! In a word, a prick, Jeremy." She nodded, confirming her choice of that particular dirty word. "Don't you see that?"

I didn't defend myself. Smiling, I just watched her across the shower door.

"I don't know why you're grinning like that. You should be ashamed. I can think of no possible justification for your behavior—unless of course she just *showed up* here or something and then *insisted* on sitting around while you chatted away all afternoon with her rival on the phone . . ."

Still smiling, I raised my eyebrows.

"Oh, that's it, I suppose?" Les cocked her head and her hip in a sarcastic pose.

I nodded slowly. "That's it, except for one thing. Hannah called first, so she knew *exactly* what to expect *before* she dropped by." I paused dramatically. "She didn't happen to mention that, I suppose."

Les was flustered. She looked away from me and made a face in the mirror. "I didn't give her a chance, I guess." The steam was starting to clear. I saw that Les was wearing a peach-colored summer dress and pale lipstick, and she'd lightened her hair to a soft shade of red. Hesitantly, she touched her hair.

"I like it," I said.

Les was still watching herself in the mirror. "I feel like an ass. I'm sorry to come bursting in on you this way."

"That's all right. I think it's rather sweet, and intimate, in a strictly brother-sisterly way."

Les smiled. Our eyes met in the mirror. "Do you really like it? My hair, I mean?"

"Love it. You look like a spring flower. You look like one of those Easter chicks that comes already dyed in the shell."

"Thanks a lot. You know I'm thirty-one years old."

"And you never looked so good."

Les turned to look at me directly, handing me a towel. "As for you . . . you look like some muskrat that's just crawled out of Long Island Sound. You're not really that tall, are you?"

"No, I'm standing on the ledge."

Through the shower door, she looked me up and down. "Even so, I always thought of you as . . . littler."

"Kind of like Matthew?"

"Well, more like a little brother than a son, but at any rate *younger* than you obviously are."

"Exactly how transparent *is* this glass?"

"It's clear enough. I've got to go."

"What was it you wanted to talk to me about?"

Les's expression was blank.

"You said you were trying to call me earlier. Why?"

"Oh, that." She turned, putting her hand on the door. "It's nothing really, just something about the bus. I've really got to go now."

"But I'm just getting out . . ."

Les gave me a sidelong glance. "Then I'd *better* go."

I dressed quickly and caught her just going out the front door. Probably she'd stopped to have a word with Hannah, who gave me a terrified glance on my way past.

"You're all dressed up. Who's the lucky man?" I asked Les, walking her out to her VW bus.

"You'll meet him, eventually."

"A mystery man? Nobody I know? Describe him then."

"He's not as tall as you are, but he's . . . swarthier."

"Sounds sexy. Is he black?"

Les gave me a sharp look. "No."

"Is he a doctor?"

Les opened her car door and hoisted herself in.

"What kind of tail would he have? At least you can tell me that."

"Cute. You'll meet him this weekend. We'll do something."

I held onto the door handle of the car. "You'll call?"

Les nodded. "If I can get through... Yes, I promise, I'll call. Now don't be clammy. I really have to run." She reached out and touched my chin. "We're not demonstrative," she said.

"De-monsterative?"

She smiled. "Whatever." Then she started up her motor. I watched her through the tinted glass as she drove away.

seventeen

Two days later, on a Friday night, the telephone rang at three A.M. I answered it on the third ring even though I'd been asleep and the phone was halfway across the house. I didn't think it would be Sara, and I wasn't surprised to hear Barbara's voice. "Mommy's been in an accident. The hospital just called."

"Stanford Hospital?"

"Yes, I think so. They asked me how old I was and whether there was anyone I could call. I said I had an uncle—"

"You did just right. I'll call you from the hospital. It might be thirty minutes or so. Will you be okay?"

"Oh, yes, I'll be fine. I'm just worried, is all."

The road was slick, glossy black before my headlights. It looked like a calm inlet reflecting back the smeared lights. I could see the stars. The sky was clearing. The rain had come and gone in the few hours I'd been asleep, and it hadn't even stopped the sprinklers from watering the median strips. They were on timers, apparently. This was the first rain we'd had in two months.

These thoughts settled on my brain on the way to the hospital, but I didn't think about them, not in any conscious sense. At least I didn't reason. All possibilities were suspended. There was no other traffic, not a single car. I drove fast and at a steady speed. All the lights were green my way. At the emergency desk I introduced myself and asked to see my sister, Leslie Jakes. It sounded wrong to say her married name.

The nurse blinked rapidly and asked me to sit down. Then she slipped into the back. I was alone in a vast waiting room. There was no one in sight, not even behind the counter. Nor could I hear anything except the tap of my shoes as I paced.

The nurse returned to the counter. "The neurology resident will be with you in a moment, if you'd like to sit down."

I stood, troubled by the conditional. After a few moments, a dark-haired woman of my sister's age approached me. She had her hands thrust deep in the pockets of her long white doctor's coat. "Mr. Jakes?"

"Morgan. Jakes is my sister's married name."

"Your sister's been in a very serious accident," she said. "She sustained massive fractures... to her head. We're treating her now. As much as is possible. We'll do everything we can. But unless her condition improves, more than we expect it to, there will be no point in surgery." I didn't say anything. The resident looked me closely, clinically in the eyes. "Do you understand? We won't operate unless her condition improves."

Her manner was cool and impersonal. The resident seemed neutral, and some part of me couldn't abide that emotionless stance. I searched her eyes, and then responded, blinking back the tears. "You mean she's going to die?"

"Yes, I think so," she said without dropping her eyes.

The room was suddenly smaller, much smaller than a moment before. It was another room. I heard my voice, though I hadn't willed it, ask, "Can I see her now?"

The resident seemed startled by the question, which let me know I could see her if I insisted. "She's unconscious. You don't want to see her," she said.

Again my voice without volition: "Yes I do. It's important, I think."

She hesitated, seemed to be trying to stare me down. "You wait here, and I'll check," she said finally. The resident walked off with her hands in her pockets. I turned away from the counter where she'd gone. In what seemed like only an instant, the nurse reappeared. She touched my elbow. "You can see your sister now. Are you sure that you want to?"

"Yes."

The nurse led me past the counter, the same counter I'd approached when I first came in. Then she drew back a curtain and motioned me past. I went in. Leslie had been so close all along.

Her body leaped and shuddered on the table. Her nose and mouth and ears were pouring blood. A sheet covered part of her body. There was fresh blood on the sheet as well. A young man was stationed at my sister's head, pressing towels with one hand to catch the streaming blood. He glanced up at me; he looked ashamed. With his other hand he tried to hold her to the table. Her whole body heaved with each convulsion. He was keeping her body from flipping away.

eighteen

I called Barbara with a quarter because it came to hand quicker than a dime. "I'll be right over. I'll tell you everything when I get there." I may or may not have seen the emergency-room nurse on the way out the door, but I remember her at some point saying, "If there's any change, we'll call."

Between the hospital and my sister's apartment, the road passed through Stanford campus and the longest traffic signal for miles around. When I reached it, it was red. I stopped. I waited, but then I couldn't wait any longer and drove on through. A few miles farther, another red light. I ran that one too.

Barbara opened the door before I'd even knocked. "I don't want to wake Mat," she whispered, leading me into the dining room. "Do you want anything? Coffee? A glass of wine?"

I shook my head and sat down at the dining-room table, pulling another chair up close to mine. "You don't have to be a hostess. Sit down here next to me." Barbara sat on the edge of the chair. Her hands fluttered, ready to fly. I put my arm on the back of her chair, took a breath and began, "Your mother's badly hurt. She hit her head in the accident. She has multiple fractures of the skull. They won't even operate unless her condition improves. Barbara, she might die."

"Is she awake?"

"No, she's unconscious."

Barbara sat on, perched on the edge of her chair, the tears plummeting into her lap. "I just wish I hadn't yelled at her before she went back out. I *yelled* at her. I was so mad, I didn't want her to go. I don't know why I didn't want her to go. I just wish I hadn't said—"

"You were probably right not to want her to go out, but that's nothing now. Your mother always knew how much you loved her. She knew." I put my arm around her shoulders. "We'll know more in the next couple of hours. If anything changes, they'll call."

"I want to stay up."

"Of course you can."

Barbara put her arms around my neck and squeezed me. Maybe she was childishly grateful, maybe more maturely so, or maybe she was just comforting me, hearing more in my voice than in my words. Barbara could be so old and young at the same time. "Now would you like that glass of wine?" she asked.

"Yes. I'll get it though."

"No, let me."

Barbara came back from the kitchen balancing two glasses of red wine, one large, one very small. The ruby liquid lurched back and forth as she walked. For the next hour we sat together waiting for the phone to ring. At five Barbara finally agreed to go lie down, but only after I'd promised to wake her if the telephone rang. When she went to bed, I noticed that she hadn't even touched her glass of wine.

The hospital called at five-fifteen. "Your sister's vital signs are improving. Do we have your permission to operate? If we don't relieve the swelling inside the skull—"

"Yes, yes, operate! Do whatever you have to! Do you need me to come down and sign?"

"No, your permission over the phone is all we need."

When I hung up, I turned toward Barbara's room. I was going to wake her, but she was already there in the hall. "What did they say?"

"They said *maybe!* They said they're going to operate! They said she's got a chance!" Barbara hugged me around the waist. Then, for the first time, I cried.

Barbara went back to bed, and at five-thirty I called my mother. It was eight-thirty her time, she'd just have gotten up. I told her that Leslie was very badly injured in a car accident, that she was going into surgery now. She repeated, "Now." Then I told her to book a flight and call a neighbor to drive her to the airport and watch the house. She repeated, "Watch the house." I told her after she'd done all that and knew her flight to call me back at Leslie's number. Mother repeated not "Leslie's number," but "Call you back," so I knew she'd be all right.

Hope is the most treacherous of human emotions. At three-thirty that morning, I had seen my sister dying, her body fighting on without her mind, and I'd accepted the fact, passing directly into a state of shock. Now, two hours later, I was still in shock, but my mood was as buoyant as a musical. I felt light-headed from the mildest dose of hope.

The sun came up at six. Objects in the darkened living room took on shape, dimension, and finally color and life. I moved, almost waltzing from room to room. The world was a beautiful place; anything could happen, everything could hardly help but turn out right.

At six-fifteen the telephone rang again. I thought it would be my mother calling back, but another woman's voice said, "This is Stanford Hospital calling. Am I speaking to . . . Mr. Jeremy Morgan, brother of Leslie Jakes?"

"Yes, that's right," I said simply, though in my exuberance I could have said much more.

"Mr. Morgan, we understand your sister is in diminishing condition following her fatal head injuries, and we wondered if you'd consider allowing your sister to participate in the Stanford Hospital heart-transplant program?"

I didn't answer.

"Mr. Morgan . . . Mr. Morgan, are you there?"

Then I spoke. "You're either premature or *horribly wrong*. Who is this exactly?"

"I'm with the administrative staff of the Stanford heart-transplant program. We recognize that this may not be the best moment for you to discuss this subject, but you must understand that timing is of the essence in situations of this kind. You know, many donor families find great solace in knowing that through their generosity and sacrifice they may have helped to save a life and, in a very special sense, that their loved ones may be said to live on as part of another life—"

The skin tightened across my face. I tried to hang up, but my hand was shaking so much that I missed the cradle. The receiver clattered off the table, swinging on its cord, battering on its down-strokes against the hardwood floor. I felt a chill run through me. Nonsensically, I pictured the pinched eyes on the face of the woman who worked in the hospital gift shop where I'd stolen the card. Nonsensically, I felt as if I'd just been talking to Death herself.

I was on my knees retrieving the telephone when Barbara opened her door. "Who was that?" she asked.

"Nothing. No one. A fool," I said. "An institutionalized fool."

"Was it a wrong number?"

"Yes. Very wrong."

Like God, hospitals work in mysterious ways. In as many hours, I'd had three encounters with Stanford Hospital, and each had left me transformed. I felt as though I'd been a child before.

The first encounter had put me into shock. Go into shock, do not pass Go. Don't even say the word, Go. The resident had told me the truth, and then she'd let me see it. She had made a quick and clean incision: shock rushed in like a frigid anesthetic.

My second encounter had been sweet, and for a little while I'd soared. I trusted this lesson the least of all. The hospital had called and given me hope, something slender to clutch onto and something to give to Barbara and my mother and Mat when he woke up. Nothing more.

The third encounter steeled me. I felt that I was being tested,

Dean Crawford

or prepared. I could feel the steel like pinions, pulling the skin taut across my cheeks, and knew that I needed it, would need it even more later on. When Mat woke up, I told him exactly half the truth I'd told Barbara. Then I fixed him breakfast. Afterward I called Dr. Eckles, the chairman of the endocrinology department, Leslie's boss. I called him at home.

Dr. Eckles was a honcho at the hospital and a luminary in his field, waiting to receive his Nobel Prize for work well done thirty or forty years before. I knew all this from Leslie, who had compared the Nobel Prize first to Calvinism, then to systemic cancer. Les had laughed when she told me this—a lifetime before.

I introduced myself fully to Dr. Eckles since Les had also told me he was vague and I'd spoken to him only once before, the day Les and I met in the hospital for lunch, the day I'd seen the gift shop woman I'd just spoken to on the phone. "Oh, yes," Dr. Eckles said, pretending to remember me. Then I told him only the barest facts—that Leslie had been in an accident, suffered head injuries, and was going into surgery now. I didn't tell him anything in medical terms, feigning even more ignorance than I had. "Who's her neuro-surgeon?" he interrupted me to ask.

"Oh, I don't know. Whoever's on call, I guess. They wouldn't tell me that." I knew Dr. Eckles would be down there when Les came out of surgery, if not before.

He met me in scrub clothes when the operation was complete. He didn't tell me much, only that Leslie was alive, and he told me that in the doorway, out of earshot of Barbara and Mat. Afterward I left with the kids to pick up my mother at the airport. I must have mentioned that to Dr. Eckles.

When we returned, he was still in the hospital. He'd left word at Intensive Care that he wanted to meet Mrs. Morgan, and they paged him as soon as we arrived. Dr. Eckles appeared in suit pants and a long white coat. Mother took one look at him, saw his wrinkled face and white hair, and tears welled up into her eyes. He wrapped a stiff but chivalrous arm around her shoulders, and she softly sobbed. I hadn't seen my mother as a daughter in some years.

For the rest of the afternoon, we waited outside Intensive Care, waiting for visiting hours to begin at five, waiting for some word. I took Matthew to the bathroom four times, and twice Barbara came along as far as the door. My mother didn't move except to raise her eyes expectantly whenever someone in a white coat passed through the waiting room. At five we were allowed to go in, but only my mother and I. "She's in number six," a nurse came out to tell us. "But the children can't go in, not unless they're fourteen and I don't think they are. That's our strictest rule," she added like a kindergarten teacher, smiling at the kids, who did not return her smile. "But I can find someone to watch them if you like."

"Thank you, but they can watch themselves," I said.

There were two patients in room number six. At first we stood in the doorway; we didn't know which one was Les. Both patients were entangled in tubes and wires. Both had respirators clamped over their mouths. Both were dwarfed by their equipment. Then I noticed that one of them had white hair above her respirator mask, and her feet reached hardly halfway down the bed. I guided my mother toward the other one, but even then I had to look closely to recognize her as Les. She was a young woman. Her arm was Leslie's arm. The freckles on her shoulder were Leslie's freckles. I stopped comparing there.

Leslie's chest heaved like a bellows with each breath. When I realized that her heaves were those of the respirator, breathing through her, my mind filled up with horror like the amplified noise of the machine. Then it began to subside. Leslie wasn't there, I reminded myself. She couldn't feel a thing.

She could feel nothing. The mask covered more than her face. Bandages covered more than I could see, more than her scalp and her chin and all of one side of her face. The bandages were covering her brain. My mother could sit at her bedside and cry. I stood, I couldn't cry. My mother suffered. I could see that she really loved my sister. That brought tears to my eyes, but I wiped them away. My mother grieved. I could see that. But her love and her grief were not mine.

Mother wanted to be at the hospital for both the morning and evening visiting hours as well as the doctors' rounds. (She called them vespers, twice.) I didn't want to be there at all, but I went with her and stood by. She needed someone to drive her. She didn't know the roads. She couldn't drive my van. And while I allowed her her manner of grief, she allowed me mine. She never objected to the way I drove, not even when I veered around cars and ran red lights, in traffic, in the middle of the afternoon.

Leslie's condition improved for the first two days after surgery, then it began to decline. They operated again on the third day, once again to relieve the pressure of the swelling inside her skull, but this time it didn't seem to make any difference in her "vital signs." Barbara and Mat came often to the waiting room, but they were never allowed inside Intensive Care. Barbara was only two and a half years underage, and we might have been able to slip her in. But not Mat, who wasn't even seven yet. And we felt that sneaking his sister in and not him would have been too hard on Mat. Maybe we were right, maybe not.

"It's not fair," Barbara said bitterly. Mat echoed her.

"No, it's not fair," I agreed, but after the third or the fourth time they repeated it, I told them that their mother wasn't really in that hospital room, that all they'd see in there would be tubes and bandages and a mask over her mouth to help her breathe. I told them the only reason I visited her was because Grandma wanted to. Grandma had to, for reasons of her own. Then they understood a little better. Grandma's grief was great, but it was no more theirs than mine.

The doctors made their rounds before the afternoon visiting hour at five. Every day following their rounds, a different resident came to speak to us in hushed tones. He never had to ask for us, he always knew who we were. Usually he came in a long white coat. Once he came dressed as a lawyer in a three-piece suit with a watch fob dangling from his vest. The residents who spoke to us were either short or tall, light or dark, but what they said to us was always the same: "All we can do now is hope." "We've done everything known to medical science." "It's all up to Leslie now." "It's up to God."

Dr. Eckles met us in the waiting room from time to time, as did his two residents in endocrinology, Dr. Chandi and Dr. Mark

Gold. We learned that Dr. Chandi was from India. He was a tall, handsome man. He smelled of Canoe cologne and smiled constantly except in those moments immediately after something very sad had been said and then he frowned. I preferred Mark Gold, who avoided us as much as he could. He was shorter, less handsome, and he never smiled. He wouldn't even let me catch his eye. I called the first resident "Dr. Chandi," the second "Mark." I liked Mark instinctively and suspected that he was shifty only to cover himself, only because he could be touched. Even so, I didn't spare his feelings when I wanted an answer. "What exactly is the prognosis, Mark? What does it say on the chart?"

"Only a miracle . . ." he began, then stopped himself. Mark was shorter than I and certainly swarthier. I wondered, was he the mystery man? I must have been looking at him too closely. I was about to ask him if he'd seen Les last Friday night when he caught me looking. "The prognosis is bad," he snapped. "It would probably be better if she died."

In that week, I learned a number of more or less esoteric terms, becoming knowledgeable if not exactly expert in several narrow fields: the probable effects of massive brain contusions, the "vital signs" by which one measures "life," the various requirements of insurance companies (both medical and life), the most expeditious ways of approaching a Social Security office, and the California laws for setting up a conservatorship. My concentration was tunnel—I felt as though I were looking at the world down a long, dark tube—but it seemed to me pinpoint at the time, the best it had ever been. I had a mission, for once in my life. In the service of my sister and my sister's kids, no institution (and very few red lights) could stand in my way.

For a little while, I felt like an Israeli, galvanized to help my kind survive. Later, I might become just another Jew in Diaspora again, more the exile for having lost my sister (my consciousness, my twin) along with the Promised Land where I'd had a sense of common purpose to be served. But that would be later on. For now, busy was what I needed most to be. I drove briskly, urgently, as though there were something behind me, following steadily, catching up. Sometimes it even had a face: the woman from the gift shop, trying to retrieve the stolen Hallmark card. Sometimes a voice: "... knowing... in a very special sense, that their loved ones may be said to live on as part of another life—" But more often it was just an urgency, hot on my heels at all times.

Leslie's "vital signs" started to decline that Sunday night, two days after the accident. On Monday they operated for the second time, and we spent all day at the hospital waiting for some word. Mother wanted to keep a vigil. So did I, but I couldn't sit. I roamed the hospital corridors, going over and over the events in my mind. Les must have been with someone earlier on the night of the accident; yet no one had come forward, and I didn't know who to ask.

On Tuesday and Wednesday, I was grateful for errands—to the insurance offices, the lawyer, Social Security (three times), the police department to pick up a copy of the accident report—ferrying my mother and the kids back and forth to the hospital in between. I had to be on the move. I even drove across the bay to Newark, to clean out Leslie's bus. The insurance company was storing it in a sea of wrecks that extended out into the baylands. At the office, they gave me a map and a number and wouldn't look me in the eye. I wondered how much information was towed in with each car. The cars were arranged in straight rows of twisted metal. When I got to Les's VW, it didn't look so bad from behind, just dirty. It didn't look as bad as some of the cars on either side, and some of those people must have survived. Then I saw that the front had been crumpled like an aluminum can. Inside everything was covered with pieces of glass the size of hailstones and everything was scrambled. I found Les's suede coat and a sweater, a stuffed rabbit (Barbara's), Blazes' leash, and dozens of empty Ballantine beer cans (Jay's favorite brand) that Les had been meaning to take to the recycling center. The cans were everywhere. I started gathering them, gently packing them back into their torn paper bags. I thought I might drop them off for her, since I'd be going right by the Palo Alto Recycling Center. Then I realized that everything in this car was already destined to be scrap metal.

While my mother was visiting my sister's body, animated only by machines, and the kids were waiting in their own shell-shocked ways, I tried to find Mark Gold. Dr. Mark Gold didn't answer my telephone messages. I couldn't find him in the office marked "Dr. Gold." For an hour at a time, I stalked the west-wing labs. I wanted to ask him a question. I would have asked it cold. Wasn't Leslie en route to meet him when she was killed?

Returning home on a Friday night, my sister showered at one A.M. Then she made two calls. Barbara woke up. She and her mother exchanged sharp words. When my sister went out again, it was after two.

She drove down Middlefield, the street on which she lived, to Oregon Expressway, which she'd driven a hundred times before. Oregon was the only direct route to her bank and the shopping district, or to her brother's house, or to the nearest bar. That night the road was slick and glossy black, alluring in the way it shone. There had been a rain shower in the hour or so she'd spent at home. The road looked refreshed; so did her situation. Earlier in the evening maybe she'd been drinking, but now she felt better. The lights were green as far as she could see, bright orbs above her head, smears of color on the pavement. She drove with ease, she knew the road. She wasn't wearing her seat belt. She was going about forty-five miles per hour when she hit the Alma underpass curve.

Maybe another car pulled out in front of her from the half-hidden entrance ramp. Maybe she just felt she was going too fast and hit the brakes too suddenly too hard after she was already turning. Or maybe there was something wrong with the car. Her brakes may have pulled; her steering, locked. All things equal, the curve can be taken at forty-five.

Alma underpass is a lonely place at any time of day. The concrete walls and abutments are unusually high, and the dip is further shaded by a railroad trestle in addition to the Alma bridge itself. Still, it only takes a moment to drive through. If you call out the window while you're in the curve, you'll be out by the time the echo of your voice returns.

Alma underpass is actually an ancient locale. In the course of its construction in 1959, the excavation crew discovered an unusually large tooth and pelvic bone. Dr. Earl Packard, then only a research associate at Stanford, now president of Hewlett-Packard and one of the richest men in the world, identified the remains as belonging to a mammoth that died in the Ice Age about twelve thousand years ago.

At Alma underpass the road also changes names. Behind is Oregon Expressway, running flat across the valley to the bay. Ahead is Page Mill Road, which starts to climb just beyond the curve, eventually winding its way up to Skyline Drive. Page Mill is an old logging road. They say the horses used to burst their hearts trying to brake their loads of timber on the steep descent. That was in the days when these hills supplied redwood to the world. Old hill roads are a standard feature of many Western towns, but it would take a sharp eye to recognize the character of the past, of glacial-moving afternoons, in this one, Page Mill Road. Its lower slope is lined with service stations and "clean industry," the software and electronics companies of Silicon Valley, which was once known for its apricots and prunes. Higher up, the road leads to houses, very expensive houses, which look down on the valley and the bay. My sister was driving to meet someone at a service station, beside an all-night restaurant, on Page Mill Road.

First her car bounced off the concrete wall on the outside of the Alma underpass curve. Then it hit the water-filled bunker around the bridge supports, head-on. Her car recoiled, spinning halfway around. Her body was thrown sideways within the cab of the car. Like an egg, her head struck the metal of the wheel well on the passenger side and smashed. Leslie must have had a moment more of consciousness. Her consciousness must have felt the warmth descending from her scalp across her temples and her eyes. Her consciousness must have cried out, voicelessly, "I must not die! I must not die!" even as it felt the warmth and the darkness descending, quenching it, consciousness itself.

• • •

The hospital called on Thursday morning to tell us that Leslie had died at four-fifteen the night before. They told us that her heart had stopped. They didn't tell us that they had made no effort to resuscitate her since her electroencephalograph reading had been flat for several hours and the night staff had only been waiting for the morning to ask permission to unplug. Leslie's body died on Matthew's birthday, April seventh. Her brain had died before. We arranged for the funeral on Friday at noon.

Mat slipped into his first trance on Thursday afternoon. My mother was at home with him. Barbara and I were at the grocery store. When we got back, Mother met us at the door. She said, "I can't reach him!"

"Reach whom?" I thought first of the telephone since I knew that night I'd have to make some calls. Whom did she want to reach? Dr. Eckles? Papa? Fog?

"Matthew!" she said, gesturing toward a small boy who sat Indian-style on the floor, staring as though transfixed by the television set, except the television was behind him and he was staring at the wall. "Don't you *see?*" Mother continued, rolling her eyes, raving a bit herself. "First I called to him, 'Do you want some ice cream?' and he didn't answer, so I thought the must be sleeping. But then I heard him. He was *moaning.* The poor child was whimpering as though he were afraid. That's when I came out here—I was in the kitchen—and saw him shivering. Then I saw his eyes. Don't you see his *eyes?*"

"Yes, I see them." His eyes were wide, unblinking, glazed like a sick animal's.

My mother turned toward Mat again. She extended her arms. "I can't *reach* him," she said a second time.

"You don't need to reach him," Barbara said. "He's right here." She sat down behind her brother and folded him up in her legs and arms. They sat like that for five or ten minutes, an eight-legged creature, like a spider or a Buddhist god, until Mat started to squirm. Barbara tickled him, he giggled and thrashed, and soon they were on their way to play in the other room.

Barbara smirked at us on her way past. "That doesn't prove anything!" my mother called after her. Then she turned to me. "They were always close, as thick as thieves. That doesn't prove a thing."

I nodded. "You're right, it doesn't." I looked at her, my mother, wringing her grandmother's hands, leaking tears from her small girl's eyes, grieving like a widow. This woman had buried her mother, father, husband, and tomorrow she'd have to bury her daughter too. This woman was my mother. I couldn't reconcile her roles.

Mat lapsed into other trances from time to time. Barbara could reach him. My mother could hold him. The child psychiatrist we found could draw him out, playing checkers by the fifty-minute hour. But I could do very little for him, perhaps because I was afraid of him, perhaps because I saw him as me.

The night before the funeral, I made three calls and would have made four if I'd known a number where Dudley could be reached. I called all the recent men in my sister's life: Jay and Sultan in Connecticut and Aaron in Omaha. First I told them I had some bad news, then I told them the worst, ending with the how and when details. Two of them screamed when I said it. I'd thought it would be kinder not to mince my words, but the truth was I felt a rush of satisfaction when I heard from their voices their pain. Let them hurt. Leslie loved them. Maybe if they'd loved her better, she might have stayed home that Friday night. She might have still been alive.

Aaron was the one who didn't scream. His first words were calm. "I'm sorry to have to ask you to do this, Jeremy, but you'll have to say that again."

I didn't mind. The words slid right off my tongue. "Leslie died early this morning. She was badly hurt in an automobile accident last Friday, and she'd been lying in a coma ever since. The injuries were to her head," I added. "She suffered massive contusions to the brain and, of course, multiple fractures of the skull."

"Yes, yes. Oh my God," he moaned. His voice broke. I wiped away the dust from around the telephone dial while I waited patiently for him to digest the news and ask for more. "I'll come to the funeral," he said, getting control of his voice again. "When will the funeral be held?"

"Tomorrow at noon." I wet my fingertip and started wiping each number in the dial. "But Aaron, no one expects you to come so far."

"I'll be there," he promised. "Tomorrow at noon."

That night I dreamed about Leslie at the party again. She was sitting on the kitchen counter with her long legs crossed, just as I'd seen her in the dream seven months before. I entered the room, and she turned toward me. I noticed the other men in the room. All of them were curly-haired and swarthy with the hair coiling out of their button-down shirts. All of them looked like Aaron or Mark Gold. "Yes, that's what I told you," Les said to me, betraying some impatience in her voice. "That's what I wanted you to do." Then she turned back to the men in the room. I tried to walk toward her, but my legs wouldn't move. I tried to speak, but I couldn't make a sound. Inside I was screaming, "Yes, I will!" but I couldn't get the words to come out of my mouth. I woke up not knowing what it was she'd asked me to do.

Of the men in my sister's life, Aaron was the only one to show up for her funeral. He wore a black three-piece suit (and a button-down shirt) even though it was a hot day, very hot in the sun. I wore white, which Fog once told me is the custom in Hawaii. I didn't own a black suit and wouldn't have worn one if I did.

The service was held outside in the gardens of a Catholic chapel, presided over by an old priest whom Les might have liked. He'd lost the pastorship of his fancy congregation because of activism against the war. He'd suffered, in more than just his priestly way. It was a nonsectarian service and blessedly short.

A lot of people came. Relatives I hadn't seen in years. Jacques and his girlfriend, Frankie. Margaret of course. Drs. Eckles, Chandi, and Mark Gold along with a woman who turned out to be his wife and a number of other people from the hospital staff. I thought I recognized the emergency-room nurse and a nurse from Intensive

Care. I was hoping to see that first resident, from the emergency room, but she wasn't there.

Dr. Miller was there, my mother leaning on his arm. I shook his hand; he said something in Hebrew. I thought, God and I don't speak the same language anymore.

Then I spotted Mark. I accosted him as soon as he arrived. "Mark, I'm not trying to make trouble or anything. I just need to know. Did you happen to see Leslie last Friday night?"

"The night of the accident...?"

"That's right."

"I didn't see her."

"Then you spoke to her on the phone?"

Mark looked me in the eyes for the first time. "Yes. I did. She called very late, maybe one A.M. She said she needed to talk to someone. She wanted to come over. We decided..." He glanced at the blonde beside him. "This is my wife, Sandy. Sandy, this is Leslie's brother, Jeremy. We decided that it would be better if I met her someplace else instead. We live way up in the hills, you see. It's a hard place to find in the dark. Leslie was supposed to meet me at a service station on Page Mill Road. I waited an hour and a half. We weren't going out together, or having an affair, if that's what you think. Your sister and I were just friends."

I remembered how Les hated to be "just friends." "Do you know who she was seeing?"

Mark shook his head. "She'd seen someone that night, earlier. I don't know who..."

I believed him and thanked him for the information. Afterward I wandered through the crowd looking for other not-so-tall swarthy men. Jacques and Aaron were the only ones. Of course, the mystery man might not have come to the funeral. Why should he? I didn't really care if I found him or not anymore. In passing, I thanked Jacques and Frankie for coming and walked over to stand at Aaron's side. The service was about to begin. "Thanks for coming all this way," I said to him.

"You don't need to thank me. I wanted to come. Who are all these people anyway?"

"Friends, acquaintances, Irish cousins. I don't know a lot of them myself."

"So what are they doing here then?"

"My mother called them, I guess."

Aaron took my arm and drew me toward him. "It's you and me and the kids. Maybe your mother too, but that's all. We're the only ones here who really knew her. We're the only ones who can really grieve."

"I don't know about that. These people knew her. They must have cared, or they wouldn't be here. Who are we to judge?"

Aaron stared at me for a moment, teetering on offense, then he added, "All right, okay. Maybe that's the right attitude. Maybe that's right." He put his arms around my shoulders, a gesture which must have been hard for him since he was so much shorter. That fact, more than anything else, was what made me cry.

We cried together, Aaron and I, until it came time for the old priest to deliver his message. He said only a few words of his own, and they weren't memorable. As he admitted, he had never met Leslie, though he knew she meant a lot to us, the people here. Then he read, "To everything there is a season, and a time for every purpose under heaven." I walked through the crowd as he was reading and found myself standing by Barbara and Mat when the old priest delivered the last line, "What gain has the worker from his toil?"

Mat burst out, "Who are all these *people*?" He was red in the face. He was looking squarely at me.

I put my arm around him. "Friends, relatives, people who might not have known your mother very well but still cared enough to come."

Mat dropped his head, retreating back into his slump.

"I know this is hard for you," I said.

Barbara answered for both of them. "It's not hard for us. It's just . . . nothing," she said.

nineteen

arbara and Mat were separated by court decree. Hank Jakes sued for custody as soon as he received my letter informing him of Leslie's death. The court fight was protracted, each side mustering lawyers and psychiatrists to write petitions, give depositions, testify.

"Children are resilient," the judge told us, peering down over his half-glasses. "And both parties are deserving, as far as I can see."

"What about what the children deserve?" our psychiatrist said from the witness stand, although no question had been asked.

The judge smiled playfully. "Is the medical profession trying to tell the bench what it can and cannot do?"

"Yes," our psychiatrist said, combatively.

The court retired to the judge's chambers. The two families were exiled to the hall. Hank and Maria stood at one end; Barbara and Mat and Mother and I at the other. It was a long hall. Mat screamed when he heard the decision. He filled the hallway with his screams. He wailed and clung to my legs, embarrassing everybody but me. I was proud of him and dropped down on my knees to hold him to my chest. At seven he could still howl like an animal caught in a snare. He could howl for me.

When the social worker approached us, two shapes cleaving together like a starfish and its stone, I stared her down. She was a woman shaped like an urn, but I felt no pity for her, no forgiveness.

Her role in the scheme of things was to uphold the children's welfare in court, and she could have done it if she hadn't caved in to the judge. "Do you think Solomon would have really gone through with it and chopped the child in half?" I wanted to ask her. Then I did.

"I'm sorry," was all she said. Then she touched Mat's back, his shell. "Matthew?" she said gently. "Mat?" He responded to her only by altering the rhythm of his wails. They rose in pitch until he'd torn the fragile membrane of her concern. I watched the tenderness drain from her face, revealing the bone beneath. Mat was my voice, screaming for me. Wail, Mat, wail! Drive this cadaver away.

Hank waited patiently at the other end of the hall. I turned Mat's voice to blast him, but he didn't flinch. He didn't turn away. Maria hung at his side, stealing glances. Then she turned her back, maybe to hide a triumphant smile. Mat would have to call her Mom. "Call me Mom," she'd remind him over and over again, cementing the suggestion with a pasta grin. Eventually, he'd give in——a betrayal that he'd never be able to comprehend.

Mat was facing the wall, but still he seemed to sense his father approaching. He screamed even louder than before. Maybe he heard Hank's footsteps rapping down the marble hall. Maybe he felt them shudder through my body and the floor. Hank took the boy's shoulders and tugged, but Mat wouldn't let go. Hank reddened, and Mat howled again, piercingly, as though to press his small advantage, voicing a wordless scream as wrong in these halls of deliberated behavior as the judge's ruling seemed to me. I smiled in spite of myself, and Hank saw it. "If you'll give us another minute, I'll bring him down the hall."

"Yes, thank you," he said softly and walked back to his end of the corridor.

The process took much longer than a minute, but Hank waited patiently. Mat had to wail and cling to each of us in turn: Barbara, Mother, and the psychiatrist who'd beaten him so many times at checkers, then come to court to fight and nearly won the day. After the others, Mat clung again to me, and though I knew I was chosen, the best rock for the moment for his starfish love, I was also aware of just who would have to hand him over to Hank.

• • •

Mat left the next day for Southern California, a sub-suburb out in the desert below L.A., and Barbara flew home with my mother to Tory Hole. Brother and sister pledged to write, and even the court had decreed Christmas and summer visitations. But of course they'd grow apart.

Barbara would be popular in Tory Hole society, more acceptable than either her mother or me. She might grow a sable's tail or she might one day decline the cotillion, but her first boyfriend would be English, a student at Choate. Would he love her and leave her like a typical male? That I'd never know. Barbara wouldn't tell me, and I would never ask. Throughout high school, she'd call me up at night to chat, and only after we'd spoken about small things for a while, would she ask, "Was it this way for you? Was it this way for my mother too?" relying on kinship to carry her meanings, just as her mother and I had.

Conversations with Mat would be more rare and more distant. Sooner or later, he'd adopt his father's accent. He'd learn how to hunt. Barbara would object. She'd say it was cruel and inhumane. She'd say she still wanted to become a vet. But eventually she'd go to Barnard, where there are no courses offered in animal husbandry or animal anything. And they'd fight. They'd fight about Maria, their father, their mother, and me. Their visits would be less and less frequent. "I've got exams like you wouldn't believe," Barbara would say over the long-distance phone. "I've got to have a draft of my senior thesis in by January fifteenth, and I haven't even *begun*."

"Dad won't let me come this time," Mat would say. "You must have been disrespectful to him on the phone."

As for me, I watch and listen, hearing the tones in their voices, not the words; watching to see if they'd grow up to look like Les or me; listening to half a conversation and trying to imagine the whole. I'm the static that rises between them in their silences on the phone, the cord that binds them to their mother, her closest living facsimile.

No, I'm not even that anymore. All I am is alone: the bachelor uncle, the inattentive son, the brother without a sister moon, feeling sorry for himself.

Les is buried in the Oakland hills. From there, you can see all of San Francisco Bay, both the bridges, the fog building up on the headlands of Marin, pointing its chill finger at you through the Golden Gate, the Berkeley tower, even Oakland (San Francisco's moon), where both my mother and my sister were born. On a clear day, you might even pick out Belmont, where I was born, and Palo Alto, which I still drive through once or twice a week on my way to somewhere else. For a while there, I used to have a girlfriend who lived on the other side of the Alma underpass, and I'd ask, "What do you say, Les? What about this one?" as I made the dip and the curve. Sometimes I even said the words aloud, but I never got any replies. I'm not crazy enough to hear replies. I never even heard the echo of my own voice coming back to me before I was safely out of the curve.

Les, suddenly I don't know how you'll feel about my telling, which is funny since I thought I knew how you felt about everything else, or convinced myself I did. I knew you'd give your daughter a dragon's tail even if she wanted something fancier, and I knew how you felt about Pete Pardieu and the others you never told me about and what you were feeling while you waited in January on the bus station bench, which was actually a photographer's studio in March, waiting to catch the bus back home, waiting for your life to begin. Life is long, I heard you say, live it up. In my arrogance, I even thought I knew what you were feeling at the end, when the car bounced and then your head bounced against the wheel well like a rubber ball, except your head wasn't made of rubber, and your consciousness drained down from your scalp like so much blood, covering your eyes, dousing itself. But now my conceits fail me. Life is long enough to raise a lot of doubts. I never used to have so many, not when you were alive, not when you were just dying or just dead. Oh, Les, it's already been so long.

There is one thing I'm waiting for. I wouldn't miss it for the world. Barbara will be coming out from New York on the train. Mat will have been visiting Sunshine, living now in the next town east of

Tory Hole so he'll be coming by car. He'll arrive first and be feeding the ducks, descendants of the ones Papa used to feed, crouching by the frozen pond when Barbara pulls up in a cab. She'll get out at the head of the drive. She'll see her little brother as she pays her fare, but he won't see her yet. Maybe he won't even notice her walking up, and she'll be able to catch him from behind.

"Poncho!"

"Chico!" Mat will turn, and they'll embrace. Then I think they'll kiss. In fact I'm sure they will, for they'll be more demonstrative than we.